EASTER SUN

EASTER SUN

By

PETER NEAGOE

COWARD-McCANN, INC.

PUBLISHERS :: NEW YORK

A Note about Peter Neagoë

By Donald F. Sturtevant

Since its publication in 1934, Malcolm Cowley's *Exile's Return* has remained the staple item of the literature concerned with the American expatriate movement after World War I. The importance of the book is a curious matter and can hardly be credited to the scope or penetration with which Cowley treated the expatriate intellectuals or their attitudes or problems. *Exile's Return* is short, impressionistic, and essentially autobiographical. Its chief value is its communication of the youth, excitement, sense of mission, and of course the disillusionment that motivated the many American artists who went abroad to live and work during the twenties and early thirties. Many of these artists and writers were better known to each other than to the American public from which they sought to escape. Not all of them were memorialized, as it were, in *Exile's Return*. One absentee, a relatively unknown painter and writer, who first arrived in Paris from America in 1926 and pronounced France to be "agréable et favorable à l'inspiration," was Peter Neagoë, an American of Roumanian birth, forty-four years old.

After a full life of artistic endeavor and literary accomplishments, Peter Neagoë died in the hospital at Kingston, New York, on 28 October 1960, at the age of seventy-eight years. In addition to his paintings and published works, he left a considerable mass of literary materials—manuscripts, letters, working notes, and such—which his wife, the well-known painter, Anna Neagoë, wished to preserve and make available to interested readers, researchers, and scholars. Encouraged and counseled by her life-long friend, Mr. Martin Kamin, a member of Syracuse University Library Associates, Mrs. Neagoë chose to donate her late husband's literary papers to the Library of Syracuse University. At the same time, she generously endowed a fund from which an annual award is to be made to a graduate scholar in the Department of English for research in the Neagoë collection.

These papers are indeed of special value to literary students and historians of the arts. First, Neagoë's novels and short stories concerning Roumanian peasant life and folklore have been regarded and identified as classics of the pastoral genre. Second, by virtue of his important role in the American literary community in Europe, Neagoë's letters and notes provide an interesting and intimate view of the whole expatriate movement. Third, the papers document the long-time effort of a serious, dedicated artist of the Old World, transplanted to the New.

An initial examination reveals a few general facts of biography and career which lend themselves to elaboration in a more detailed study at some future time. Peter Neagoë was born in 1882 in Transylvania during the reign of Francis Joseph I, Emperor of Austria, King of Bohemia, and Apostolic King of Hungary. In a country populated largely by peasants, Peter's family was exceptional: his relatives worked generally at intellectual occupations. Peter's father, a man who spoke and wrote many languages and dialects, was official notary for the district, responsible for resolving judicial disputes among the peasant population and aiding them with their minor legal problems. The small boy's introduction to literature came when he began to write love letters for the illiterate young domestics employed in his father's household. In return for reading and writing letters for the adults of his village, he had related to him many of the Transylvanian stories and legends which were to form the raw materials of his later works as a pastoral novelist and short story writer.

Mrs. Anna Neagoë at Syracuse University
Reader's left to right: Dr. Wayne S. Yenawine, Director of Libraries,
Mrs. Neagoë, Vice President Frank P. Piskor, and Mr. David A. Fraser,
Chairman, Syracuse University Library Associates Board of Trustees.
(Photograph by Harold J. Nisnoff, Syracuse Univeristy Audio-Visual
Center)

At the age of seventeen, Peter went to Bucharest where he studied at the Academy of Fine Arts, completed philosophy courses at the University of Bucharest, and began to gain a reputation as a writer of journalistic pieces and stories for various publications. He early showed what was to be his essential and continuing subject of interest— the development of characters out of his own experiences cultured by his vivid imagination. He wrote mainly of the peasants and the tillers of the soil of the Carpathian region and of the shepherds and the mountaineers of the Transylvanian Alps.

At twenty, consumed by a desire to see and experience the New World and to discover—as he later said—a greater freedom and field of action, Peter left for America, full of eagerness and ambition. In New York City he continued his art studies at the National Academy, and it was through his connection with a local association of his fellow students that he was first plunged into American literature. He never quite recovered from it. Many years later he wrote: "Although quite an advanced sapling, I believe I struck roots in American soil, for now my heart is here. Then too while I know four other languages well, I think and write in English. When I started to *dream* in English, I realized this was my language."

Following his marriage in 1911, Peter Neagoë devoted his time fully to his art. He painted and wrote, and for a number of years he and his wife divided their time between New York City and a home in the Berkshire Hills. Finally in 1926, they embarked for France and settled in Paris, where Mrs. Neagoë painted and exhibited and Neagoë's short stories began to appear in such magazines as Whit Burnett's *Story* and Eugene Jolas's *Transition*. While in Paris, Neagoë conceived the idea of editing an anthology of expatriate prose and poetry. This project brought him into close contact with virtually all the American writers living on the Continent and resulted in the publication of *Americans Abroad* in 1932. Some of the most interesting items in the Neagoë collection are letters to and from such figures as Kay Boyle, Ezra Pound, Henry Miller, Laura Riding, and others who participated in this enterprise.

Malcolm Cowley made clear in his *Exile's Return* that the artists who alienated themselves from America in the twenties faced the problem of reintegration in the thirties. He suggested that one means of reintegration lay in the artist's acceptance of the problems of society and an identification with movements geared to social reform. It was a desire for such reintegration that brought many expatriates—Peter Neagoë among them—back to the United States throughout the middle thirties. In May 1933, Neagoë was interviewed on shipboard by a reporter of the New York *Times* on his return to America. Poor economic conditions had, he declared, thinned the American writers colony in Paris and had forced many to return to this country or to decamp for the lower-standard Spanish peninsula. But the major force behind the return, as he sensed it, was that the "exciting things are happening here now. There is more literary activity; the writing here is becoming more and more important. And the economic changes which, it is almost certain, will be reflected in a changing literature make the time and place 'fascinating." Neagoë felt that these conditions might "weed out the formula writers, as readers turn to literature of individuality and force." Writers, Neagoë added, will have to be more concerned with social aspects, "the elemental motive power that moves human beings, and less with the little bits of cake that end always with wedding bells."

The year after his return to the United States—1934—saw the publication, simultaneously in this country, France, and England, of Neagoë's first novel *Easter Sun*. A year later, a collecton of short stories was published under the title *Winning a Wife and Other Stories*. This book included the pieces contained in an earlier volume entitled *Storm*—published in English on the Continent—which had been banned in the United States, and subsequently released at about the same time James Joyce's *Ulysses* was allowed legal publication in this country. In March 1936, Neagoë's second novel *There is My Heart* was published in New York.

Neagoë said he had some years previously actually worked alongside the peasants characterized in *There is My Heart;* and when asked about their portrayal in this volume and in some of his other writings, he said:

> I lived with these people many years, long after I had left them to their own fate. They insisted on following me out into the world. I decided to recreate them in my stories and novels. *Easter Sun* came into existence in Santa Fe. I worked twelve to fourteen hours each day during ten weeks and did not feel tired at all because the characters were most willing, old friends that they are, to respond to my call. They came and acted, lived, or rather re-lived their lot for me. Ten weeks, and there was the novel, the first draft of it, 110,000 words, written in long hand. The air and sunshine of New Mexico was like the air in the foothills of the Carpathian Mountains, in Transylvania, where my characters were born and raised.

IV.

An examination of the Neagoë papers shows that the books generally received from very good to excellent reviews and notices. Still, none of the volumes sold particularly well. Neagoë's publishers had one of those literary curiosities on their hands—an author who, in spite of sympathetic, even enthusiastic critical recognition, remained unread by the public. The situation is lent poignancy when one reads the encouraging reports of publishers' readers and subsequently the critical reviews and then compares them with the matter-of-fact publishers' bookkeeping reports of low and negligible sales.

Peter Neagoë became perhaps more disillusioned with the America of the forties and fifties than he had been in the twenties. To a nation engaged in war—engaged too in the brutality, cynicism, and materialism which are by-products of armed and bloody conflict—peasant literature, even *good* peasant literature, may understandably have seemed remote and divergent. In spite of the shifts of literary taste that occurred during this period, Peter Neagoë continued to write his own kind of literature. In 1949 he published *A Time to Keep*, an autobiography of his boyhood in Transylvania. It was an evocative chronicle of a happy, old-world childhood seen through the eyes of a sensitive boy, now grown to a mature writer. His final novel *No Time for Tears* appeared in 1958. Neagoë's published works are no proper gauge, however, to his real productivity. Included in the Neagoë collection are manuscripts of several unpublished novels and plays, as well as some 240 manuscripts of unpublished articles and short stories.

From his first short story in the twenties to his last novel in the late fifties, Peter Neagoë's was a folk literature. He steadfastly refused to indulge in fashionable, meretricious, or merely profitable literary effort. He wrote, as he once said, what he thought and felt. And his thoughts and feelings were, throughout his life, rooted deeply in the Roumanian life and spirit he knew so well. In an article written for *Travel* in 1934, Neagoë eloquently described the enormous attraction his people held for him:

Writing about the Roumanian peasant, one is not tempted to go into his history and the history of his country. There is a strong actuality about him, which gives the visitor a feeling that this peasant belongs where he is as much as the cultivated plains, the hillsides clad in vineyards, the beech, oak and spruce forests, the mountains, the rivers, and the brooks. He is an integral part of this land; he grew out of it. In his nature is the gaiety of spring, the warmth of summer, the mellow sadness of autumn and the un-compromising somberness of winter. He loves life with all his heart. Being a creature of the soil, the peasant extracts from it his daily bread. His beliefs are derived from mixed myths, tinted here and there with Christian beliefs. Those myths are earth-born, and are suited to men rooted in the soil. His proverbs and the maxims for his conduct grow from the earth, with the trees, the flowers, the herbage. The villages, the hamlets, and the house he lives in are integral elements of the landscape. He has mythical rituals where-with to gain the favors of the seasons; the seasons are embodied in some symbol reminiscent of pagan deity. He works well, though without haste, in a rhythm adapted to the pace of the seasons.

And it was Peter Neagoë who did his best work, both artistic and literary—without any haste, in a rhythm adapted to the pace of his own seasons.

Reprinted from the Courier, June 1963, with permission of John Mayfield of the Syracuse University Library Associates.

EASTER SUN

I

ONE-EYED John was in a rage, swearing and beating his oxen with a chain. The animals fidgeted, lashed their tails against the sharp stings.

John swore mighty Roumanian oaths, cursing "the forty thousand little saints slain by Herod at the birth of Christ." He cursed the clouds and the thunder, he cursed the moon and the sun, reaching up to the Lord God Himself.

He swore on, even after the oxen were yoked. His wife groaned: "The very sun stands still when he swears."

"Come on, lazy louts! Come on before I get after you!" he roared at his sons.

Michael, a young man of nineteen, and Nicholas, some two years younger, were on the way to help their father haul the wood from the forest. The father often struck his sons with the whip, even at their age. In drunken moments he had threatened to kill them.

On this autumn morning One-eyed John was more certain than ever that God and the saints were racking him. The prayers of a burdened, hard-working man, as he was, should have moved some saint to intervene for him with the Heavenly Father, he thought angrily. But the years passed with no favorable sign from heaven.

Surely the divine powers conspired against him. And this morning brought new proof of it. Three days ago his daughter Ileana went to the city and had not returned yet.

"She is lost! My girl is lost!" John growled. "The devil has got her in his claws. Taken her soul. Uses her beauty to trap other souls."

Even Danila, the priest's son, is caught by the Unclean One, John thought. Danila follows Ileana like her shadow. He threatens to kill himself because she does not care for him. He does not study any more. His parents are broken with sorrow. They begged him to give up the girl, they cried on his shoulder, embracing him, both at once. They prayed to God for his salvation and gave an extra dole to the poor, whispering: "For God's sake and for the saving of our boy." Yet Danila follows her and wastes away.

One day when Ileana was not at home, the priest came to One-eyed John. The two men went into the girl's room. The priest sprinkled holy water in every corner of the room and on all of the girl's things. But the room, though small and clean "as a candle," was filled with a charm that made the priest shudder. Approaching the bed he noticed the strangely patterned coverlet, woven by Ileana, and was struck by its beauty. Only one possessed could weave such designs, the priest thought, for never in his life had he seen such blending of colors. It dazed his eyes. Then also, there was a subtle scent in the room,

which troubled the priest. He went from the bed to the
narrow deal table. Years of scrubbing and care had made
the wood of the table as smooth as fresh skin.

The poor priest felt Ileana's presence more and more,
until he could have sworn that she was there, all dominant
though invisible. He felt the unholy poison of her charm
drilling softly but insistently into his very soul.

Unconsciously he laid his palm on the cool surface of
the table and stroked it absent-mindedly. A sharp thrill
ran through him. It awakened him, as it were, and he
drew his hand away quickly, crossing himself and making the holy sign over the table also, murmuring, "Good
Lord, save our souls. Amen."

One-eyed John, who watched him spellbound, crossed
himself also and left the room, as if suddenly remember-
ing something.

Left alone, the priest stood in the middle of the room
as if riveted to the floor, but he turned his head this way
and that, staring at the walls and the scant pieces of
furniture. Then a light seemed to come to him and he
began to pray. His lips moving in prayer, he went to the
windows and traced with his finger-nail several little
crosses on the sills. He did likewise to the threshold. This
devout procedure would stop the Evil One from entering
the girl's room, he thought. But when he got home the
priest remembered that he had left the chimney open to
the devil; for he forgot to trace the protective crosses on

it. This troubled him exceedingly and took his sleep away. He spent his nights tossing and groaning beside his wife, who slept quietly, still as the image on the icon.

Veronica, the priest's wife, had a cheerful nature, to which she owed her fresh complexion and the firmness and suppleness of her matronly body. Looking upon her cheerful face comforted the priest, for even when Veronica cried there was more love of living in her eyes than sadness. And now, when sleep had left him, he derived what little comfort he could from looking at her sleeping form. Veronica had a way of putting her palms together, as in prayer, resting her head on folded hands. Her black hair fell over the pillow, over her white throat.

The priest inhaled the warm air of the room, rich with the fragrance of sweet-mint which Veronica always kept in the linen chest. His eyes, accustomed to the dim light of the oil lamp burning under the icon at the head of the bed, rested upon Veronica's round, full arms. Their white amplitude comforted the priest. He touched the arm gently. In a flash the deal table, that bewitched room of Ileana came to his mind. His head felt in a turmoil, with Ileana, the table, the richly colored coverlet, white, full arms, Danila, and the devil himself, all in a jumble. He crossed himself, murmured prayers, his heart bursting. He got on his knees in bed, facing the icon, and prayed devoutly. But always the chimney in Ileana's room loomed up and gaped before his eyes, like the unholy gullet of

hell. Yes, yes, the Black One, Satan, can still enter the
girl's chamber, he thought. And she is tearing my son's
soul out of him, for— "Good Lord, save us. Save us,
Heavenly Father," he groaned. Towards dawn he fell
asleep.

One-eyed John was no less tormented than the priest.
His nights were not sleepless, but dreams tortured him.
He awoke one morning worn and raw. And on that
autumn morning he noticed a new sign of God's anger.
The big apple tree in the yard had started to bloom, and
winter coming on. As if the roots of the old tree were
heated by the fires below.

John cracked his whip yelling, "Tsha, Paicu!" The
oxen jerked their lumbering bodies into a clumsy trot
and the wagon rattled out of the yard. The boys jumped
on the wagon. Nicholas bumped against Michael and
burst out laughing at his angry grimace, but a look from
John stopped his laughter.

One-eyed John noticed the boy's white teeth. Two
rows, white and even, showing when he laughed. "Just
like her," he growled. For when laughing, Ileana's lips
shaped a red triangle, in which the two rows of teeth
gleamed white. "Cursed white teeth," John swore under
his breath and cracked the whip again. He fell to thinking of his lot.

A hard lot was his, he said to himself. Yes, yes. To

the hard work for his daily bread was added the training
of the children also, because Chiva, his wife, only knew
to say to the children, "Yes, dear," or "Yes, little one,"
and other such soft words, which are of no earthly use in
training a child. So it all fell to John to mould them.
Well, with the boys he managed well enough, but the girls
—good Lord, that was a task. And a puzzling one too.

"These female children can break a saint," he was
saying to himself. "Those angel faces, what will and stub-
bornness they hide. They are stubborn and hard as a knot
in the oak. Harder even. And they have no head for brief
male reasoning. None. A boy—well, he is a little man.
You talk to him, a few words. If the words fail, a good
shaking, a slap on the face, and you get at his reason. But
talk to a girl, and see! She stands there with her arms
dangling like two ropes, looking on the ground. Never
looks at your face, no, no, or if she does, it is that frightened look in her eyes that unhinges you. 'Well, what did
I say, girl?' you ask, trying to calm the man in you. And
what do you get? Not a word. Maybe a stolen glance, a
bucketful of tears. Good Lord! the awful trial of it, for a
man to look at a girl's chin, trembling and jumping, and
the eyes squeezed together and the tears running from the
slits. Enough to drive one into sin. And all that because
of this Chiva, this wife of mine."

Chiva was a plump, ruddy-faced woman, who spent no
time in thinking. If ever a thought came into her head,

it was a simple one. A sort of stirring in the head before she stirred herself into action, for she was ever moving about from early morning until late at night. Then, to close up the day and lay it aside "for good and for ever," Chiva said her prayer. Chiva never missed her evening prayer. That was to her the sealing up of the day past. The giving of it, the offering of it to God's keeping. Her whole life was God's, but she offered it piecemeal, day by day.

As a little girl Chiva would kneel before the icon that hung on the eastern wall in her father's house, in the large room where the whole family slept during the winter. The icon represented the Virgin Mary seated on a heavenly throne, the infant Jesus smiling up to her from the folds of the drapery that formed a nest in her lap. Above the Virgin was a golden triangle and in the triangle God the Father, symbolized by an all-seeing eye looking serenely upon the world and its mortals. And, in the heavenly azure, with outstretched wings, the Holy Ghost embodied in a white dove, stood eternally poised in stillness. On the lower left corner of the icon was the Crucifixion; on the right, the glorious scene of the Resurrection. By day this icon shone like a jewel, and at night its splendor was enhanced by the light of the oil lamp burning in front of it, in the silent gloom.

Chiva inherited this icon. Now it hung in the house— on the eastern wall—where for twenty-two years she and

John had been living. Under its protective glory her four children were born. Each child Chiva dedicated to the holy spirit of the icon by raising it towards it three times, praying that the newcomer may be guided through life by the heavenly light.

Every time Chiva repeated this devotion, she perceived a divine smile on the Virgin's face, a benign smile, and the Lord looked on and approved. So she felt that herself and the children were not only part of this world, but indeed, they were part of the larger heavenly scheme. And in this spirit Chiva treated her children with tenderness, bearing with their faults and leading them with tempered words. And when, as happened with Ileana, the child took a road that she did not know, Chiva redoubled her prayers, asking guidance for the erring child and understanding for herself.

She could not comprehend her husband's anger towards the children, but her heart ached for him. She knew that John was a good man. A God-fearing, hardworking man who sweated his life-blood toiling to wrench from the earth sustenance for six beings. A good Christian he was—she knew that. But what she could not understand was why John, while trusting in God, feared the devil more than the Lord's judgment. "Get thee behind me, Satan," was enough to get the devil out of the way, Chiva assured John. As to herself, she had him, the devil, routed by crossing herself three times and repeat-

ing, "Pfew, Satan, may the holy cross kill you." This she
did when, at moments of great exhaustion, the devil came
to her with temptations. It is true, she avowed, that once
she distinctly smelled the brimstone, after the Evil One
vanished. "But what of that," she told John, "as long as
you can chase him away."

Chiva had dedicated Ileana to the holy icon, but the
ways of God are unfathomable. Ileana showed strange
traits since her early years. Never did this child obey
thoroughly either father or mother, for even when doing
what she was told, she did it in her own way, much to
John's annoyance. Chiva only sighed, stepping in front of
her husband to shield the child from his blow.

As time went on John came to consider his first child
more and more as a tribulation, added to his none too easy
life.

As Ileana grew her beauty grew also, so that the old
peasant women never passed her without spitting three
times and mumbling the words against the evil eye. "This
child is too beautiful," they said. The babbling of the old
women increased John's resentment to the child, especially
because Ileana paid not the slightest attention to the
women but went her way proudly, smiling or with grave
countenance.

At the age of seven Ileana began to embroider. She
learned with Anutza Pradu, whose work was known far

and wide. Anutza was a middle-aged woman at the time
and had taught many village girls to embroider, yet she
marveled at Ileana's aptitude with the needle. "I have
never in my life seen the like of her," Anutza said. She
taught Ileana the designs that came down from time
immemorial and are yet as pure as ages ago. The child
learned quickly, respecting the designs to the minutest
detail, but occasionally she used color combinations of her
own. Of these Anutza did not approve, being respectful
of tradition.

But at the age of fourteen Ileana invented some patterns which the young generation adopted eagerly. The
collar bands, the embroidery on the sleeves and cuffs,
Ileana kept in the traditional designs. Where she took
liberties was on the sides of the shirt-opening, running
down about six inches from the collar-band. On the
sides of this slit in the bodice of the shirt Ileana com-
bined colors that enhanced the tint of the flesh visible
there. "Your skin is dark, Lina, you can stand more red
than Varvara, whose flesh is like milk," she would say.
And her young friends welcomed her suggestions.

Ileana showed the same unusual skill in weaving.
Their guest room, which they called the "big room," was
hung with strips of linen for pillow cases, bed covers,
towels (which only rarely touched a face) into the tex-
tures of which Ileana wove marvelous patterns of silk or
choice wool. She could spin a thread as thin as gossamer.

She used her grandmother's distaff and hickory spindles worn smooth as air by the old woman's fingers.

On summer evenings when the moon was full, girls and boys gathered in front of Ileana's house. The spindles purred for hours, interrupted by laughter and the singing of folk songs. Occasionally the youngsters forgot time until some elderly person called sleepily, telling them that midnight had come. Often it happened that one of the company would hear the clock strike the hour in the house. He would hush the crowd and count the strokes aloud. When the clock rang out the midnight hour, the girls would reach in their sleeves for the hemp-seeds and thrust a few in their mouth, all a-shiver. But chewing the hemp-seeds would scare away the dragons who might come after midnight, in the guise of handsome young men and "play with the souls of innocent girls." Of course, these dragons got to the soul of the girl by means of seducing her in true mortal manner. There were instances of the kind known in the village.

The boys were more courageous, but even they felt the spell of the hour, and presently the company scattered, girls and boys rushing to their homes.

The girls noticed that Ileana never chewed the hemp-seeds and they began to whisper among themselves. The old peasants say that whispering is dangerous because it is like a lighted match dropped on dry stubble. It proved so about Ileana. The whispering about her spread like a field fire until somebody said: "That girl must be possessed." Had Ileana been homely or maimed or in some way deformed, it would have never come to this. The whispering would have died down after a while. But because of her beauty and unusual gifts the gossips felt that, considering his black character, the devil paid rather lavishly for the possession of her soul. They needed this anodyne for their jealousy and envy of Ileana.

And also, Ileana had too great a power over the young men, the gossips said. "They trail after her with no eyes for other girls and she gives them less than her finger-tips." Truly, Ileana treated the young men with equal indifference, which only served to attract them the more. Even her own brothers, Michael and Nicholas, had a sullen respect of her—"a rare thing among brothers and sisters, because a man is a man after all, no matter how beautiful the woman." Besides, it is just as rare that a brother should realize the loveliness of his sister when he is as young as Ileana's brothers were, the villagers held.

At the age of sixteen the village girls make their *début*, so to say, at the Sunday dance. In the winter the dance is held in the large room at the inn; in the summer they dance in the barn. The barn floor is smoothed with clay which gets hard as cement, yet it is not like stone under foot. With a little sprinkling it is made very good for dancing.

The Sunday of Ileana's first appearance at the dance

is memorable. It was in the summer. The two gipsies were playing and the floor was packed with dancers. The wide shirt-skirts of the girls flared out about them as they whirled around, stirring the shadows of the barn into vibrant motion.

The young men, true to old custom, improvise in rhymed recitative, paced with the music, while they dance. In this way they speak out their hearts. Considerable skill is required of the young man to sing his feelings in this manner, or else he will be laughed at by the whole assembly.

Now, on that Sunday, the gaiety spread from the barn into the garden, where the older peasants sat at long tables, drinking vodka and watching the dancers, now clapping hands, now beating time with their glasses. In the midst of that clatter Ileana appeared, followed by her mother.

Usually the girl coming to her first dance looks confused and is awkward. She blushes, trips and torments the flowers in her hands by squeezing them or even tearing them petal by petal, utterly unconscious. It is natural and amusing, the peasants say. But what did Ileana? She walked like a queen, looking straight ahead of her, above the heads of the assembly, and on entering the barn she merely put up her hand and smoothed the blue cornflower in her hair, in that golden hair of hers. "Who ever saw a thing like that," the gossips whispered. The dance continued, to be sure, but "there was a moment's halt on the floor as if they all had turned into stone," said the gossips.

However, the talk about Ileana's being in league with the devil had not yet, at that time, broken out openly. So when the fiddlers stopped, the girls fluttered about her, giggling and chattering. They examined the embroidery on her shirt-sleeves, felt the fabric, rubbing it between the fingers, and one perky girl picked up Ileana's front apron to look at the intricate knots of the fringes. Ileana let them do as they wished. Then the boys gathered around, forming a circle about the girls. They pushed each other, pinched and teased the girls, occasionally aiming a remark at Ileana, as if from behind a fence. The girls chided when they were pinched, or giggled at a droll remark from a boy, or answered pertly, but Ileana, if she merely glanced at a boy, the fellow jumped with gladness for the reward. Such was the light in her blue eyes.

Ileana's mother sat down with some friends, who had called her. Old Mira, the midwife, was at the same table. As soon as Chiva sat down, Mira turned to her saying: "That daughter of yours, Chiva, she's as lovely as the day. My, my! Look at her. I remember, Chiva, when she was born. For a first child she gave us no trouble at all. No, no. She came into the world smiling, one might say. Her face was plump and round as a melon. A little angel.

Yes, yes! I remember as if it was yesterday." Smiling, Chiva sighed remembrance.

At the next table were six or seven men, talking noisily.

"The wheat is fine this year," said a tall peasant.

"So it is, on the flats," answered an old man; "but on our hill it was washed by the spring rains. It's as thin as my beard."

"Well, Mitru, you are older than I, but I always told you that on your side you should sow winter wheat." This from a red-faced man who looked well-to-do. As the old man just looked at him, puffing his pipe, the red-faced peasant bent close to him, emphasizing: "Now, haven't I?" At this the old man pulled his pipe out of his mouth, spat and said: "You did." Then he wiped his beard and smoked on.

"Talk is talk and work is work, and God knows how to manage both," shouted One-eyed John, who came up behind Ghitsa Strong, the tall peasant. The latter turned and looking over his shoulder he put up his hand, saying: "Welcome, John. Shake hands and pull up a stool."

One of the peasants called for another quart of vodka. They drank silently, emptying the glasses at one gulp. Then John spoke up.

"You see, good men," he began, "there is this: We are here in this world—men, women, children, beasts—everything. Good! Above us is heaven. God rules there

and rules over us. Good! Below us (he pointed) is hell,
the devil there, high and mighty and meddling with us
here. Now, that's as true as day-light. Well, here I am—
a peasant, a simple man. Good! I get my daily bread in
the sweat of my brow. Good! The Lord made it so. I
work, I sweat, I work more, I sweat more until I drop,
limp as a wet rag. Even the oxen stop, with their flanks
going like bellows. I fear they would burst. Good and
well. But look here, listen well. Heaven is above, hell is
below and we are in between, on the earth. Now—to God
I pray; the devil I fear. Yes, I must fear him, the black
enemy of mankind. Good—I fear him. But—I've thought
it all out in my mind. Here is what I say: this world
would be fine without the devil. That is true—eh, abso-
lutely. So I ask you all, why was the devil made?" John
paused, took another glass of vodka, then he continued.
"Well, as I said to you, friends: do we or don't we need
the devil? Listen well. Listen to me, friends. I say, no!
God and all the saints, no! No, no, no! We don't need
him. Amen." Concluding, John struck the table with his
fist.

There was a short silence, then the men burst out
talking, pell-mell, all at once.

"No, we don't."

"Don't what? That's blaspheming."

"I leave it to the Lord."

"God save us. I also sweat and work—I—"

"We do. All of us. What? Why don't we need the devil? We'd forget the Lord—"

"The Lord made him."

"Made him black as the flue. Blacker—"

"The Lord be praised. Hallowed be His name. Amen!"

"Amen! Amen!" cried all the men.

With that they felt relieved and they settled down to drinking. Presently the tall peasant started to sing:

"Buds, oh darling buds, when you burst,
  The blossoms come!
Shines the sun, the sun on blossoms.
The wind blows the blossoms off, but fruit is there."

The others chimed in, repeating in chorus:

"But the fruit is there, the fruit is the-e-e-ere."
  The blossoms come!

2

UNTIL her eighteenth year Ileana was much courted, but gradually the belief that she was in league with the devil took root with the villagers, and the young men were, between the devil and her seductive person, at a loss what to do. She was now twenty and still unmarried. There were nevertheless some young men in Aciliu and in the neighboring villages willing to brave the devil for Ileana, but she was indifferent. Besides, these brave ones were really not brave enough. Those of her own village would dance with her, speak to her and seek chances to meet her alone in the fields or when she was fetching water from the spring, but they were too easily thrown into confusion by the girl. Her words seemed to them double-edged. Even Anghel Bradutz, a tall, wide-shouldered young man with a small black mustache and eyes that flamed up or darkened with lightning rapidity, had not enough wits to match Ileana's. The young men from the neighboring villages saw Ileana in the city, on market days, and they were no more equal to the task of winning her than were those of Aciliu.

To all these young men Ileana's beauty was what light is to the moths. Directly they saw her they went to her, but only to be baffled. For they could not measure up to her intelligence. What they could not understand was, why so beautiful a girl should take pleasure—as it seemed—in using her head. The usual way of girls, as they knew, is to listen to a man, to blush, to smile, burst out laughing at his humorous remarks—a gratifying thing, indeed—but not to stand up and talk back as an equal. Such conduct in a girl puzzled them beyond comprehension.

Being routed in that manner, these young men sought solace in the whispered tales about Ileana. "Surely it is not natural, such ready speech in a girl. Yes, it may be unholy," they said. And they came to admit that Ileana's wit was of the devil.

Then again, Ileana's beauty increased every day. That was strange, and more strange even this thing about her eyes. Up to her eighteenth year Ileana's eyes were blue as the sky. Then, as if over night, her eyes became of a velvety violet, her eyelashes turned black, and when she looked at one there flashed from her eyes a light that sent darts into the heart. And her voice changed also. It became full, rich, and sounded more like the deep notes of a flute than a human voice. Hearing her talk one experienced a strange sensation. It warmed one to the marrow, like sunlight. She barely moved her lips, and when she smiled the words issued from her mouth like the warbling of some wonderful bird. Even when her face was set and stern, the lips almost pressed together, the words flowed nevertheless in a variety of modulations, enough to befuddle a saint. And when she sang in church, no man could keep his mind on the prayers. Even the flames of the candles flickered and trembled.

Ileana went often to town, on market days. When Chiva could go, they went together, otherwise she went with her father. But of late John would only drive to town when he had a load of grain to sell. So Ileana would go alone.

On this day neither Chiva nor John was going, for they both had pressing work on hand. Ileana dressed in her Sunday clothes, put two chickens in the basket and started off. Her mother said: "Well, daughter, if you sell the hens at a fair price, buy the silk you need for your new shirt."

The sun was just rising above the crest of the hill when Ileana arrived on the flats, outside of the village. It was one of those summer mornings when a human being feels that earth, sun and heaven are his. The dew on the grass sparkled, the skylarks sang, and the light spread on the plains a flood of gold. Ileana took off her boots and walked in bare feet on the wet grass alongside the road. She trailed her feet to soak them in the dew, then she took to brisk walking. From the east came a light wind, as if blown by the sun itself.

Ileana gave herself to the wind. Her shirt flared,

bulged out, flapped and clung against her legs as if alive.
Her puffed sleeves swelled out, her back apron a streamer.
Through the slit in the bodice of her shirt the wind entered intimately to her breasts. The lively, playful morning
breeze behaved as if it wanted to undress her. Ileana un-
braided her hair, shook it and gave it to the wind.

The cool, damp carpet under foot, the strong air, and
now the timid warmth of the morning sun filled Ileana
with joy. Great, young joy. She began to sing. First
softly, a song without words, a song on which she walked.
Then the song grew in her, quickened and became strong,
taking all her voice.

The hens started to jump in the basket and she became aware of them. Annoyed by their restless weight,
she changed the basket from one arm to the other. The
hens flopped their wings and scolded. Ileana stopped
singing. She apostrophised the hens: "Yes, I've fed you a
whole year, even longer, with good grain, and now if I
sell you I shan't get enough for what we need. Maria
needs a shawl and a ribbon, mother lost her thimble, my
shirt needs silk for the embroidery. Then we need
matches, salt and soap, and blueing for the laundry. Yes,
and dye also. I need the price of four hens, but we could
only spare two and you are heavy enough to carry eight
miles."

"I wonder why they built Aciliu in that hole," Ileana
mused. "Even the sun rises later in the village than here

on the plains. Here I can see far, far away, in all direc-
tions. It makes me feel free. Oh Lord, there I go thinking
again and thinking makes me sad. Mother says thinking
isn't good for women. It isn't good for anybody but those
born for it, like the priest, the notary and the lawyers and
the judges, she says. A girl should get married and not
think, mother says. She must get a husband and children
—God bless them—and more work than your two hands
can do. If you think, you'll never get your work done,
she says. She wanted me to marry Anghel. Oh Lord! He
smells of sheep and of cheese. 'Fool of a scatterbrained
female,' father scolded, 'that man is a man. He has a
thousand head of sheep or more. You'll bathe in milk.
You'll feed on the fat of the land—you fool of a female.
He's big, strong as a bear. He'll give you male children.
Sturdy male children. He limps, yes. But he got that
fighting a wolf. He killed the wolf, Anghel did, you silly
female.' I told Anghel: 'Good man Anghel, if you care
for me, leave me in peace. I can not marry you.' He
looked at me with his big eyes—just stared at me and
said nothing. Then suddenly he jerked up his arm and
touched his eyes with the sleeve and ran away. He never
came again. He did not come to the dance either since
then. But I would like a man."

Ileana stopped, set her basket on the ground, shook
herself and stretched, as when getting out of bed. She
breathed deep, long breaths. Her lips were moist, tears

came into her eyes. There was a throbbing in her temples. Something welled up in her, rising to her throat. As if a hand were choking her. "Oh, God!" she cried. This outcry did not comfort her; it was the cry for a mate. For a man such as Bujor, or Padure or Ciungu. Those Haiducs. Those heroes who took from the rich and gave to the poor. Men with strong blood in them, as her grandfather Stan had told her. They were in her fancy ever since she could remember. Planted there by her grandfather, when she was a little child, and these men grew with her. They were in her blood and from within her they shamed the young men who courted her. For these young villagers were not like Bujor, the brave, handsome Bujor who took a young girl, Mironica, from the village and on his horse they flew into the mountains, to his cave which was richer than a Sultan's palace. "Your eyes are my heaven and my soul," he told Mironica. He gave her two male children. He slew bears and fed them the meat and rubbed their bodies with the kidney fat of the bears to make them strong.

Ileana resumed her walk and now she thought of home and of her grandfather who was seventy-five years old, but he was hale, sturdy as an oak and yet spoke to her and to the other children only with kind words. The old man never chided John when he was raging, but tried to quieten him with wise words. Ileana wondered at her father's uneven temper, because some days he was mild,

gentle as a lamb, but more often he was sullen and quar-
relsome. And he drank and then scolded for nothing and
raised his hand against whoever was near him. Only Maria
he never touched. The little girl was as sensitive as a
poplar leaf. Everybody she called "dear," and God she
called "dear Lord." These thoughts made Ileana cry. She
felt that herself and Maria were strangers in the family.
Even to the village they were strangers. She looked at the
great expanse of the plains, her heart ached with yearning.

Arrived on the state-road Ileana braided her hair,
put on her boots. She put on her straw hat, for the sun
was warm. Loaded wagons drawn by oxen moved slowly
over the dusty road. She went past them, on the wind side,
to avoid the dust. A young man smiled at her from the
top of his wagon, then he winked and pointed a place
near him, on the sacks. "Walking's faster," said Ileana.
The young fellow cracked his whip, smiled broadly.

3

I N the market place Ileana set her basket down between two peasant women who also had fowls for sale. She spread a rag on the pavement and placed the hens on it. The women were chattering noisily. On the opposite side of the narrow alley, through which the buyers circulated, were the Saxon women. They looked like large cones of garments, topped with round heads, broad smiling faces, framed in hair as light as the straw of their hats. They were selling stuffed geese, huge birds which lay with open beaks, their eyes half-covered with an opalescent film. The Saxon women sold ducks also, and hens, and an occasional rooster whose plumage shone in the sun. Further down were those who sold suckling pigs, pink, sleek animals that squealed, squinting small eyes.

The whole row was taken up by women vendors. The men were on the outskirts of the market place, where grain, forage and cattle were traded.

Where Ileana was the buyers were mostly city ladies. The better-to-do of these ladies were followed by stocky peasant servant girls carrying large baskets. The vendors called out loudly, praising their wares. "Here, good lady, fat hens! It'll roast so tender (pointing to a small pig) it'll melt on your tongue; (pointing to a goose) it's all fat and liver!"

Ileana said not a word. She watched the crowd. Very few men passed through this alley. Occasionally a lady would stop in front of Ileana and after glancing at her would stoop down and dig her fingers into the squawking hens. The two women near Ileana sold out and hurried off to do their own marketing. "Good luck to you, pretty one," each said to her on leaving. Two hours passed and Ileana wondered how much longer she would have to wait for a buyer. She almost burst out laughing watching a very fat lady who had several tiers of chin and a crop of moustaches under a flat, pasty nose, when suddenly a tall peasant emerged from the crowd and stood in front of her. He was a man of twenty-five to thirty, very sunburnt. He looked at her for a considerable time before he spoke. As he spoke he touched his moustache. His shirt-sleeve fell back from his tanned hand, revealing an arm as white as a girl's.

"Good morning, lovely one," he greeted.

"Good morning," answered Ileana.

"Fine hens you have there," the young man said looking straight at Ileana. She felt her eyes caught by his and held. She noticed his handsome face and the haughty posture of his head. Several ladies looked at the young man from the corners of their eyes and even slowed their steps.

As he was speaking to Ileana, in a deep, mellow, yet assertive voice, an elderly woman came up. She set down

her two baskets and wiped her face with the creton apron
which covered the woolen one. Ileana saw she was a
peasant woman, but one who did not work in the fields,
for her face was rosy under the large straw hat.

Without looking at the woman the young man said:
"Take these fine hens, *lele* Sandra."

"How will I carry the fowls, Serafim? The baskets
are heaped with things. Where could I put them, Mother
of the Lord?" She bent over the baskets, muttering to
herself.

"Did you ever see such nice hens, *lele* Sandra?" asked
Serafim, pointing to the hens.

"Oh yes, they're nice, but how will I carry them, I
ask myself. All I have is two hands, God bless you, Serafim, only two, and with these baskets full—" The woman
shrugged her shoulders.

"They must be worth more, but—will you take four
florins? What is your name?"

"My name is Ileana. But—four florins—" She blushed
crimson.

Sandra picked up the hens and weighed them in her
hands. She pinched their crops and felt them, her fingers
spreading the feathers and digging. One of the hens
squeaked, flapping its wings. "Hush, you old beast," muttered Sandra. She put them down near her baskets.

"If they would follow me like other decent animals,
I could tie a string to them and lead them, but hens are

such stupid creatures, Mother of the Lord," Sandra mumbled.

Serafim paid no attention to her. He searched in his wide, ornate leather belt, then held out four silver coins to Ileana. Sandra bent forward to look at the amount. Ileana tied the money in the corner of a handkerchief and stuck it in her sleeve.

Serafim came very close to her. Touching her arm he said: "If you would help *lele* Sandra—she can't carry the hens. I would myself, but see—I have this yoke and pitchforks."

Ileana took the hens, saying: "Willingly, of course."

Sandra picked up her two baskets and started off at a good pace. At intervals she called over her shoulder: "This way, girl, this way." Ileana followed on the woman's heels, yet Sandra kept repeating: "This way, girl, this way."

The sidewalk was crowded and because of the cumbersome things he carried Serafim followed the women at a little distance. He walked in the street, on the rough pavement, where fewer persons circulated. All the time he watched Ileana, craning his head.

A girl among a thousand, he thought.

At the bridge Sandra stopped to rest. Serafim caught up to them, just as she was saying to Ileana: "From here it is not far. Have you never seen the big house with the tile roof, near the state road? The one with the big tamu-rac in front of it, and the pigeons cooing underneath the roof of the large gate?"

"Yes, I have," answered Ileana. Then she smiled, saying: "The Raven's Nest they call it."

"Of course, that's it. The Raven's Nest. Serafim's name is Corbu—raven—that is to say," explained Sandra. "That's why people call him the Raven also."

"Am I as black as that, Ileana?" Serafim asked, mopping his face. He took off his hat and wiped the sweatband inside it. His hair was as black as a raven's feathers.

"Oh, no—not as black," answered Ileana, glancing at Serafim. Sandra buried her face in the apron, rubbing it. She mumbled something, but neither Ileana nor Serafim made out her words.

Now the three walked together, the streets here being almost empty. "We shall be home in a few seconds," said Serafim.

"With your legs under me I would be there already," Sandra retorted, puffing.

"Better if you were on wheels," laughed Serafim. Ileana glanced at Sandra's red face and smiled.

"Am I a lumber cart, then—that is to say," snapped Sandra, jerking the baskets on the crook of her arms. Then she said: "There it is, the gate. Look at those pigeons, girl. One must run through or they drop something on one's head."

Ileana looked at the large oaken gate, studded with

forged nails. A small door ornate with nails was cut in one of the wings. A cross formed part of the ornament in the upper half of it.

Serafim opened the door. As they entered the large courtyard a big mastiff ran towards them, barking heavily. Ileana stopped frightened. "Hector, be still," shouted Serafim. The dog jumped on him, whining.

"Listen to the big brute whistle," said Sandra, irritated. She kicked at the dog because he almost knocked her down.

"Anna, where are you?" she called, walking past a wide stone staircase. A young peasant girl came running. "Take them, my arms are falling off," snapped Sandra. The girl took the two baskets.

"Give me those hens now, girl," Sandra said. "Shall I let them loose here or what shall I do with them?" she asked, turning to Serafim.

"Let them loose—very well—so they'll run in the shade," answered Serafim.

"I will go now," said Ileana. "Good health," she greeted, turning towards the gate. Serafim took her hand. "Oh, no! Come in and rest yourself a little and eat with us."

Sandra untied the hens and swung them in the air. "So!" she shouted, clapping her hands. The hens flew noisily towards the barn. Two large roosters scolded, running towards them.

"Thank you, but I have some purchases to make yet

and I have to meet some of our villagers," Ileana said.

"It is early. You have time for everything. Stay and eat with us," insisted Serafim. He held Ileana's hand. She blushed, at a loss what to say. She did not resent his retaining her hand. His voice was pleasant and he spoke so clearly. His words were rich as his hands were strong, but not coarse. He did not speak like the city people, yet he chose his words and used them more correctly than the peasants.

Ileana noticed that while holding her hand firmly, he did not squeeze it, nor did he pull her as he invited her to stay. He merely repeated: Stay and eat with us."

Sandra had followed the girl who took the baskets, and now she was heard saying: "Broil the fish on the embers, but watch you don't burn them. Did you boil the eggs? Slice them in the bowl—on the table, not before. They get blue if they stay long in the sorrel soup. Bring the sour milk from the cellar, Anna."

Yielding to Serafim's invitation Ileana went with him into the kitchen. A large, clean kitchen, where Sandra was spreading the tablecloth. She looked like a very busy housewife now, with her flowered handkerchief in place of the straw hat, tied carefully under her chin. Serafim called to her: "*Lele* Sandra, I am going to show Ileana our garden. Call us when the table is ready." Without looking up Sandra answered: "There is time for the garden, of course. The fish is wriggling in the bucket yet. I'll shout for you when everything is ready." Then she mumbled under her breath.

Serafim and Ileana traversed the yard, crossed through the barn—the floor was hard and smooth—emerging through a small door into the garden. In the barn the sparrows fluttered and chirped noisily. Ileana heard the stamping of horses in the stalls near by. The light in the garden seemed to her stronger than in the yard for having just come out the barn, which was dark. In truth the garden was lighter than the yard owing to the shimmering green. A strong fragrance of vegetables drenched the still, warm air. They walked through an alley of raspberry bushes, the bees humming about them.

Serafim put his arm around Ileana. Bending to her he said: "You are very lovely," and holding her close to him he put his hand on her breast. Despite her surprise Ileana had somehow expected his embrace. His voice quivered with desire, his eyes burned. She struggled to free herself so she felt his strength the more. The strength of his arm, and the force of his passion. In her effort to escape him she tore the silken string that held his collar band closed; her hand slipped into his shirt, touching the curly hair on his chest. With a little cry she withdrew her hand, panting: "Oh, let me go."

"And this damage to my shirt?" Serafim whispered, holding her tightly.

"Leave me in peace—it is your fault," chided Ileana.

"No, no! It is your fault. You are too lovely. Let me kiss you. Like this, put your hand in my shirt." He slipped his hand to her breasts.

"Kiss me then—and let me be," stammered Ileana.

Serafim kissed her on the lips. She suffered his embrace, his burning closeness, his lips on hers, eager, hungry for her, and his passion melted her will. Her strength was leaving her, the wish to keep it was gone already. She felt enveloped by this male who came on her like a hot wind. Close to his breast, tightly held in his arms he was carrying her.

The grass was soft, above spread the canopy of thick foliage and it sank down on her and it rose from her with his breath, his breath on her face, on her neck, from the heaving of his chest, warm, passion-filled, and she groaned on the sinking and rising of it, in the exquisite melting of her body. "Oh—oh—mother—mother mine!" She was not speaking—it was her breath, her answer to his living weight—she breathed into him, she was in him. He drank her. He swallowed her in the furnace of his passion. She was no more Ileana, she was Serafim. "Serafim—mother mine—Serafim," her breath articulated and she heard the foliage say those words, the foliage, sinking and rising, rising and sinking. And then —then the green canopy descended on her.

4

SANDRA called from the garden gate. She called repeatedly: "Serafim, come! Serafim, where are you?" He heard her, her voice coming nearer the shelter where he and Ileana were. Sandra called and scolded: "Has the ground swallowed them, Mother of the Lord? To make me tramp after them in this noon heat." Serafim whispered to Ileana: "I will bring the food out here. We shall eat alone —we two." He got up. Rounding some bushes and a patch of high corn, he came on the path—behind Sandra. "You have a healthy voice, *lele* Sandra. Where are you going?" he asked cheerily.

"Oh! you come like a ghost. Where am I going? That's a fine question! I'm looking for last Monday— did you see it, Serafim? Where is your hat? Look at your trousers! Did you kneel in the grass to say your prayers? Ha-ha-ha! Well, where is the girl? Come in, the fish'll get charred on the embers. Is the girl flown off? I've set a plate for her."

Sandra turned, looking about. Serafim smoothed his shirt, looked at the green spots on his trousers. Then he grasped her hand, crying: "Come, *lele* Sandra, you'll faint from hunger. Look at you, you'll fall in my arms." "Ptiu," Sandra made, wrenching her hand away, mumbling:

"Where can that girl be?" But she followed Serafim, muttering to herself.

In the kitchen Serafim washed his face and combed his hair. Sandra, her hands crossed over her apron, stood watching him. Serafim turned to her suddenly, crying: "Goo-goo." Then, very earnestly: "Spit out three times, *lele* Sandra, or you'll cast the evil eye on me." But as Sandra only stared at him without even blinking, he feigned jabbing his finger in her eye and cried, "Boo-hoo." At this Sandra did spit out three times, but instead of saying the abracadabra against the evil eye she crossed herself and ran off. Serafim caught her. *"Lele* Sandra," he said, "put up the food for me and Ileana, I'll carry it to the garden. We are going to eat there, the two of us. It is lovely in the garden, *lele* Sandra."

Sandra put on a broad smile and sang out sweetly: "I understand, my lambkin. Yes, yes. The little pigeon is tired. Here, here, in the blinking of an eye." She ran to the table, to the cupboard, the fireplace, the oven. Serafim planted himself before the mirror, curled his moustache and smiled at himself.

"Ready—everything," announced Sandra after a short time. Serafim took the basket and went off. Sandra came running after him with a blanket. "Take this, Serafim, for the little pigeon to sit on—and you too." Serafim lifted his arm—both his hands being taken—Sandra put the blanket under it.

He found Ileana standing under a big apple tree. With wondering eyes she watched him coming. He smiled and hurried toward her. "We'll eat alone, my little heart. What are you looking at with such big eyes?" he asked. Ileana wrinkled her forehead, then she smiled. She took the blanket and spread it out on the grass.

But when they sat down her eyes assumed again that expression of wonder. Serafim began telling her about Sandra's drolleries. Then he said: "She is as good as new bread. Her heart is as big as that barn. But her tongue goes its own way. By itself. Here, little heart, take this piece—you see, she gave us the middle part of the fish, and look at these potatoes. She boils them so they never burst, and yet are mealy to melt in your mouth."

He is good-hearted also, thought Ileana. Serafim took a choice morsel of fish, blew on it and held it to her mouth. "Open your mouth—don't close your eyes," he said laughing. Bending forward he wiped the corner of her mouth, gently, with his finger.

Ileana ate without fully relishing the flavor of the food. Her thoughts seemed unwilling to light on anything present. Not even on Serafim, who offered her now a morsel of fish, now of potato, always blowing to cool it. Her thoughts were on her home. They were there in the days that had passed and in those nights when the fire of love flamed up in her and tore her out of sleep. Like a strong hand. Those nights when everybody slept but herself and the nightingale—she consumed by desire, and the nightingale stirring the night with its clear song. The nights when Anghel Bradutz, the limping giant, or Danila, the priest's son, should have come to her, to quench that fire in her. On such nights loving was no sin. She had known then that loving was no sin. Now her father came to her mind, frightening her, for she understood his look, it gravely revealing to her that he knew what had happened to her. He shook his gaunt, gnarled finger at her. And so her thoughts and her feelings became jumbled, and rushed on. Then came voids—total eclipses of feelings and thoughts—gaps in her awareness of reality. And Serafim, the garden, her very self sank into that void —vanishing—only her heart fluttered above the precipice like a bird lost in storm.

Then her awareness revived, cuttingly clear. Coming with the revelation that she was no longer Ileana of this morning, Ileana of the days and years past. She was another. A stranger to her parents, to her brothers and to her sister. A stranger to everybody save to herself. And she felt alone, like a dead tree on a snow-covered plain. Even Serafim, especially he, did not know her. She had yielded herself to him—but it was not he who took her, because he knew her not. It was the mate that had come to her, on the noon, in the summer warmth of the garden. It was life that came, warm, crushing almost, penetrating her entirely.

Serafim fed Ileana as if she were helpless. The same fork, now to her mouth, now to his. Ileana took the food, glancing at Serafim now and then, yet her eyes seemed not to see him.

Serafim filled two glasses with wine. He held up the glass for Ileana to look at the tiny bubbles rising in the wine. "Smell it, my little heart, smell it," he urged. He held the glass close to her face. The fragrance of the vineyards was in the wine, and the chill of stone-vaulted cellars burst forth from the powdery drops that sprayed her face.

"Let us drink to your health and happiness, my little heart," he invited. They drank. Ileana wondered if she were happy—really. The aroma of the cool wine was part of it; the good feeling of quenched thirst and of hunger satisfied was happiness—almost. Serafim's words, the deep vibrant voice that carried them—they were in the happiness. Yes, and the sudden outstanding of the garden in clarity, in light and color, in this pattern spread before her eyes was happiness.

Serafim picked strawberries, large, luscious berries, black-red with ripeness, and put them in her glass. He crushed them in the wine to yield their fragrance, their earth-flavor, so she might drink them. He held up the glass to her lips and she sipped the wine, thinking, "He is attending to me like a mother." Now he was no longer a stranger to her. "He is like Bujor," she said to herself, "he was in my thoughts all my life." As she drank, in small sips, he caressed her hair, then he embraced her and kissed her wine-moist lips. He played with her hands, patted them, pulled her fingers, bent them and straightened them and pretended to bite them—one, then two at a time. He put her palms on his face, then kissed them, in the middle and near the wrists. He pressed her tightly to him, fondling her breasts. He whispered in the shell of her ear, his lips and breath warm. Shivers pattered over her throat, ran through her body like new blood. He whispered: "Good angels brought you to me—my little heart." Her eyes trembled, wondering at his words. "I was always here," she thought. Then her vision rose, emerging to the sharply outstanding reality of the moment—and she understood. These words of his made her understand that she was a self apart from this man— that they were two beings apart—he with ties of his own, as she with hers, attaching her to parents, to home and to the village. Ties that held them apart—hopelessly apart —yet this handsome man, this ardent mate was at this moment close to her. He was in her very being. She felt him in her innermost, with his strong life added to her own. Then she doubted her feeling, and it was as if her dream had come to her, strong as reality, but it was her dream. She spoke to herself and to her dream at the same time. Clearly she heard her own words: "My mind is all mixed up."

As if her mouth spoke by itself—she felt her lips moving.

Serafim again raised the glass to Ileana's lips. She sipped the wine and sucked the berry-meat into her mouth. Then the pattern of the garden stretched out of shape, and she said: "Serafim, I'm getting drunk. I've to walk home, across the plain, but I'm getting drunk. My hands, look, they pull my arms. They are so heavy. Look." She lifted her hands, but they fell limply at her side.

Serafim laughed, playing with the ringlets on her nape, kneading the smooth, firm flesh of her neck and biting it, and laughing more at her soft wriggling and pouting. Then he kissed her mouth, while she pinched his face ineffectually. After a while Serafim reached for the wine bottle, so she, being free, commenced to speak. "I must buy things for home—don't you see, Serafim— but I am getting drunk. And to walk on the state road and across the plain—the plain—the plain is wide—wide —the road across it—from end to end—straight—like a shingle in the grass." She laughed, repeating: "A shingle in the grass. It is not a shingle, it is a road. Across the plain. The cows graze there. It isn't a shingle—it's a road." She laughed, swaying backward and forward. Serafim laughed with her.

This laughter lightened her mind. She began to sing softly, the song smoothing the laughter from her face. Her voice, clear and beautiful, flowed evenly. It cheered

Serafim. He put his arms around her, leaned his head against hers and sang with her. She began without words, but he strewed words in the melody and she picked them up, so the two repeated them in unison:

"You will gather flowers, dear one, in the herbage,
And I will gather strawberries in your bosom."

5

SANDRA came again to the garden, calling: "Serafim
—you hear—Serafim? The men have come to load the
sacks." She pattered towards them on the garden path,
calling. Serafim answered bruskly: "Go, *lele* Sandra. Go
tell them—when I come they shall see me."

"Ptiu! Wise words from an empty head," mumbled
Sandra turning on her heels. But when she ran off like
that, Serafim remembered about the wheat that was to
be carted away, and the good profit from the sale, and
that it had to be loaded and sent off. He sobered up. He
shook himself like a horse out of harness.

"I must go, Ileana. You see that I must go, don't you?
They will load the sacks—you wait for me here—and I'll
drive you as far as the plain. The sun is high yet—wait
here." His voice was almost commanding.

Ileana watched him walk away hastily, his head gliding over the raspberry bushes. When he was gone she
lay down on the blanket and closed her eyes.

After an hour or so Serafim returned to find Ileana
sleeping. For an instant he was annoyed thinking that he
had to drive Ileana to the plain. But when she opened her
eyes and looked at him, his annoyance vanished. He
drove her into the city to make her purchases, then to the

road on the plain. At parting he gave Ileana a large linen
handkerchief, embroidered heavily. It was scented with
mint and quince, for Sandra kept sweet-mint and quinces
in the linen chests.

"I'll come to find you in the market, little heart, next
week. I'll think of you day and night," he said.

The plain glowed with the late afternoon sun. It lay
like a soft carpet, wide as the world, under a clear blue
bell as wide. Ileana walked briskly on the clay road, with
her boots on. She felt terribly alone on this endless plain.
That was her first relation to it, and it seemed a long
time ago since she had seen it. Yes, there was a great
distance, a vast stretch of time, between the morning and
the present. Ileana did not try to understand that feeling.
She hurried on, as if running away, as if avoiding that
understanding, which in truth was chasing after her,
threatening to overtake her. And suddenly it did reach
her, like a strong voice, shouting at her: "Give account.
Where have you been?" She stopped, mechanically reaching into her sleeve, whence she pulled Serafim's handkerchief. She spread it and looked at it, at the fine embroidery that made it heavy. Then she scanned the plain, near
and far, as if in search of something, murmuring: "Oh
Lord, I have sinned," and began to cry. She started off
again, and hurrying along she cried freely, the handkerchief crumpled in her hand.

She heard singing. She glanced back. A wagonful of peasants came on, but the trotting of the horses she could not hear, only the singing of the peasants, louder and louder, as the wagon was nearing her. Quickly she dried her eyes. She moistened a corner of the handkerchief in her mouth and rubbed her face with it. As the wagon came near she stepped off the road. A man hailed her: "You may crowd in amongst us." The women also called: "Fly in, big girl." But the driver did not stop, he only clicked his tongue, winking. He was more than gay, he was drunk. Ileana waved to the women who stretched their arms out as if to catch her. The song of the peasants trailed after them for a long time, then it was torn, and after a few soft snatches the song was lost. The wagon grew smaller and smaller with the distance, then it also vanished, for it sank with the road leading into the bowl where the village lay. Ileana cried no more.

6

ILEANA arrived home in time for the milking. The two cows stood in the yard, chewing the cud, waiting to have their udders eased. Ileana changed her Sunday clothes, took the stool and a large pail and began milking one of the cows. Her head against the warm flank of the animal, she inhaled the odor of the milk foaming in the pail. On the evening air trailed the scent of wood-smoke.

Chiva was busy with supper. The cabbage soup was boiling in a large kettle suspended over the fire. In another round-bottomed kettle bubbled the *mamaliga* over a tripod. This thick corn mush was almost ready for "stirring" because the bubbles were large and burst with little puffing noises. Little Maria followed her mother at every step, chattering and asking questions. Chiva's perspiring face smiled occasionally as she answered, but she never stopped one instant from her work. She set the plates on the table, the large earthen bowl, the wooden spoons, and the knives and three-pronged iron forks. With her teeth she snapped off a bit of thread from the spool for cutting the *mamaliga*. She put the thread near the round board on which the *mamaliga* would be laid.

When Ileana brought in the milk Chiva helped her

strain it through a cheese-cloth in a wire sieve. "How was the market, daughter?" she asked.

"Good, thank God," answered Ileana.

"How much did the hens fetch?"

"Four silvers."

"What? Four silvers?" asked Chiva, amazed.

"Yes! They were fat and quite heavy."

"The Lord be blessed! Why, daughter, that's twice what we expected." Ileana only nodded, saying nothing.

7

NIGHT had almost fallen when the men came in. One-eyed John washed his hands noisily. Filling his mouth with water from an earthen jug until his cheeks swelled out, he spluttered it over his soapy hands. The boys helped each other, spilling water in turn from the jug. They washed face and neck, smoothed their hair with wet hands. John did not wash his face. He just passed his wet hand over his eyes and twirled his moustaches several times. They left a muddy pool outside the kitchen door.

The family sat down to table, each member in the habitual place. John crossed himself and all the others did likewise. He bent his head murmuring: "Lord God, bless our daily bread as Thou hast blest the loaves and fishes in the desert. Amen." The family repeated Amen in chorus, all crossing themselves.

They ate noisily. John sat on the bench against the wall, between the windows, the boys on each side of him. Chiva sat opposite her husband, Ileana at her right and Maria at her left. When something was needed Ileana got up and fetched it. John did not look at her at the table, but when she got up his eyes followed her, peering from under bushy eyebrows. Once he seemed about to say something, but he only pulled at his moustache. No one spoke a word. At length Chiva said: "John, the two hens fetched four silvers. Think of it, four silvers!" she exulted.

"So," muttered John, glancing at Ileana. He pulled from his belt the pipe and a pouch made from pig's bladder. He stuffed the pipe, put a bit of punk on the flint and with a leaf-shaped steel struck the stone rapidly, several times. When the punk took fire he blew on it until it glowed and laid it in the bowl of the pipe. He began sucking at the stumpy stem vigorously.

The boys went out to see about the oxen. In the yard Nicholas began to sing at the top of his voice. Ileana was cleaning away the dishes. Chiva leaned on the table, her arms folded, sweet fatigue in her body, her mind blinking sleepily. John sat leaning against the wall, staring into vacancy, smoking furiously. Occasionally he spat on the floor, behind the bench, and stroked his moustache. Suddenly he jerked up his head. Michael, sitting on the kitchen door sill, was playing on the shepherd's fife. Nicholas and Ileana hummed the tune. The girl's voice rolled like a bird's trill. John's face brightened. The melancholy music was occasionally rent by the clatter of dishes being ranged on the shelf by Ileana. John scowled each time that the noise cut in. Then he stretched, sighing. He leaned over the table: "Go to bed, Maria, you're falling asleep sitting there. Go, child. Say your prayers! Don't fall asleep without your prayers," he said.

The little girl, her face already expanded with sleep, got up slowly, mumbling: "Good night, dear father, good night, dear mother," and staggered out of the room. John tapped the ashes from his pipe, striking it against the corner of the table. He looked at his wife for several moments, then he said: "How is that about the four silvers for the hens, Chiva? I don't understand it. Who would pay so much for two fowls, even in the city? How is that, about the four silvers? Did the girl tell you?"

"No, John. I did not ask her, but then—they were fat and heavy. That she told me," answered Chiva.

"They weren't fatter nor heavier than those I sold last time—for two silvers. And I haggled with the woman. She pinched and dug her fingers into the poor hens for a long time and weighed them in her hand before she paid the money. And then she growled, 'You peasants rob us city folk, you do, yes, you do,' lashing me with her look. And here—the girl gets four silvers! I can't make it out, woman. No, I can't make it out! But I think about it. You never use your head."

Chiva wondered what there was in this about using her head. She was surprised at the good price, in a way, but then she thanked the Lord for it and that, for her, closed the affair. So she did not answer John, simply because she knew not what to say. But to soothe his irritation she smiled. John frowned at her, refilling his pipe. But instead of lighting it he snatched it out of his mouth and slammed it on the table, demanding: "What's happened to the silvers, woman?"

Smiling as before, Chiva answered: "Ileana bought soap and matches and blueing for the laundry; and she got some silk for her shirt laying there unfinished, and wool for Maria's aprons." Her face flushed as she added: "And she bought a shawl for me, for Sunday wear."

"So! Basta! That's all," snapped John. "I work like a beast of burden to feed the fowls and then—we buy knickknacks, adornments for the women folk. We men —we can have the crust of dirt on our skins. Our skin is tough and that's good enough for us, working until we drop, in all kinds of weather. Michael will go into the army soon, then I'll have to do his share also. These hands of mine. How many lives do you think I have, woman? One of these days I'll drop, like a dog, dying in the mud. And—" But he did not continue. He fell silent suddenly. He was tired, very tired. He might not have spoken at all but for the momentary vigor which the singing of the children gave him. But now that they stopped singing John felt more tired than before. He could not talk. Even his thoughts became jumbled. So he sat there, scowling at his fists on the table. Gradually, however, as an object coming out of a fog, from his jumbled thoughts emerged Ileana. With her unholy beauty and her unholy voice she

came out and stood clearly in the center of his turgid
thoughts. She bewitched somebody to buy her two hens
for the price of four. Yes, yes—the work of the Unclean
One, the devil. Yes, yes. John groaned aloud.

Chiva watched his haggard face and his creased forehead, now all sweated. His large fist on the table, black
and knotted, his pipe at his elbow. Her heart cried in
pain for him, for his troubled soul. He was, indeed, she
felt, not only husband to her, father of four children; but
somehow, a child of hers. She cried inwardly for help
from heaven, help that she might give him, to cleanse
his soul of dark thoughts. A long time, while watching
John, she prayed inwardly for this heavenly help. Then
her face brightened and she spoke to him: "John, this was
a good day of God. A blessed day. We got up with the
sun. You went into the fields with the boys and worked.
I stayed at home, I washed the week's laundry, hilled up
the potatoes in the garden, took the hemp to the swamp,
laid it in and weighted it down with stones. Then I
chopped wood for three days—yes, three days at least it
will last me, and after all the chores about the house I
prepared supper. Now my body is tired. I can't hold my
eyes open. But God gave us sleep to rest us. Let us go to
bed, John. Tomorrow, on a new day from the Lord, we'll
get up new ourselves. Come, John. Come to bed. The
children have gone to sleep already." She rose and going
up to John put her hands under his armpits as if to lift

him from the bench. John groaned and got up, leaning on the table.

The coarse hempen bed sheets smelt fresh from the sun. John and Chiva crossed themselves, said the Lord's prayer and lay down. For a short while Chiva heard John's breathing and the clock's tick-tack. Then she fell asleep.

8

THE early morning, when yet the sky held some of the night in its depths, when the dawn came slowly over the fields and gardens, melting the shadows in its path, was ever new to Chiva. Standing in the garden gate, facing the east, whence the light came, she prayed, imploring for the new day, light in the soul and cheer in the heart of all mankind and of each member of her family. Then she would kneel on the ground and bow down, touching the earth with her forehead three times, while crossing herself. After that the day began. The hens came clamoring for food. The pig squealed, the oxen stirred in the stalls, rattling their chains. The cows, never shut in in the summer, came to the kitchen door, chewing the cud or licking their muzzles with their long file-rough tongues. They stood there waiting for the pinch of salt which Ileana gave them in her palm before she milked them. The boys were combing the oxen, pulling angrily at the burdocks caught in the animals' tails. But the oxen, curving their heavy necks, rolled their eyes contentedly.

John was greasing the hay wagon, his mind dark. Again those dreams have tormented his sleep. He was muttering to himself: "These axles are bone-dry. No wonder they squeaked so. Might have caught fire. Bah! Couldn't catch fire. Those oxen will never heat up the axles." Things were in his way wherever he moved, so he kicked at them, flung them about. He picked up a scythe; it was dull as a stick. He took a small anvil, stuck it in the ground near the barn and sitting down began hammering the edge of the scythe. The strokes resounded in the yard. The rooster scolded at the noise. John spat out, hammering away furiously. This reminded him of the old peasant saying, "An unloved woman is like an unwhetted scythe." Sluggishly his thoughts reverted to Chiva. It was a long time since he had approached his wife. Always too tired. She was warm in bed, her body full and warm as the oven, but he was too tired. Often she caressed him, timidly, perhaps sleepily, saying: "I hope, John, you'll have a good night's rest. I've prayed for you. I always do, John." "Much it helps," John muttered. "At twenty, at thirty, even at thirty-five I wasn't worked out, but now—"

Ileana walked by him, her shirt-skirts flaring out as she walked. "Look at her," muttered John, "that swaying of hers—her haunches—" He watched her from under his thick eyebrows, thinking again: An unloved woman is like an unwhetted scythe. "Let her get married, by thunder, let her get married," he growled. "Let her get a man and ... Those haunches of hers. Like a fine, young mare. Her shoulders too. Swelled out, her haunches, like—like a grape." He battered the scythe with the hammer, then he mumbled: "Get thee behind me, Satan!"

9

THEY had breakfast, warm milk and cold *mamaliga*. The boys gobbled noisily, their wooden spoons clattering against the earthen bowls. When they had finished John and the boys went out. The oxen were yoked, waiting in the middle of the yard. "Smear some tar around their eyes and muzzles, Michael," John said, pointing at the oxen. "They'll be eaten up by flies. Quick, get to it, boy," he shouted. Michael smeared the tar from a wooden bucket, with a rag. Around the eyes, he was careful, using his hand. The oxen blinked. Standing up in the middle of the wagon John called to the oxen: "Tscha, Paicu! Hie, Pondor," and swung his whip over them. The beasts pulled off, heavily.

The hay was good that year. The windrows were heavy, a rich purplish green. John and the boys stirred the hay a little to shake off the dew. "One hour of sun will dry it," Michael said. By the time they got to the end of the field they could begin loading where they started.

The three of them worked well, with their wooden forks, the prongs smooth as ivory. Work in the morning was always pleasant, particularly to the boys. It stretched the muscles until they tingled. Then came the first prickling of fatigue and they looked forward to the noon hour. When noon came, they sprinkled their faces with cold water from a spring. They soaked their bandanas and swaddled their heads and put their large felt hats on the wet bandana. They sat down in the shadow of the loaded wagon and ate the lentil or bean soup from an earthen pot, each scooping it with a wooden spoon. They had fresh pickles also, pickled in brine, seasoned with cherry leaves, caraway twigs and thyme. To finish the meal they chewed a piece of hard bread, thick-rinded but sweet, with the flavor of the whole wheat. Then they stretched out, covering their faces with their hats, and slept half an hour.

John closed his eyes but did not sleep. He lay there, the warm waves from the sunny fields rolling over him. They came, warm and fragrant, rustling the hay under his head, ever so gently. Occasionally a bird cried near by, then all was still. In the torpor of fatigue and the full stomach John's thoughts were lazy but persistent. They rested on Chiva, lazily. Yes, the good woman worked hard, almost as hard as himself, John thought. Yet—her body did not dry up or shrink. It was full and warm, Chiva's body. She moved about the house cheerfully, her face always flushed, her skirt tucked up in her belt, so her strong calves showed. Sleepily, John thanked God for this life-companion He had given him. They were yoked together and they pulled and pulled through the years. His parents came to his mind. In their old age,

when, after many years of pulling together in the yoke of
their lives, they were tired, so tired that when going to bed
they prayed: "Lord, we are ready, send the messenger
Gabriel to gather us unto Thee, Amen," for they longed
for the long, long sleep. They went peacefully, each saying when his turn came: "Son, I leave you in God's care.
Live righteously, until your hour comes."

John did not wish to go yet, but life was hard. Hard
enough for the body, yet harder for his soul. His soul was
very burdened. He sighed deeply, his thought on Ileana
now. And he appealed to Chiva for support, and lo!—as
he appealed to his wife she became blended, she became
one with Ileana, her tucked up shirt revealing the young,
firm calves of Ileana. They flashed pink as she walked,
her full thighs swaying.

John sat up quickly, rubbed his eyes and crossed
himself, gasping: "Get thee behind me, Satan!" Then
his very insides got stirred up as if a storm had broken
out in him, to issue out of him in a hoarse laughter. The
laughter still shaking him, he muttered: "An unloved
woman is like an unwhetted scythe." Sweat broke out
over his whole body as he jumped up. Grabbing his fork
he shouted: "Get up, lazy ones, don't sleep away the day!
Set to—load her up!" But the wagon was loaded already,
so they rolled the hay into hillocks, John working furiously, muttering: "He's after my soul, the black enemy
of man."

10

SERAFIM CORBU was one of those peasants who use cunning and intelligence to promote their own interest. He had both in good measure. As only son of a rich peasant from Sugag he was well fed in his young years, well advised by his parents, yet pampered. He always had money in his belt, and on Christmas and Easter he was dressed in new clothes from boots to hat. He grew up into a strong, handsome young man. The girls and the young women admired him and desired him. Aware of his attractiveness he assumed a reserved, even cold attitude towards them. But he burned the more for them, being of a passionate nature, and selfish to boot. So when he was alone with a young woman, he never curbed his **desire.** He could not endure being thwarted once in the throes of aroused passion. If cunning, cajoling and flattery proved futile, he used force. Thus it happened that before he was called to do military service, he had violated several girls in the mountains and stolen into the life of three young couples.

Luckily the girls were engaged and married their "chosen men" soon after the occurrence. The young women "had only God and their conscience" to witness their sin. And so all would have gone as smoothly as oil,

but for the fact that one of the young women fell des-
perately in love with Serafim. In her wild jealousy she
spied on him and found out about his relations with the
other two women, both married as she was herself. So
one day, driven by jealousy, this young wife threatened to
reveal everything, not only to her husband but to the
other betrayed men also. Serafim, though strong as a
bear, was not hero enough, not even in fancy, to meet
three enraged husbands. He called upon his cunning.
Facing the situation squarely, weighing it carefully, he
decided that pleading with the woman would aggravate
matters. He must subdue her. Knowing that she loved
him, he decided to be firm with her. Yet he must assert
himself in a manner agreeable to the woman. And as he
was soon to leave the village for the army, he decided
that if she were pacified now, his absence would take
care of the rest. So he took the woman by the hand, made
her sit down; not on his lap—that he thought too hasty
—but on the bench, at his side. He spoke to her in his
deepest voice.

"Look you, Radutza," he said. "I speak from the
heart. You are as lovely as a day of spring. You are
healthy and strong. You have good mountain blood in
you. But you get weak in your head because of your
jealousy, and so you can't see my love for you. Now, just
hear me, dear. Did I ever come to you empty-handed?
Have I ever come like a thief—to steal? Was ever my

heart cold when yours was burning? Did I ever betray to
any mortal soul, by sign or by word, what was between
us? Have I spoken your name but in whispers and to
any living creature but yourself? No, by all the saints,
no! So, then, why this and that, angry words and threats
from you? You want to do so and so. I will tell the world,
I will tell their husbands. I will this and that, you throw
in my face. Have I changed in my love for you? Are my
eyes angry when I look at you? Is my heart cold when I
embrace you? (Here he took her around; she did not
resist.) Am I weak in my love to you? (Here he put his
hand to her breast.) Did I chew up your lips and leave
you with your desire to burn you up? (Here he put his
face close to hers, his lips almost on hers, but not kissing.) Don't I quench the fire in you? (Here she quivered.) Don't I give you all the manly force in me?
('Serafim!' she panted.) Then—(firmly)—why do you
rage in ugly words? Why do you sour your blood? Why
do you maim your face with such anger? (She hid her
face against his chest.) Don't you know that it will
dry up your love? Don't you know that your breasts
—now firm as apples and white as snow—will shrivel
up and get to look like corn husks? (Here he strained
her to him.) I love you, Radutza, from the nails of your
toes to the tips of your hair. Now, I will say, it is true
that I went to Stancutza and to Veta—but when? When
your husband was at home with a broken leg. And whom

did I seek in their arms? You! You! For while I loved
them I closed my eyes to cheat myself. But did I suc-
ceed? No, no, no! They don't kiss as you do, they don't
embrace as you do, they don't cling to me as you. They
haven't your fire—neither of them. Neither of them
groans, nor cries, nor bites, nor scratches as you do. When
I leave them I am cold and hungry for love, but when I
leave you the marrow in my bones sings. When I leave
them I feel cheated and robbed. I lose good nights which
the Lord gave me to love in. I lose the days too, because
they are heavy and I cannot work, or eat, or drink, for
the thought of you."

Radutza was open to his words as the day is open to
sight. The creases on her forehead vanished. Her lips
filled with blood. The corners of her mouth raised. Her
eyes lighted up. She put up her radiant face, whispering:
"Are your words true, Serafim? Yes, yes—they are. I believe you! My dear love! My life! The light of my eyes!
I am yours—soul and body—I am yours!" She was his.

Soon after this reconciliation Serafim left the village
for the army. "The saints will keep us for each other and
protect our love," he said to Radutza when taking leave.
She was pale as wax and cried. But Serafim found in the
city servant girls, young peasant lassies, gullible and thirsty
for love. He forgot Radutza or else he did not miss her.
Then he became friends with a young fellow, son of a
well-to-do merchant. Both had money to buy tit-bits, and

the life in the army, with little work and full bellies, made them stronger even. They planned for their future. The merchant's son said to Serafim: "You have a good head, you're cunning as a fox, why should you spend your life in a mountain village? Get money from your father, buy a house on the outskirts of the city and trade in wool and wheat. You can get rich, with a head like yours."

"Yes, yes, you are right—by Saint George—you speak like a judge," Serafim said to his friend. And when his father came to see him, he told him of his plans. The elder man was cautious. He shook his head, saying: "My boy, would you leave your father and mother to a lonely age?" But the young men took him to a restaurant, fed him roasted chicken, white bread and strong wine. They became gay, sang together, and the old man cried from happiness. They won him over, both talking at great speed, and they even kissed him when they were good and drunk. When he came again they showed him a place owned by an old Saxon. The place was for sale, but the Saxon was not quite ready to leave it. "Not yet, Roumanian men, not yet. Maybe in a year, maybe in two," he said.

Serafim's father was a shrewd peasant. He looked at the house, at the stone barns, at the buffalo-cows, whose milk is sweet and thick as cream, at the big garden and at the granaries built on stone pillars, without a twitch on his bronzed face. But when he saw the vaulted cellars, cool and drenched with the odor of many years' vintages, cellars such as he had never seen before, he pulled his son by the sleeve, betraying his covetous feeling. That settled it. Serafim and his friend had little to do after that to get him to put up the money.

So, when Serafim left the army, they bought the place, deeded to his name. His parents came to see him, twice a year, and stayed one week each time, but they preferred living in Sugag. They were proud of Serafim, however, because he managed well, was prospering and gaining not only wealth but reputation as a shrewd wheat merchant.

On the very day when Serafim met Ileana (he had seen her twice before that, but she was with her mother and he with his future father-in-law) he settled the last points about the dowry of his future wife. His prospective father-in-law was rich and the bride's dowry considerable. Yet each time that Serafim visited them during the year of courtship, he extracted more from the girl's father.

Saveta was comely enough, but the constant haggling over the dowry made her parents opine that Serafim was as interested in her possessions as he was in her person. However, Saveta being their only child and in love with Serafim, the parents gave in to the suitor's demands. Besides, Serafim never came empty-handed. He showered

gifts on Saveta, craftily aware that his generosity was
"taking money from the belt and putting it under the
pillow," as Sandra said. For Sandra knew her employer
"to the core of his heart." She knew that second to himself Serafim loved women, knew that "when he set his
eyes on one, she was his." In her heart, being past the
years of snatched carnal pleasures, she admired him,
though outwardly she grumbled, as becomes a trusted
servant.

II

W H E N Serafim returned from accompanying Ileana, Sandra bustled about the house, with a serious mien, mumbling to herself. If Sandra knew Serafim, he was no less able to read her every gesture. He smiled watching her and, to increase her irritation—so she would burst out in words—he set to playing his tricks. Whenever he heard her coming into the room he ran to the mirror, stood peering into it, smiling at himself, twirling his moustache and patting his hair. Even when the table was set for supper, Sandra waiting for him to sit down, Serafim did not budge from the mirror. That was the last straw. Sandra burst out at last: "Fine, fine! You are swelling in your feathers like a turkey-cock. Licking yourself like a tomcat. All you need is a red fez on your head."

Serafim laughed. "Then what? I would be a Turk or a monkey, hain, *lele* Sandra?"

"Mother of the Lord, you can be both with no harm to your cockiness," snapped Sandra.

"Is that so?" cried Serafim rushing up to her, and taking her around he whirled her about several times, then sat her down on the chair at the table.

"Oh—oh—you wild buck, let me be, let me be—for

shame!" she cried. That meant peace. Serafim quit hovering about her instantly, becoming serious. As serious as the saint on the icon and as stiff. Stiffly he sat down and stiffly crossed himself, beginning in a sing-song: "Our Father who art in Heaven, give us this day our daily bread." Sandra folded her hands, mumbling after him, her head bowed.

They ate in silence. It was usually at the evening meal that Sandra reported to her master about the household affairs. Serafim trusted both her honesty and her judgment. He enjoyed even her scolding about his "women chasing" and her various "resistances," for he knew that one can only lean on characters that resist. He waited. Sandra would at length do her duty. He was not mistaken.

Carefully wiping her mouth with the corner of her clean apron (she always put on a clean apron at the table) she began: "You have been licking your chops the whole evening, Serafim. This time it's a nice, tender pigeon. And sweet as ripe grapes. Oh, yes! You see her in the market. You trap her. One, two, three. You tie her in a knot, never thinking about your soul—or about Saveta. What would she say if she knew how you chase a white shirt if there is a girl in it?"

"I am not married yet, *lele* Sandra. And then, how is she to know?" queried Serafim with mock contriteness.

"That you are not married yet we know, but as to her

getting the gossip about you—well—do you think the people around here are blind? They all know what's hiding under your clothes. When you see a young woman with good breasts your Adam's apple begins to dance, even if you are in church. Your mouth waters more than you can swallow. You ogle her, you edge to her as the rooster in the henyard, fluffing your feathers. Now this beauty of a girl today. She has more sense in her little finger than most women in their heads. How you got her in your snare is a wonder to me. Yes, a wonder. Yes, Serafim—a great wonder. But I have a mind to warn her, because you'll ruin her soul. Mother of the Lord, forgive me that I did not whisper in her ear, 'Little one, this buck will tie you in a knot before you know it.' Yes, I have sinned, knowing and not speaking."

"Lele Sandra, you are a mother to me," Serafim said softly.

"Oh, good Mother of the Lord, listen to him! A mother—eh? Then why do I stand like an old broom in the corner and let you go your sinful way? Why?"

"Because, *lele* Sandra, you love your boy," answered Serafim, smiling angelically.

Sandra jumped up from the chair, snatched the bowl off the table and ran out. In a minute she was back again, her hands scurrying over the table, gathering forks, spoons and plates, clattering noisily. Serafim caught her hands, looking at her, melting with affection. *"Lele* Sandra," he said, "when I am eighty I will sit in the chimney corner, repeating the ten commandments the whole day and at night—if I wake up. I promise you, *lele* Sandra, on my heart."

"And you think you'll find grace—eh? Am I eighty? Am I dried up like a plum of last year?" snapped Sandra.

"Oh, yes, *lele* Sandra, sure I'll find grace. Christ loves a sinner because He loves to forgive. No, of course, you're not dried up, *lele* Sandra, you are full of sap. Now—didn't I see Ciucur tickle you under the chin but a few days ago and you never raised a finger? No, no! You held your hands hidden under your apron, giggling. You see, you know one thing and I know another. But Ciucur is a good man. He's no more than forty-five, not a day, and he's hairy as a bear. This house is big enough. I'll buy a large bed for the two of you and—"

Sandra blushed, snatched away her hands, crying: "Ptiu on your words—ptiu, ptiu! If that cross-eyed bear touches me again I'll scratch out his straight eye," and picking up the dishes she ran out of the room.

12

CHIVA, after John's scolding about the price of the hens and the way in which the money was spent, thought a little about it, but to suspect anything she was unable. With her everything was preordained by God and if she wondered sometimes about things that came to pass she soon got over it, with no comment. When they were annoying, she prayed to the Lord to take them away and smooth out the path of their life, and for the good she thanked Him. Now, Ileana's luck in selling the hens for a good price was a matter of gratitude, not worry, and she took it as such. So on Monday, when Ileana prepared rather hastily to go to town, Chiva only said: "Daughter, don't spend the money for the eggs and the butter but for what we need mostly—you know."

Ileana agreed and left. On the way she was overtaken by two young women from Aciliu, just as she was pulling off her boots. The women greeted her cheerfully, for going to the market put them in a festive mood. The young women thought it was a fine idea to walk barefoot, though taking off the boots and putting them on was not easy. They had to sit on the ground and the grass was wet. "Just lift up your alls, and sit on the pads you were born with," suggested Ileana. They laughed and did as they were told. Now the three walked lightly, chatting and laughing. Presently they started to sing. The morning freshness exhilarated them and soon they set to running and jumping, jostling, pinching each other and upsetting each other's hair. Ileana was agile, yet she had her arms pinched and her hair ruffled by the two young women.

They were married women and when they had enough of playing, they began talking about men. As they knew what they knew, they spoke with relish, especially after they noticed that Ileana blushed. To embarrass her still more they went into delicate details. If words proved inadequate they made use of little ejaculations, varied in pitch and color. Ileana turned her head away, she even covered one ear with her hand, the other being taken with the basket and the boots. She could not help hearing all that her companions said, nor could she master her excitement. But thinking of Serafim she felt ashamed, as if for him, because the prattle of these two young women seemed to refer to him and herself also. Yet she knew that outwardly she betrayed nothing of these intimate feelings, her companions being thoroughly abandoned to their freedom and noticing her embarrassment only as that of any girl who had no experience in matters of intimate love.

13

O n that Monday Serafim went to the market with a ready plan. His "city wagon" was at the inn. He left the horses hitched, tying them to a manger to eat their oats. He made his purchases, brought everything and put it away in the wagon, so all should be ready. Then he went to find Ileana, never thinking of Sandra's words for one instant. He was burning to see Ileana. He arrived just in time, for she had sold her ware and was ready to leave.

"So you would have gone without seeing me, little heart," chided Serafim.

Ileana turned crimson, her heart a-flutter. "I have to buy some few things and get home early," she said. She was happy that Serafim stood so close to her now, for she had wondered all the time whether he would come, though at moments she was certain he would come. What she was not certain about was her feelings: strong passion for him and a strange fear of him. Of his uncanny force, of his power to take her before she realised it. She was of course full-blooded and lived always close to the life of mating, as peasants do, seeing—ever since she could remember—how life was begotten. Yet her own love-life, she thought, was to be guided by herself. For, could she not keep the young men of her village at bay, as she pleased? Yet Serafim came—and just took her.

Serafim leaned to her ear, whispering: "We will go together, my little heart, then I'll drive you to the plain."

"No, no—I better go alone. Someone from Aciliu might see us," pleaded Ileana. Serafim only scowled and waved his hand, saying nothing. But he grasped her hand.

The women vendors watched them interestedly. This striking couple held their eyes as if charmed. The Saxon women jabbered loudly, nudging each other and laughing. They looked from under their large straw hats, trying to understand. They admired the handsome young man more than the girl, though they were fascinated by her grace and beauty.

His face lighting up, Serafim whispered: "I'll wait for you at the steps of the German church," and pressed Ileana's hand.

"Yes, yes," answered Ileana.

"Remain with the Lord," he said aloud.

"Go with God," she answered, and they parted.

The Saxon women followed Serafim with their eyes until he was gone. When they turned to Ileana she was slowly making up her basket, as unconcerned, it seemed to them, as if she were all alone in the place. When she picked up the basket, walking off in the opposite direction from Serafim, the women craned their heads to watch her.

From the steps of the Cathedral Serafim could survey
the big market place. It was filled with wagons, lambs,
calves, pigs, goats and sheep. On the yearly fair-days the
outskirts of the place were occupied by tents, but on the
weekly market days there were very few tents.

Most of the trading is finished by noon, so now, it
being almost midday, the animals were being moved, and
there was much noise. By two or three in the afternoon
the place is practically deserted.

The sidewalks were yet crowded. Under the eaves of
the church the pigeons fluttered and cooed. A flock of
them lighted on the market place, dodging the passers-by.
Now and then city folk, women and some elderly men,
mounted the steps and went into the church. Serafim
walked to the door, looked into the gloom for a while,
but did not lift his hat nor cross himself. Then he turned
and, walking over to a pillar, leaned against it. But presently, noticing Ileana approaching, he hurried down the
steps, murmuring, "There she comes."

"Have you filled your basket, little heart?" he asked.
"Let me take it, my hands are empty. We'll go to the
inn, the horses are hitched."

"Yes, yes, so I shall get home early," Ileana said.

"Oh, no! You shan't walk in this heat, my little
heart. You'll get drenched with perspiration. We are
going first to eat, together," Serafim protested. Ileana did
not answer, but let him take the basket.

14

T H E wagon clattered over the cobbled city streets noisily. They sat, Ileana and Serafim, on the upholstered driver's seat together. Now and again Serafim glanced at Ileana, but she was looking straight ahead of her. They did not speak much.

Having passed the bridge Serafim swerved the horses to the right, along the river bank. "Are you not going home?" asked Ileana.

"No, my little heart, we are going to my vineyard. It isn't far and it is lovely there," he explained.

Now they turned into a white road shaded by apple trees. The foliage was covered with dust, but on both sides of the road, as far as the eye could see, the corn shimmered green. After a short drive on this road they took a lane cutting through the fields. The wagon rolled noiselessly.

"There it is," said Serafim, pointing with the whip. They were facing a low hill covered with grapevines, the rows mounting from the foot of the hill to the very top. Finally they came to a small grove of silver poplars. Serafim drove off the road into the shade. Ileana remained in the wagon while he attached the horses to a tree, took the bits out of their mouths and gave them an armful of hay. The horses strained to nibble the fresh grass. Serafim loosened one tress of each horse and chained both hind wheels to secure the wagon.

"Come, my little heart," he said, holding out his arms.

Ileana stood up, but instead of jumping into his arms she sprang down on the other side of the wagon and ran behind the trees. Serafim chased her. Ileana eluded him, now by circling a tree, now by swinging suddenly to one side. She felt exhilarated by her success. In a flash it came to her that she was, in this particular thing at least, Serafim's equal if not his superior. She decided to match her wits against his. She stopped. He caught her, took her in his arms and tried to kiss her.

"No, no—wait, Serafim," she said, resisting. She did it laughingly, but she was as strong as she was quick. Serafim entered into the spirit of the play, but repeated discomfiture irritated him at length. He wanted to have her: he was giving the day to satisfy his desire. Was she going to play cat-and-mouse with him? He would see who was the cat. He left her, running to the wagon whence he took a blanket and the basket of food. "Now, little sprite, there is the vineyard and a short way up is a cabin, in a clump of peach trees. It is cool and nice there. Let us go. We'll eat and—come, little sprite, give me your hand."

Looking about, Ileana pointed to a shaded place

where the grass was soft and thick, saying: "But look at this lovely spot—why not here?"

"Because the sun does not stand still and the shadow moves," answered Serafim.

"We can move too," laughed Ileana.

It was Serafim who yielded. He spread the blanket, opened the basket and laid out the food. There were hard-boiled eggs, black olives, fresh butter wrapped in vine-leaves and a wet linen cloth in a covered wooden bucket; chopped nut-meat rolled in honey, two roasted pigeons, and fresh bread.

Serafim poured out two small glasses of plum brandy from a wooden flask. "Eat a few olives, little heart, and drink this—it will whet your appetite," he said. He sat opposite Ileana, pretending only a host's concern. Gallantly he offered her the glass. Ileana took it ceremoniously. "Good luck and health," she said, with a graceful swing of the arm. She's a devil, thought Serafim, answering: "May God preserve you." He imitated her gesture. Ileana took a sip of the brandy. Gingerly, with two fingers, she picked up an olive. Instead of putting it into her mouth whole, as the peasants do, and spitting out the kernel, she nibbled it. She broke small pieces of bread, delicately, as she had seen the city lady at the notary's do. Serafim watched her silently. He imitated her every gesture. But when they came to the pigeons, he picked up the little bird, tore it apart in his hands, snapped the bones and crunched them, smacking his lips and wiping his mouth with the back of his hand. He spoke with his mouth stuffed with food, laughed uproariously at his own remarks and gesticulated, now with a piece of bread in his hand, now with some part of the pigeon. Ileana smiled affectedly, with tightened lips, picking with the fork a shred of meat which she had carefully carved off the bone. Or she broke morsels of bread from the slice near her. When she sipped the wine she barely touched the glass with her lips. When she spoke she chose her words, uttering them slowly, in the gentlest manner.

Serafim drank in big gulps, leaving his moustache dripping, spoke loudly and opened his shirt collar, exposing his hairy chest. Ileana with delicate tugs pulled down her sleeves to the wrists. She is a devil, thought Serafim again and again. When he had eaten his fill he stretched his arms, clenched his fists, assuming a fierce expression: "I can fight a bull now," he cried. Ileana smoothed her apron, looked at him seriously, folded her hands as if in sudden wonder and said: "But you are heavy in the head, Serafim."

Serafim narrowed his eyes as if to stab her with a look. Slowly his lips stretched into a smile: "Sober as the bishop, little sprite, and clear as dew up here," he said, tapping his forehead.

"Tell me then a lovely story," said Ileana.

"Aha! A story? One story? Ten stories! A hundred

stories! I can spin them out thin as spider's thread for
delicate little girls. Or I can make your blood curdle.
Yes, with words, only with words. What shall I give
you?" he asked boisterously.

"Have your own choice. I will listen without blinking," answered Ileana.

Serafim began: "There was a miller, Mitru he was
called, and he was a man among men. He could eat a
ham at one meal and never belch. At twenty he was married. His wife died giving birth to his first child, ten
months after their wedding. It was a girl. Mitru brought
her up on wheat. He chewed the kernels into a paste and
fed the little one, from his mouth, as birds do. And he let
her suckle from an ewe. He held the baby under the ewe
and it suckled, wriggling its toes. She grew and grew.
He called her Balana, because she was fair, her hair light
as straw. At sixteen she was taller than his shoulder. She
could carry a sack of wheat under her arm and swing it
into the hopper. The young men came like bees to a tree
in bloom. They stayed in the mill till late in the day. At
night they came like moths to a torch. But Balana singed
them with her scorn. She wanted a man like her father.
But there were no such men. The miller sneered at the
young men, yet he let them come. A year passed, two
years. Balana was a woman now, for she was eighteen
already. She used to bathe under the large sluice, at night,
when all the water spilled over it, because then the six

wheels were still. She bathed naked. The young men
watched from hidden places on the bank, lying like rab-
bits in the bushes or behind willow trees. They saw the
moonlight on her wet body as she stood up on the beam
across the sluice before plunging into the foaming water.
Then she went through the air like a trout and the
water swallowed her, but soon her head came up like the
sun rising from a lake. Then all of her emerged, her
body like white salt, all a-shimmer. One night a young
man, the bravest, fell prey to his passion, which drove
him like a whip. He came out from his hiding and faced
her. Balana stood still, covering neither her breasts nor
the shame. But her eyes burnt into the very heart of the
young man. He was brave. He did not flinch nor tremble.
'I want you,' he said. 'Then take me,' she answered. He
stepped up to lay hands on her. She threw out one arm,
grabbed him and whirled him into the water, so quickly
he knew not how it happened. The swirling current swallowed him. She waited. He came up, then sank again.
She jumped in and pulled him out. 'When you grow up,
come and take me,' she said. She was naked as a nestling,
yet never tried to hide it. The young man went into the
mountains to feed on bear's meat and smear his body
with the fat, so he may get as strong as Mitru the miller.
Then, soon after that night, the miller came to his daughter. 'Balana,' he said, 'we are going to the mountains to
live like the eagle. These are weak folk!' They left. In

the mountains they lived like the eagle—free. They
shunned their kind and lived in the wilderness. One day
Mitru said: 'Our seed must not perish.' Balana answered:
'It must not.' So Balana became with child from her own
father, like the daughters of Lot. And she was wife of
him who made her and mother to his two sons and two
daughters. Then Mitru lost his sight. His eyes were open
and clear, but he did not see. Balana washed them with
the milk of her breasts; she blew her breath in them,
warm from the open mouth, or cool from puckered lips,
yet Mitru remained blind. She came into his bed at night
with sweet words to soothe his pain. 'You are my dear
wife Arghira,' he said, 'the Lord be blessed, for you came
to me with His forgiveness.' And Balana spoke her sweet
words until Mitru fell asleep. Now that he was blind,
Balana's voice deceived him; for though she could not
know it, her voice was her mother's. And from that time
on Mitru called his daughter Arghira. He died in late
years, happy, and the children called him father and
Balana mother, and never knew otherwise. They were
strong boys and girls and they loved the freedom of the
mountains. They learned from folk who came their way
to the high mountains that where people lived in crowds
there were those who stole and grew rich on their neighbor's sweat. Then these children of Balana and Mitru the
miller grew angry and went to punish those who stole
from others. They were the first *Haiducs,* and if they are

not dead they must be living still, hiding in the mountains."

Ileana listened entranced. She never stirred but looked straight at Serafim. When he finished she sighed.

"How is my story, little sprite?" Serafim asked proudly.

"It is beautiful. My grandfather told me stories of the *Haiducs,* but this one he never told me. Do you know Bujor's story?"

"No, that I do not know, but his name I have heard," Serafim answered.

"Then, if you want, I will tell it to you," Ileana said.

Serafim was burning with desire of her, yet "let me take her in her own way," he thought, and preparing to listen, answered: "Tell me the story, little sprite, I have ears to listen."

Ileana began: "Bujor was a famed mountain brave who fought the servants and the paid men of the rich, and what he took from the rich he gave to the poor. They knew not where he came from, nor if he was peasant-son or son of a *boyer,* for when he talked to a peasant he used simple words, but when he spoke to a *boyer* he used high words, in Greek or Turkish or the French tongue. He was beautiful as the sun and his horse was like a winged dragon, with eyes of burning coal. He came like the wind and disappeared like a spark. One day Bujor came to the village and took a girl, one of those who came to him with flowers—for all the girls in all the villages brought him flowers—and carried the girl away into the mountains, to a cave richer than a Sultan's palace. In the day he carried her in his arms, out into the sun, and played with her golden hair and kissed her eyes. 'Your eyes are my heaven and my soul, Mironica,' he said to her, for her name was Mironica. He gave her two male children, beautiful as angels. He slew bears to feed them with strong meat and rubbed their bodies with bear fat to make them hardy, not only strong. And his men, who loved Bujor, their chief, as the light of their eyes, taught the boys to wrestle, to throw the knife and to ride the horse. Then Bujor gave Mironica two more children, who were girls and beautiful as the full moon. They lived in love and happiness in their mountain cave and among the old oaks of the forests, where they knew their way in the day and in the night and could hide away, if any noise they heard, as if the earth had swallowed them."

Ileana paused, her face aglow with the verve of her story. Then she continued: "But one day Bujor's comrades returned to Mironica without him. They told her that Bujor was trapped in a *boyer's* house while he was hushing to sleep a little fellow who was awakened by the cries and noises in the house. The armed men of the *boyer* poured into the room like a flood and chained Bujor and led him to the dungeon. Mironica did not cry. She put on man's clothes and bid one of the *Haiducs* cut her tresses. He cut them with a knife. Then she put on the peaked astrachan cap of the *Haiducs,* took knives and pistols in her belt and kissed her children. She stabbed her arm and dipped the point of her knife in the blood, swearing to free her husband.

"It took all her heart and cunning and two full years of time to dig him out of his grave, and at last Bujor came into the light. But he was blind!

"Mironica brought him to the mountains, but Bujor could no more see her beauty. He touched her face with his bony fingers; touched her eyes and her hair, then he cried. The first time in his life, he cried.

"Mironica kissed his tears away and with her hair she dried his face. 'Angel of life, angel of my life,' Bujor kept saying, his thin hands smoothing her hair.

"Then one day Bujor said to Mironica: 'Sweet life of mine, take me up to the mountain-top, to our first day of love.' They went, Mironica leading him by the hand. 'Let us sleep here this night, sunshine of my soul,' he said. When morning came Mironica opened her eyes. Bujor was on his knees praying, his face to the rising sun. Mironica knelt beside him and prayed also. When Bujor finished, crossing himself, Mironica did likewise. Then she spoke to him and he answered, but his voice was strange to her. He said: 'Sunshine of my soul, the angel Gabriel is calling me. Take my hand and lead me to the vulture's peak.'

"Mironica took Bujor by the hand and led him to the vulture's peak. His hand did not tremble, but his fingers closed tightly on Mironica's. The vulture's peak is a naked rock, way up in the clouds. When they reached there Bujor stood up straight on the edge of the rock and said to Mironica: 'Now, my dear life, I will fly to the angel who is calling me. This is my hour. I will watch over you from heaven, where my soul is going, by the grace of God.'

"These words out of his mouth, Bujor crossed himself and jumped into the great depths. Mironica saw Bujor's dear form flying through the air, his black hair raised on his head like flames. Then, eager to join him, Mironica lifted her face to heaven and cried, 'Join me to him, oh Lord!' and flew after Bujor."

Ileana sat silent and pensive. Serafim watched her for a long time. She now revealed a beauty unknown to him in woman. The beauty of exaltation through the mind and the soul. Not that he understood that inner light, but the outward expression of it in a girl like Ileana was bewitching, for it revealed, added to her usual beauty, a richer and deeper nature than he had fancied. So that to him it was as if, having found a treasure already gratifying, he discovers that it is much greater. But with the increase of its worth, in a case like the present, the worth of the possessor, especially in a character like Serafim's, is rendered smaller. That Serafim could not endure. At

length he spoke: "There are brave men now also, but
life is changed." He moved over to her and took her in his
arms. "I am like Bujor," he whispered; "are you like
Mironica?"

These words from Serafim established the equality
between them: for himself entirely, because now he felt
it; for Ileana, they brought her back from her story to
the present.

The horses stamped and snorted, the sun having
reached them and the flies grown vicious. Serafim caressed Ileana and she did not resist him. Thinking of him
as Bujor, a man among men, her passion kindled.

15

Serafim drove Ileana to the edge of the plain. He drove fast, because he wished to be back in the city before evening. Ileana hid her face as best she could under her straw hat, whenever they passed a wagon or peasants on foot. As they neared the plain they caught up with a peasant driving a pig tied to a rope. The pig jumped suddenly, squealing. The horses shied so unexpectedly that Ileana fell back against the seat. The hat slipped off her head. With a cry she reached over and rearranged it. Two Saxon women looked up, seeming to recognize her. They nudged each other and laughed. Ileana was glad that they were women who did not know her. They had merely seen her in the market place. But one of them called after them: "Happy journey, young ones." The horses were galloping wildly, neither Serafim nor Ileana hearing the woman's words.

Serafim had all he could do to quieten the horses and bring them to a stop at the plain. Ileana jumped out. "Saturday, then, my little heart," Serafim whispered. Ileana nodded, hurrying away.

16

THE sun was setting when Ileana reached home. The hens were noisy in the yard, waiting for their evening feed, but the cows had not yet come from pasture. Chiva was coming from the garden with an armful of dried linens, and Maria ran to meet her "big sister." "What have you brought me, dear sister?" she asked eagerly, clapping her hands.

Ileana gave her a doll made of ginger cake. It was painted red, yellow and blue, decorated with white frosted sugar. The little girl kissed Ileana's hand; then pulling her down to her, she kissed her cheeks, twice on each. She whispered shyly, "Have you something else?"

"Yes, darling, I have," smiled Ileana. "I have a lovely ribbon for you. I will give it to you in the house." They hurried in. Ileana placed her basket in a corner and quickly changed her clothes. "How nice your shirt smells," Maria said. "Like your own Sunday shirt," answered Ileana. "It smells of sweet-mint, doesn't it?" She hid her face in the clothes chest, laying her shirt and aprons at the very bottom, where lay the bunches of dry sweet-mint. But Maria, as if out of the blue sky, said: "No, dear sister, it smells like some other flower," and she bent over the chest, sniffing.

"Hush, child, you are so excited you don't know what you are saying," Ileana reprimanded.

"Oh, yes," Maria cried, jumping up and down, "I am excited to have these nice things." She held up the ribbon and the ginger cake. Then she kissed each in turn.

Chiva laid the wash on the cradle and hastened to the fire. Her face was flushed as usual from hurrying. Stirring the lentil soup in the kettle she asked: "Was it a nice market, my daughter?"

"Very nice, mother. A great crowd of people," Ileana replied.

"Oh, yes, there is always a big crowd on such fine days. Have you sold your ware at a good price?" Chiva asked laughingly.

"Not bad," answered Ileana, rinsing the milk pail. She was milking one of the cows, when she heard her father's voice at the gate. The loaded wagon had stopped there. Michael had opened both wings of the gate, but John did not drive in. Ileana heard women's voices. She looked but could not see them in the shadow of the gate. Suddenly she recognized the voices of the two young women who accompanied her to town. They were talking both at once and giggling, while John only grumbled in monosyllables. At length the women left. John drove in, walking beside the oxen. He passed Ileana close by but did not look at her. Ileana felt her hands grow weak. The cow turned its head, chewing the cud slowly, looking at

her. "What could they have said to father?" Ileana
thought, and with an effort finished the milking.

John tramped into the kitchen with heavy steps,
frowning and muttering to himself. The boys came in
after him. John turned, shouting: "Have you unyoked the
oxen?" The boys said yes, in one voice. Chiva hurried
past her husband with the steaming bowlful of soup.
Glancing at him she thought: "He's in a tantrum again."
Maria took her place at the table, watching her mother
with timid eyes. She feared her father in his fits of anger
and dared not look at him.

Ileana strained the milk, rinsed the pails, hung them
on a pole in the yard and came to the kitchen. Chiva
seeing her pale, the color in her cheeks faded also.

John was already seated in his place on the bench
against the wall, under the icon. His clenched fists on the
table, he scowled at the soup. Chiva came in, ladled some
soup into Maria's bowl, and sat down. All were at the
table save Ileana. "Come to supper, Ileana," Chiva called.
"Yes, mother, I am washing my hands," Ileana answered.
Presently she came in. They waited for John to bless the
food, but he did not move. The boys looked at each other
uneasily and glanced at their mother, but never stirred or
said a word. Maria, spoon in hand, waited, but she had
tears in her eyes already.

At length John made a jerky movement with his
head and crossed himself. He mumbled the prayer, all

the others joining in the Amen and crossing themselves.

The soup was very hot, but the film of fat on it kept the steam from rising and John was deceived. He burned his mouth. He spat out the soup violently, cursing: "Heaven and thunder! She puts boiling oil on the table to scald my guts!" glaring at his wife.

"It's just a little fat from the rind of bacon I put in, John," Chiva said quietly, stirring the soup and blowing on it. "Eat now, John, it's very good. You must be hungered out—all of you." She encouraged the boys with a nod.

John picked up his spoon again, scooped jerkily the soup, blowing at it angrily before taking it into his mouth. His eyes disappeared completely under his eyebrows. His forehead was a maze of furrows. His nostrils spread out, quivering, his moustache bristled. A big vein on his neck throbbed ominously, thick as a rope.

Maria could only swallow a few mouthfuls of food. She coughed and started to whimper. John snapped his fingers loudly, without turning to the child. The little girl stopped whimpering instantly, but she turned white, her lips trembling.

The meal over, John crossed himself again, mumbling, and remained sitting on the bench. The vein on his neck was still beating. Maria hid in a corner. The boys went out to see to the animals. Chiva and Ileana cleared the table. John lifted his elbows to let Chiva gather the crumbs and wipe the table. After a long time of sitting silently he grumbled something and, getting up, went resolutely to the cupboard. He took the bottle and drank. The strong vodka made him screw up his face. He paused, took a long breath and drank again. Replacing the bottle he went and sat again at the table. Presently he began muttering: "I am her father. I must settle this. The Unclean One is in this—yes, yes. But I must settle it, Lord help me." He called: "Chiva, come here!"

Chiva and Ileana exchanged glances, and Chiva went into the room. "Now, woman," John grinned, "sit down here. Let me—I will talk to you." Chiva sat down, her eyes on John. "Look here, Chiva, these women, two young women told me about the girl going to town," John said, still trying to smile.

"You can't go, John, and I have too much work to lose a day—so, surely Ileana has to go. You know she would go if we don't," Chiva said.

"Good, that's one thing," John continued. "But when she gets into the city she sinks into the ground. Nobody sees her again. Maybe she changes into—into—what can she change into I want to know? But nobody sees her again. She is there and she is not. Those women, two of them, went with her. They get into the city, all three, walking together and suddenly—the girl vanishes. They look to right, to left, everywhere, but no girl. That's what they told me."

"John," Chiva began, leaning towards him across the table, "the city is crowded. Ileana is a big girl, she knows her way. She always has a thing or another to sell. She goes her way. What else?"—she concluded simply.

John struck the table with his fist, shouting: "What else—eh? That's all with your silly head—what else! But I ask you—how does the girl vanish like that from the sight of two sober women? Then she appears on the plains—out of—the Lord knows—the air, and walks along as natural as the others. I want to know this. Good Lord, woman, you have no heart. I can't sleep, I can't find peace in my mind, and you say—'what else'. And the good priest told me that his son is melting away, yet the girl, God save us, gets more beautiful each day. My head is splitting with troubled thoughts and I have no one to lean on. No one to speak to. I speak to you—but, God save me, your head is empty." John sighed, groaned and shook his head dolefully. Suddenly he jumped up and rushing to the cupboard snatched up the bottle and drank.

Chiva watched him, then she cried: "John, John, you will kill yourself!"

"Woman, I want to burn my innards. I want to burn here (he struck his belly) as I am burning here (he slapped his forehead). Yes, woman, yes. And,—and—" he clenched his fists, "I want to chase the devil out of my house. Out of my house, you hear, woman, out of my house! I'll drink (he took the bottle and emptied it) and chase the Black One out of my house," he shouted.

Chiva rushed to him, for he began tearing his hair, roaring: "Out of my house, Satan!" He shook her off, tore his shirt, rushed to the table and pushed it over, smashed the window with his fists, whirled a chair against the wall, the blood streaming from his cut hand.

Chiva ran out, crying for help. The neighbors were rushing into the street, hearing the noise and Chiva's calls for help. Several men came into the yard. "Quick, good Christians—come, John's in there," Chiva pleaded. They rushed in to John. John was standing in the middle of the room, a wild look on his face, but he was pale as death. His shirt was drenched with sweat.

The men approached him, talking kindly, trying to lay hands on him. John swung out at them. "I am not mad, no, no, no! Don't put your hands on me! It is the Devil, you hear, the Black One, the Unclean One!" he roared, staring about him. Noticing Chiva behind the men, he shouted: "She there, she says—'what else'—but I'm after the Devil. Out of my house, out of my house!" he yelled and fell to the ground.

17

THE men took John and laid him on the bed. Chiva washed his hand and they stopped the bleeding with spider webs and salt on the wound, then they bandaged it tightly with a strip of linen cloth. In the yard the women whispered among themselves but dared not go into the house. Michael and Nicholas stood at the door, but Ileana had gone into her little room with Maria, who dared not cry aloud.

"They should call the priest," one of the women said, and everybody began to repeat her words. But the men came out saying that John was asleep now. He had drunk too much and got into a fury, "but now he is sleeping peacefully," they said.

"It is not all clean," a woman said. As if awakened to the truth, the peasants crossed themselves and went to their homes.

The priest came in the morning, being advised of John's plight. Besides, he had great compassion for John, feeling also that while doing his priestly duty in helping him, he was easing the burden of his own heart. He found John standing near the barn, pale, his haggard face twitching. He looked at the priest with dazed eyes

and to his soothing words he nodded and several times
sighed as if his heart were bursting. The priest was saying: "John, the Good Lord sends trials to His best beloved. Remember that. (It gratified the priest to include
himself with the Lord's best beloved.) We must pray,"
he continued, "and say always 'Thy will be done,' and
help will come to us from heaven."

"Amen," said John in a broken voice. Then, as if
fearful of being heard by someone, he leaned towards the
priest, saying: "But, Reverend Father, it is the Devil's
work. The Unclean One is after my soul." He turned
and looked behind him in terror. "I am lost, Reverend
Father," he groaned.

The priest, struggling to keep his composure, laid
his hand on John's shoulder. Firmly, his eyes on John's,
he said: "My son, these are not good Christian words you
are saying. There is one God. He is our Father—His
name be blessed unto eternity. Your soul is His." He
crossed himself and John did likewise, with bowed head.
The priest continued: "You must be a good father and a
good husband, so that your life may be long and blest
with peace." Brokenly John bent and kissed the priest's
hand. Of the two men, as they parted, the priest was the
more comforted.

18

JOHN went with his sons—soon after breakfast—to the cornfields. They were hoeing the corn, working well, keeping abreast, each at his row. The sun was hot on their backs. The corn was high, affording a flickering shade to half of their bodies, but the back and arms were sweated.

The stirred-up soil mingled its fragrance with the sweetish scent of the plant. The long, sickle-edged leaves shimmered in the light and rustled with a rasping sound when a breeze came.

"Sweating is good, it cleanses the body," remarked Michael.

"It makes me feel lighter," answered Nicholas.

"Because it washes away the tired feeling," explained Michael.

"But dogs don't sweat," said Nicholas.

"They get the relief through the mouth. You see how it drips from their tongue when they are hot," Michael said.

"But it smells strong—the sweat," said Nicholas, his nose against his sleeve.

"We must rub it off our body. Rub it hard. It is the first sweat. After the rubbing it will be pure as water," Michael said.

The boys took off their shirts and with a coarse linen
towel, rubbed each other dry. The shirts they laid out in
the sun to dry. John watched them, then he pulled off his
shirt also and let Michael rub his back with the towel.
When the shirts were dry Michael advised cooling them
in the shade before putting them on. With the dry shirts
on they felt new vigor in their bodies.

In a nearby field women were singing. Their voices
rolled pleasantly over the corn. The boys took up the
song, first quietly, then with full lungs. Singing speeded
up their hoes. John worked on in silence. The singing of
the boys cheered him, however, and after a while he
began to hum. It seemed to make the hoe lighter in his
hands. The women in the adjoining field raised their
voices also—so they sang together. It was a song addressed to the corn, saying: "Corn, beautiful corn, suffer
the hoeing as the beloved submits to kissing." Then they
sang a *doina*. It starts out sadly, this song of the shepherd
who, having fallen asleep, loses his flock. He awakens
to find himself alone and in his sadness the thought of
his loved one, who is far away, makes him sadder still.
No sheep, no sweetheart—and the dark pines mourn with
the shepherd. Singing his sad fate, he starts out in search
of his sheep. Ascending a hillock he sees his flock grazing
peacefully in the distance. His dogs run to him to report
that all is well. The shepherd gives voice to his joy—so

the song changes to a gay note. He shouts, dances and throws his sheepskin cap into the air.

Just as they finished this song they heard the greeting "Good cheer to you, good people." It was Jancu Tedescu, the hunchback village teacher. He came up to John and the boys, smiling broadly, but with a wistful expression in his eyes. The boys greeted Tedescu eagerly. John, who knew that the teacher always spoke his mind, felt uneasy, thinking he might mention his outburst on the previous night and, while counseling him, put him to shame before the boys. But Tedescu only spoke about the fine crops, about the good work they were doing and about the weather. John felt relieved. Upon making ready to leave them, the teacher said: "Well, good Christians, I am on my way. I leave you in the care of the saints, going on my way with God." The boys burst out laughing. John glared. "What are you laughing at?" he demanded.

"A funny story the teacher told us," Michael said.

"It gave me cramps from laughing when he told it," put in Nicholas. "Let Michael tell it to you."

John liked the teacher because of his straight-forward character and respected him as a learned man, and now he held him in higher esteem even. He was aware that the teacher also was bewitched by Ileana, for which reason the young hunchback was closer to his heart, as through an added misfortune. He pitied Tedescu because of his back. He said: "Well, boy, tell the story."

Michael began: "There was in a village, not far, an old Saxon, known as a great miser. One evening a poor Roumanian peasant came asking for a night's lodging. The Saxon's kitchen was full of sausages hanging on a pole fastened to the ceiling rafters, for the old miser had slaughtered a pig as big as a steer, just the day before. There were strips of meat too, pink and streaked with fat, and it made the poor Roumanian's mouth water. The miser watched him, laughing inside his stingy belly. The poor peasant was cunning and smooth as oil in speech, because poverty was his teacher all his years. He folded his hands as one wondering at a sight he had never seen. He opened his eyes as big as he could and pointing at the sausages he asked: 'Oh, my good host, what are these things, the like of which my eyes have never seen before?' The Saxon decided to have some fun with the stupid peasant. He answered with a serious face: 'Those are the hosts of saints.' 'Ay, ay,' said the Roumanian, 'I should have guessed that, had I been blest with more sense.' Then, pointing to the hams and other parts, he asked again: 'And these wonders here, good Christian, what are they?' 'Those, my man, those are the prophets and the apostles,' answered the Saxon, bowing his head. 'Ay, ay,' sighed the Roumanian, crossing himself, and he turned toward the large bacon hanging on two wooden pegs in the wall. The blanket of fat was six fingers thick. 'And this, honorable host, this snow-white miracle,' he asked. 'That,' said the Saxon, bowing to the ground, 'that is the Lord God Himself.' 'Amen,' chanted the Roumanian, crossing himself three times.

"The Saxon never asked his guest 'are you hungry or thirsty?' He gave him a tattered horse blanket and some sacks. 'Make yourself at home on the hearth (there was no fire on it). The night is cold, but my kitchen is tight as a barrel. No draft to chill your bones,' said the Saxon, and he yawned.

"The Roumanian thanked him for his generous hospitality and, as the Saxon was about to close the door to his warm room, he said: 'Good host, I have to be on my way before sunrise. Don't bother seeing me off. So I thank you now, from the bottom of my heart, for putting me up on a night like this in such a fine shelter. Good night, kind Saxon, may the blessing of heaven rain upon your household.' 'Good night, Roumanian friend,' answered the Saxon and closed the door. He went to bed, laughing at the Roumanian's simplicity.

"The Roumanian stretched himself, or rather he curled up in a corner on the hearth, and slept with one eye open. And so, an hour before dawn he got up as quietly as a shadow and cut up the bacon with his sharp knife, which he carried in his belt. He put the bacon in one of the sacks, tied the sack carefully, and divided the load in two parts as in a saddle bag. He put his heavy stick under it and swung it on his shoulder. When he was ready he tapped lightly on the Saxon's door. The old miser grumbled sleepily. The Roumanian, in a sweet voice, said: 'Bless you, good host. I am on my way with God, leaving you in the safe-keeping of all the saints.' Sleepily the old miser answered: 'Go with God, Roumanian, go. Fasten the door with the latch.'

"The peasant made no fleas, but went off as fast as his legs would carry him."

John laughed heartily, then he spat in his palms and grabbing up the hoe he said: "Let's get to work, boys! He's a fine fellow, that teacher is. It's God's pity he's a hunchback."

"But he is strong as an ox," answered Michael, with a touch of resentment.

"He can run like a rabbit, too," put in Nicholas.

"He can?" asked John.

"Yes, he can! He plays ball with the bigger boys in the school yard and steals the bases quick as a lizard. And when he strikes the ball he sends it clear over the fence into the priest's yard." Nicholas' eyes shone with admiration. John sighed. "What a pity, though, he is a cripple," said he.

"To my mind it's only a misfortune he's got, but I don't call him a cripple," Michael protested.

"That may be so, at that, for he neither limps nor hobbles," John agreed.

John and the boys set to work again, with good heart.
The boys were hurrying to see who would finish his row
first, but it was John who got to the end, for with the
teacher's coming his thoughts turned to Ileana again and
he worked as if driven by the whip. The priest, of course,
had assured him that God was taking care of them all
and watched over John's soul. Yes, but there, the women
had told him that Ileana just disappears, in full daylight.
"That is unholy," muttered John. As his thoughts dwelt
again on the devil and his black power, he remembered
suddenly Filon, the rich peasant whom he had known in
his childhood. All the villagers said that the Unclean One
abided in Filon, in that swollen leg of his, which shook
like a bag when he walked. The children ran away when
he came through the street. And Filon's face was always
out of shape, his mouth crooked, his eyes like dead coals.
At night the villagers heard him groan as if in great
pain. Children and grown folk stood at the high wall
which enclosed his yard, listening to his groans and his
wailing, crossing themselves. They knew that Satan was
torturing him. Some old women, when crossing themselves saying, "God save our souls," would add, "and the
soul of poor Filon," but even these women did not believe that Filon's soul would be saved. John was a boy of
ten when, on a Sunday, Filon went out of the church in
the middle of the service, with a wild, crazed look on his
face. The congregation understood that the devil in him

drove him out of the holy place. Most of the villagers
said that Filon should not be allowed to set his foot in
their church again, but the priest, an old and venerable
man, told them that the house of the Lord is open to all
seekers after salvation. Besides, no one could accuse the
unfortunate man of one single evil act. If ever any peasant
in need—and he had to be in great need to do it—went
to Filon to borrow a bushel of potatoes for seed or a
sack of corn, in the dead of winter, Filon gave it without
a question. Not only that, but he answered to the one
who set a term for returning what he borrowed: "When
God will help you." Yet that did not appease the mind
of the peasants. Just the contrary, because in the years
when everybody had poor crops, Filon's seemed not to
suffer. Nor was it known that his vineyards and orchard
should ever fail in a fair yield of grapes and fruit. So
that Filon grew richer each year.

John remembered the peasants speaking about the
unholy practises of Filon, as regards his grapevine and
fruit trees. He had himself heard a tall, poor peasant say
to his father: "Don't forget, Zahary, that I have seen it
with my own eyes, always after sunset or before sunrise
it was, that Filon sprayed his vines and the trees with a
green poison. He dared not do it in plain daylight. So his
plants were green, unholy green, not like the plant and
tree as God made them, and when the leaves on our
trees and in our vineyards shriveled, the leaves on his

plants remained untouched by the blight, and he had grapes and fruit as in good years."

It seems only a short time since Filon died, crying so fearfully and groaning, John was thinking. He was a young man by then and he knew that Filon's old widow would not touch the gold he left, all to her, in a small barrel hidden in the wall, but she would not touch it for she was a God-fearing woman. She told her friends that after her husband died, she would be awakened suddenly in the middle of night by the jingling of those gold pieces, yet when she looked at the place in the wall, even the spider webs were there, across the stones that covered the hole. They had no children, so when she died, a sour-looking man, a nephew, came from a town—John could not recall the name—and took gold and everything. But he must have known his uncle's fate, for to redeem his own soul he gave money to the church of Aciliu, enough to buy a holy flag, a silver crucifix for the altar and a large chandelier with crystal pendants which, when the candles were lit in it, threw a shower of wonderful light on the people beneath. Still, the village knew that this money was not put in the church treasury; the good priest would not defile the house of the Lord with it. He kept the gold pieces in a small linen bag, on top of a rafter in his own house, and sprinkled it with holy water every day. Glad he was when the time came to part with it by paying for the embellishments in the church.

His Ileana got no gold from the Unclean One, but she got beauty, such as nobody ever before had seen in a woman, for her own soul and that she may trap the souls of others with that beauty. This is what John believed. The villagers were of his mind also, though all they had in support of their belief was Ileana's beauty and her skill with her hands. Yes, and also her intelligence and her charm over men. But now the story of the two women about the girl's power to make herself invisible gave the villagers—as it did to John—another proof of her unholy tie with Satan.

While John suffered because of this belief, the fact that the entire village believed with him increased his resentment towards contrary opinions, such as held by Tedescu and Stan, his father-in-law. Tedescu, John could yet understand, because—well, he was queer in that respect, owing to his city education: that is, a lot of book learning and lack of insight into facts which to the peasants were positive ones. But Stan should know better, John thought. Still, after a time he set aside the old man also, saying: "He talks a lot of foolishness about stars and planets, and now, because of his years, is altogether back to childhood again."

These thoughts turned and turned in John's mind as he was hoeing the corn. He sighed deeply every now and again, mumbling to himself.

19

Jancu Tedescu had tried repeatedly, in a careful manner, to drive these thoughts from John's mind and straighten his ideas, but it was a hopeless task. The teacher realised that John's mental state was the result of his desperate fear of the devil, which fear was an integral part of his deep-rooted religion.

He was glad to find John at work this morning, apparently quiet. Continuing his walk through the fields he thought about the peasant's ravings of the night before and the fear he must have caused Ileana.

Presently Tedescu heard his name called. It was Danila, who came running towards him. "I've been looking for you, Teacher," the youth said, quite out of breath. Tedescu, noticing his distraught face, asked kindly: "What is it, Danila?"

The youth became pale and his eyes filled with tears. "Do you really think it is true—true?" he whispered.

Danila had often confided his feelings for Ileana to the teacher and the latter pitied him, but he had no patience with his believing the village gossip about Ileana.

"Do I think *what* to be true?" Tedescu demanded, somewhat sternly.

"What they say—about her," stammered Danila.

"What *do* they say and who is *her?*" asked Tedescu in no milder tones.

"Oh—you know—Ileana—Ileana," answered Danila meekly.

"Good, then, Ileana. What about her?"

"It is—what the peasants say—that—that—she is—Lord—I can't say it. This—about the devil," Danila gasped.

Tedescu looked him squarely in the eyes. He was ready with a sharp reply, but the next instant he felt as if he were looking into the eyes of Veronica, Danila's mother. So he said calmly, yet earnestly: "Danila, the beliefs of the peasants are narrow and often false. What they can't put to God, they put on the devil. Many of the finest types of mankind were accused of being in league with the devil, by people of such minds as our peasantry. But you, Danila, you should know better. Look into your own heart and listen to no other voice. Remember that all mysteries—so called—are born of our ignorance." He touched Danila's hand and walked away, quickly. He had too much of Ileana in his own mind to be able to comfort this youth with advice.

20

Jоhn's home resumed its air of quiet almost immediately, for Chiva—with her strong faith in the ultimate good of things—forgot her husband's outbursts quickly. She was happy also to see that Ileana was now changed. She was calm, with a quiet serenity that lighted up her face. It appeared to Chiva that even her walk was different, for Ileana seemed not to touch ground or make any noise, but glide like a shadow.

A particular eagerness, an anticipation of happiness which assailed Ileana when the market day was near, Chiva did not notice. In fact, nobody did save Jancu Tedescu, the teacher. And he coupled this with Ileana's changed mood since several weeks, trying to understand it. Being in love himself, he knew its potency. Love, he said to himself, lifts one into the seventh heaven of happiness, or it can throw one into the deepest gloom. Did Ileana love someone? Apparently—apparently—I could almost say yes, the teacher reasoned. Yet, he continued, her manner towards the villagers is as before. This plunged him into deep reflection.

21

I т was Saturday evening. The boys had swept the yard
and the street—the length of their house—and were sitting on the bench, in the street. Soon Grandfather Stan
came along. "Good health, boys," he greeted, pipe in
mouth. He hardly ever took the pipe out of his mouth,
though most of the time it had no fire. He sat down beside the boys, spat from the corner of his mouth, sighed
and pulled the hat a fraction of an inch over his eyes.

The boys loved Stan. To them he was respectable old
age, kindness and wisdom personified. He was the village
peacemaker. In all important questions concerning the
village he was consulted and he never failed to pronounce
one of those oracle-like old proverbs, fitting because usually it carried a double meaning. That, however, was its
merit, for in a debated question each side took the meaning suiting them. Stan would then speak up and recon-
cile them with wise words of his own. He would say:
"Just so, good peasants, just so; you have understood the
wisdom of this old saying, its meaning is, as you see—."
And he would give them a meaning generally acceptable.

If at such reunions the peasants reached a settlement
beneficial to all, Stan would nod approval without saying
a word. But if they all talked, "churning water," Stan

called their attention, and when the noise subsided he would say: "Good peasants, brothers mine, there was once upon a time a village, just like ours. And it came to pass that one day God thrust upon those villagers a burden like ours now. The peasants gathered—God-fearing people they were, even as we are—and set to weighing it in the scales of their minds, so as to reach an understanding. Well, they talked and talked—just as we are doing. But the knot of the affair remained tight. Not only that, but the more they talked, the tighter the knot got. And why? Look you, good people. Here it is. A rope gets knotted. One of those big, tangled knots it is. Good. Two parties set to untie it. But what do they do? They do what you have been doing here. One party takes hold of one end of the rope, the other party of the other end, and they pull and pull with all their might, each party its own end. But what happens? The knot tightens more and more instead of yielding. So, I say to you, good people, if you want to untie the rope, get you all at the same end, let the other end loose, and pull in one direction. This I say to you, as once upon a time an old man said to those villagers: 'Friends, get ye all to one side and the knot will yield.'"

And Stan could tell stories, such that his hearers would roar laughing or would cry, with a sad contentment in their hearts. He was always there where counsel or solace was needed. He cheered the sick and the dying,

ever since the villagers could remember. He knew reme-
dies for many illnesses and he knew how to help the
soul of a dying man "on the straight and narrow road,"
to his Maker. He even helped the midwife in very hard
cases of childbirth. He could cure fevers and sunstroke,
could fix a sprain and set broken bones.

Stan never missed a wedding, either, for he could eat
and drink as the best of them, but he knew when he had
enough—now in his older age. When that feeling came,
he would say to himself: "Stan, you've had enough."
After that he raised his glass with the others, toasted and
laughed as loud as any, but never swallowed another drop.
Stealthily he would pour the wine into his neighbor's
glass or back into the jug. He was always contrite for
cheating his neighbor in this way, saying, "Lord forgive
me," but he never stopped doing it.

Soon after Stan sat down with the boys, Tedescu came
along. "Good evening, friends," he greeted.

"Good may be your heart, Teacher," Stan and the
boys answered. "Sit with us," invited Stan.

Tedescu sat down. He had a large head, set between
broad, raised shoulders. His legs and arms seemed dis-
proportionately long. His infirmity would have brought
upon him a nickname from the peasants—their unconscious resentment of every deformity—but for the fact
that Tedescu had a good voice and a strong temper. Be-

sides, he had powerful arms and hands that gripped like
a trap. So his name remained simply Tedescu the Teacher.
He was much admired because he could play the fiddle,
and often at weddings or festivals he would play with
the gipsy fiddlers. Sometimes he played some to them unknown tune. Then, Tache, the gipsy, would hold his
violin to his chin, the bow poised, listening like a magpie.
Soon he would touch the strings lightly, as if feeling with
his bow for the tune, while the *cembalo* player strummed
the accompaniment to Tedescu. But when Tedescu finished, Tache would let go his bow and draw out from his
fiddle that tune, perfectly, his teeth gleaming in a broad
smile, the peasants shouting their admiration of him. And
Tedescu would slap the gipsy on the shoulder.

In the eyes of Michael and Nicholas, Tedescu was
an old man, he being in his late twenties, while they
were still in their teens. The teacher's wide knowledge
sustained their idea of his advanced age, for Tedescu
could hold abreast with Stan as to wise talking. In some
instances, as when they spoke about the stars, the moon
and the sun, Tedescu gave figures on their actual dis-
tances from the earth. He spoke about stars so far away
that the farness had to be measured by the speed with
which light travels, and that was not only beyond the
comprehension of the boys, but even Stan only nodded
his head, sagely to be sure, but without a word to say.

Then also, Tedescu knew the "wide world" of which

he could tell them things they never would even fancy,
as when he told them that as many as a hundred musicians played together in one hall. The boys marveled at
the hugeness of such a hall, holding three thousand people beside the fiddlers. As to the music, they said, it must
have rattled all the windows in the place. Then, speaking
about singers who had wonderful voices, Tedescu hinted
that Ileana also had a great voice. They trusted his judgment, because the teacher had proved himself. He trained
the village boys and girls and formed a choir—he even
put several men in it—which gained a reputation that
reached the Bishop. In the summer, when the reputed
Count Vargas came with his family to what was left of
his estate—an ancient house with gardens, within two
miles from the village—this proud nobleman would bring
family and friends to the church in Aciliu, all because of
Tedescu's choir. And he always put a piece of silver in
the collection plate.

If there were city folk in the neighborhood, they soon
flocked to the church also. So, at the beginning the village
elders murmured, saying that the house of the Lord was
no show place, but Tedescu spoke to them and they were
reassured.

This time again Tedescu spoke about the beauty of
the human voice, for he had heard Ileana singing that
very day in the early morning. While he was speaking,
Chiva and Ileana came out. It was the hour when the

day of rest—Sunday—was already in the air. The elder
peasants were gathering in front of their houses, the children, after the evening meal, came out less noisily, sleep
hanging already on their eyelids.

The women sat down quietly, and when Tedescu
finished what he was saying, they greeted him. Tedescu
felt a shiver run through him at Ileana's voice. If anything supernatural was in the girl—he thought—that came
from the angels, not the devil. Yet her own brothers,
who feared her biting words, inclined more towards the
general belief of the peasants, concerning their sister.
Despite that, they loved her in the clumsy, shy way of
rude brothers. But her great beauty they did not quite
see.

The moon came up, shedding a bleaching light upon
the village. Voices trailed along walls. In the stillness of
the night the muffled sound of voices enhanced the pre-
holiday peace.

John appeared at the gate, smoking his pipe. He
leaned against the gate, puffing for a while, not saying a
word. Nor did he sit down on the bench with the others.
After a short time he walked in, saying, "Good night."

Tedescu watched Ileana. His affectionate understanding caught every change in her expression. The
moonlight being on their side, he could see her as plainly
as in daylight. Stan mentioned the city, so they spoke
about it. Tedescu noticed Ileana's interest. She must meet

someone in the city, Tedescu surmised. When she became pensive—after they left off speaking of the city—he was sure.

Ileana forgot the persons about her, her mind having gone to Serafim. She sat quietly, yet her face radiated her happiness, and Tedescu saw it. The revealment of this truth shook him. For a moment he felt lost. All hope of ever winning her love left him. Then, because the life in him was strong, he caught it again and, leaving the family, carried it with him.

22

THE following morning Ileana went about the few Sunday chores in a holiday mood. She was humming all the time, occasionally she sang out loud. She resolved more than once during the day to hide within herself that feeling of elation behind a serious countenance, but her heart was too full. She could not. She could not, for tomorrow was Monday and she was going to town.

Ileana got up "with the night on her head," as the peasants say, and when day was breaking she started out. On the steep grade leading to the flats she overtook a loaded wagon. The peasant walked behind the wagon, having gotten off to lighten it. He was the first to greet. "Good morning, Ileana," he said.

"Good morning, Uncle Dimitri," answered the girl.

"Going to town, child?" Dimitri asked.

"Yes, Uncle Dimitri, with a basketful of ware." She laughed.

"Well, girl, your load can't break my horses. Put it here."

They walked together in the clatter of the wagon and the heavy tramping of the horses. The smell of the warm horses came in wafts, as if with their breathing.

The sky was as clear as the song of the skylarks rising above the flats. A hawk poised against the blue, a black speck in the sky. On the flats the horses stopped by themselves, having gotten there with a last effort, their legs gripping the ground. The green level plain stretched as far as the eye could see on the left, but on the right the horizon was bordered by the dark ridge of the forest.

Dimitri and Ileana climbed up and sat on a blanket stretched over bags of oats. The wagon rolled smoothly on the clay road. The hawk swooped down, after circling, but the skylarks sang unseen, lost in light. The fragrance of the fields came in little eddies, cool and refreshing.

Ileana breathed deeply the freedom of the great expanse. She recalled the time when as a little girl she saw the wide, open stretch for the first time. How in a burst of happy surprise she clapped her hands, shouting: "Mother, is this the top of the world?" She felt now also as if she could shout and clap her hands. What she would say she did not think of.

At her side Dimitri, his eyes fixed unmoving on the green tableland, his sunbaked face relaxed, filling himself with the good air, his large form seemed to expand, yet yielding to the motion of the vehicle.

"It is beautiful, this largeness of space," Ileana said at length.

"Aye, girl, so it is," Dimitri answered without turning his head.

"I have loved it all my life," she pursued.

"That's less than I, girl, seeing I am more than twice your age."

"I wish I were a bird, so I could fly above it, very high, then just glide above the blades of grass, as the swallows do," Ileana said with animation.

Dimitri laughed a short, deep laugh. Then he said: "That's a girl's wish, straight and true. When I was a boy I wanted to be the village cowherd, so as to spend my days here. But yours is a girl's wish, no doubt on that."

"So you also had a longing for the plains, Uncle Dimitri?"

"Aye, girl, I had. And now, I tell you, my going to town is a holiday, because I cross the plains, twice in the same day, morning and evening." His voice had a deep, pleasant ring like the sound of a big bell coming from afar. His words increased Ileana's wistfulness.

As if continuing a thought, Dimitri said: "A peasant's life is not an easy life. The work hardens his hands and the winds toughen his skin. But I look at the pale-faced city man and I say, 'Dimitri, praise the Lord for thy lot.' And I cross myself and thank God that I am a peasant. I look at the city man in his funny clothes and I say, 'Well, he also lives by the will of the Lord, no saying otherwise,' yet I feel sorry for him. Yes, yes, I feel sorry for him. Why? Because he spends his living days like a mole in its burrow. We peasants, now, we are with the

soil, we are of it, like what grows from it. When the
rains come in the growing season we feel the water of
heaven. I take my hat off and I say, 'Good Lord, send it
pure,' and it falls on my head like baptism, God's blessing to man. Then, after the winter, when the warm sun
of spring rises, the snow melts and the water pours from
the roofs and you can hear the earth drink it. We are
glad in our hearts. The earth drinking pure snow water,
you hear it go down into its belly. But the poor city man,
does he know aught of this? No!" He shook his head,
resuming:

"Then, when the first green blades of the corn push
through the soil, I am happier than the king. I say to
myself, 'Dimitri, you have put the kernels in the earth
with your own hands; look now, Dimitri, the Lord has
blessed your work.' But the city man, does he know aught
of this? Eh, girl?"

Dimitri turned his face to Ileana. Ileana felt tears in
her eyes. She dared not look at Dimitri who now resumed
his contemplation of the plains, in silence. She wished he
would talk more. His voice was soothing and his words
went to her heart. But Dimitri remained silent. He spoke
not even to the horses, letting them move along as they
wished. When they stopped, he waited until they rested
and started off by themselves, watching them.

He feels with the beasts, Ileana thought. As if reading her thought, Dimitri spoke up: "You know, girl, the

beasts may have no soul like ours, yet some kind of a
soul they have, I am sure. Did you notice that be it ox
or cow, horse or donkey, when the animal lies down on
its bedding, it first scratches the sign of the cross on it—
with its front leg? Yes, they do. A year ago last spring
my best cow got into the clover and I looked for her a
long time before I found her. There she lay, all swollen
up, groaning like a human. I knelt down by her head and
I said: 'Bell, what is the matter with you, my good, nice
cow?' She let out a moo that went to my heart, and
looked at me with eyes big and sad. I put my hand to
my belt, but the knife wasn't there. Now if I had my
knife, I could have stuck it into her swollen belly and
saved her. But I had no knife. So I was there like a block
of wood, scratching my head, the poor creature looking
at me sad, sad. She must have understood my trouble,
for suddenly I saw tears in her eyes. Yes, girl, as true as
the sun, the poor creature cried. Well, I could not stand
it, I bent down and I kissed her, asking her again: 'Bell,'
I said, 'my good old Bell, what can I do, you see I have
no knife?' Now what do you think, girl, she did, that
good cow Bell? She put up her head a little as if to get
nearer to my helpless bumpkin and let out another moo,
only longer and weaker than before. Then she scraped
the ground with her front hoof, meaning to make the
sign of the cross, and her head dropped to the earth. I
made the sign of the cross over the poor dead creature

and would you believe it, I couldn't help saying, 'God rest your soul in peace, Bell.' This is as true as the sun."

Ileana had listened to Dimitri, hardly breathing. His rich voice made her wonder if Serafim also felt as Dimitri did about the beasts and about the soil. Serafim's words rang in her ears, she felt as if Dimitri were, in some strange manner, involved in her relations with him. This feeling did not disturb her; it was rather reassuring, because a third person, unasked, took part in her present actions of which no other soul but Serafim and herself knew. Suddenly a thought flashed in her mind and made her speak. "Uncle Dimitri," she said, "do you believe that the devil comes among the people to tempt them and take their souls?" No sooner did she say the words than she was aghast at what she said.

Dimitri turned and looked her full in the face. He seemed as if seeing the girl's beauty for the first time. Her violet-blue eyes shaded by long black lashes were such as he had never seen in his life. Her full lips, slightly parted, were as pure as a baby's. Her skin smooth as still water. His steady gaze made Ileana blush. He turned away his head without a word, straightened the reins over the horses' backs and sat silent, staring at the flickering heat above the field. He sat like that for a seeming long time; then very quietly, as if speaking to himself, he said: "Girl, we know what we know with the feelings of our heart, not with our minds, for we peasants, we have no school-

ing. The heart has hope and has fears. We pray in
hope and we pray in fear. Good, all good comes from the
Lord, but evil—evil comes from the Unclean One. The
devil is the enemy of every Christian, but the Lord
showed us the way how to save ourselves from Satan—
may the holy cross kill him." He crossed himself, then
continued: "Yes, my child, the devil keeps watching us
and good reason we have to fear his unholy temptations.
He comes in different shapes, this we know from our
ancestors. Some there are whose misfortune brought them
face to face with the Black One, and they speak as wit-
nesses. This I know and no more."

"Might he come in the shape of a handsome man, as
people say, to steal the soul of an innocent girl?" asked
Ileana timidly.

"That he might," answered the peasant, nodding.
"But the best thing for every Christian is not to dwell
on the Evil One. Let us turn our minds away from him,"
he said firmly. After a short silence he spoke again:
"There is a *claca* at the priest's tomorrow, will you go?"

"My parents said I should, so I will," answered Ileana.

"You will be a good help, making binders for the
sheaves," said Dimitri, smiling.

"I love the smell of ripe straw and crushed stubble,"
Ileana said.

"And, girl, and the wild pea, eh?" Dimitri asked.

"Yes, yes, the wild pea and the dusty smell of the earth," said Ileana.

"You know, girl," Dimitri smiled as he was saying, "even the sweat of the harvesters is good to the smell in the fields." Ileana assented, nodding her head.

"And I don't despise droppings from the horses and the oxen, either," Dimitri added, laughing heartily. Ileana laughed with him.

Now they had crossed the plain, the wagon turned into the highway. They watched the white, hard roadway, stretching out straight after a fine curve, then bending again and again stretch out until it vanished in the warm haze, far away. The telegraph wires hummed, swallows darted over the road, some lighting on the wires. In the city Ileana left Dimitri, going to the small market place. The peasant watched her until she was lost in the crowd.

23

SERAFIM'S passion for Ileana was growing. It grew separately from his thoughts about his approaching marriage. A thing apart. But he was troubled seeking a means of keeping his relation with Ileana unchanged, after his marriage with Saveta. In the meanwhile he meant to have as much of Ileana as he could. The time between their meetings seemed very long to him. He rushed to the market place ready to seize her and carry her off in view of everybody. But when he arrived only his eyes and his trembling hands betrayed his passion.

"I need that butter and those eggs," he whispered, unable to wait for her to sell out. He hurried her off, "Come, come, my little heart." Furtively he kept looking about, for he had heard gossip that he was seen with a peasant girl "beautiful as the sun."

To Ileana he appeared superhuman because of his face, his searching look and his power over her. In her mind he was identified with Bujor the Haiduc. Or else, how could he have taken me so that I never knew how, she thought. He is more than any man, more—she shuddered—perhaps unholy. Yet she walked with him as fast as her feet could carry her.

Serafim led her through a narrow, ill-smelling passage running under stone buildings, from the market place into a street where the peasants did not pass. Ileana almost ran to keep up with him. He walked noiselessly

They drove again to the vineyard and Ileana followed him to the cabin. Without a word. The cabin smelled like a hive. There were large cakes of wax on a shelf. In a wide basin of water stood three buckets filled with strained honey, the buckets covered with pieces of linen. Some bees and wasps circled about, were crawling on the linen, trying to get to the honey. Serafim drove them out with his hat and closed the door.

Suddenly, as if awakened by the odor of wax and honey and the green-golden light that filled the room, Ileana became aware of Serafim's greedy lust and shuddered. But it only lasted one moment, for when Serafim took her in his arms she could think no more. There was the fragrance of the room, the light in it, and Serafim, his endearing words on her neck, burning, his lips on hers, his crushing embrace, his hands, and she was no longer whole—she was burning up, being swallowed in the fire of his passion. And together they were one in the center of life, in the very core of it. How could words pass her lips? She could barely breathe her sighs and the groans that were not her own but issuing through her from that burning center of life.

Walking across the plain Ileana did not feel alone. Serafim was with her. She spoke to him without uttering words, but she heard clearly his voice answering. She was in a trance. She saw not the world of reality—at this moment a wide plain, bare as an empty table. But when the road dipped into the village her fancies were suddenly dispelled. Jancu Tedescu, as if rising from the ground, stood before her. "Good evening, Ileana," he said. Awakened from her dream Ileana looked at him. Their eyes met. His strong, earnest eyes caught and held hers, yet only for an instant, but Ileana asked herself: did he see my thoughts? For Tedescu's eyes had that power of seeing deep into one's mind. So the peasants said about him and they held that God had given him this gift to amend for his being a hunchback.

Ileana said she must hurry home. Without a word Tedescu turned and walked with her. Neither spoke. Tedescu observed her. No doubt, he said to himself, there is happiness in her which she is trying to hide. Ileana thought—he is prying into my secret.

At the gate she took leave of Tedescu, hurriedly getting into the house. She put on her every-day clothes and went about her work. In the kitchen she talked with Chiva of small, familiar matters. They smiled, they laughed, their hands busy. She was content with these every-day parts of life. This was peace and calm, because her secret was hidden in her heart. This was the daily life. Her father saying the prayer before the meal, lighting his pipe after the meal, her mother helping with clearing the table, all this made up the daily life. And when the evening came, undressing in her little room to go to bed, Ileana was thankful for the peace of this daily life.

24

W ITH the first light of morning the peasants began to gather in the priest's yard. When Ileana and her brothers arrived, the boiled eggs and baskets of sliced bread were being set out on the tables. Veronica, the priest's wife, was pouring out *rachiu* into glasses, cups and in small wooden containers. A maid servant was offering the drink to the men first, then to the women. The girls only moistened their lips with the strong beverage, but the men swallowed it with relish, ejaculating a long "A-a-a-ch" after it.

Tedescu was helping Veronica. Danila tried to be helpful, but he seemed to be in his own way. His eyes were constantly turning to Ileana, who sat on the bench, amongst other girls. After this early breakfast the harvesters, fully thirty of them, filed into the street. Tedescu took Danila to the head of the column and they marched off. Tedescu started a lively song, the others joined in, and singing they got to the field.

The wheat was good—it reached to Tedescu's waist, the straw smooth, the spears heavy. Tedescu tore off a few spears and rubbed them in his hands, blowing the chaff. The kernels were like golden beads. Heavy, with a sheen on them. The priest stretched his arms over the fields, in benediction, saying a prayer of thanks, his head up. The peasants with bowed heads repeated his words in a murmur. Then they set to work.

The cutters started out in a row, with long sickles. As the right hand cut, the left laid down the cut wheat. The women who were to bind the sheaves did not have to wait, for by the time they had tucked up their shirt-skirts there was enough stalk cut for them to start making the binders. The women's legs, bare to nearly the knee, gleamed pink against the screen of wheat.

The sun came up from behind the hills. Fat, noisy sparrows fluttered about, scolding at the harvesters. An hour or so after the sun had risen the wagon came, bringing buckets of buttermilk and a cooling drink made of fermented bran, leaven and spring water.

Tedescu filled a cup and gave it to Ileana, saying: "Take this, Ileana, it is cool yet." Now again his eyes, meeting hers, had that earnest, penetrating look. She blushed as she took the cup, but soon regaining her composure she said: "To your health, Teacher."

"One moment," said Tedescu, filling another cup. "Now, Ileana!" He raised the cup so they should clink.

"But with water it is not lucky, they say," Ileana interposed.

"This is leavened, fermented, that changes it," Tedescu said. They clinked and drank. The cup in his hand embarrassed him. But he stepped nearer to Ileana and very quietly said: "I have made a wish when we clinked."

"I hope it comes true, Teacher Tedescu," she answered.

"I shall pray for it."

"That will surely help."

A cry made them turn. It was a girl, violently shaking her sleeve, jumping and calling for help. The harvesters roared with laughter, but no one went to her. Tedescu rushed up: "What happened?"

"Oh, a mouse, here in my sleeve!"

Tedescu grasped her arm near the shoulder and the fringe of the cuff.

"Pull in your hand and let it drop out," he said. The girl pulled in her hand, wriggling and shaking, and the mouse dropped to the ground, scurrying off in the stubble.

"Who did that?" demanded Tedescu.

"George, over there," said a woman pointing to a tall youth.

Tedescu ran up to him. "George Gorun, that was a fine trick, but do it to a man—that poor girl—" Tedescu took his hand, the youth shamefacedly yielding it. He followed the teacher to the girl.

"We come to make up, Suzan," Tedescu said. "He will never do it again, George promises. Now, make up, good friends."

"No," pouted Suzan. "He always teases."

"I—I won't do it again, Suzy, honest truth, never," George pleaded.

"Don't I know you, George Gorun," Suzan persisted.

"George, you'll have to convince Suzan with a kiss—everybody here knows that," said Tedescu with a sweep of the hand.

"Yes, yes, a kiss, surely, a kiss!" cried the crowd. Suzan ran away, screaming, now circling the wagon, now a stack of sheaves.

"He can't catch her! Look at his long legs! He's as swift as a fish on the ground," the peasants teased. But George kept up the pursuit and caught Suzan at length by lounging over some sheaves. They fell. The girl resisted ineffectively. When she was released she shook her fist at him crying: "He kissed me twice, the brute!"

"I had to take my breath," said George, his face all red.

The women shrieked laughing. "Give him back one," advised an elderly peasant.

"Nice advice, that—Uncle Pavel," protested Suzan. "Like this I'll give it back," she added, snapping her fingers.

"Then keep it for good measure," tittered a girl, whose cheeks were like a red apple.

Suzan ran to her and pinched her. In no time they were at each other, but Uncle Pavel separated them, before they got to hair-pulling.

At noon the gipsy musicians arrived, three swarthy, black-eyed men with long, thin moustaches. After being fed and their thirst quenched with a quart of good wine, they started to play. The harvesters were at their midday meal. Nicutz, the *cembalo* player, had a rasping, guttural voice, but he could sing. He shut his eyes like a crowing rooster, lifted his head and hammering his instrument blindly—yet never missing the right strings—he sang. The two fiddlers accompanied, one twanging his fiddle, the other pulling wailing sounds out of his. The sad folk song "wrung the hearts," as the peasants say. The spoons moved slowly from bowl to mouth and some women swallowed tears with the sorrel soup. Even the men were affected: from smiling awry their features became mournful. Danila might have burst into tears had not the gipsies suddenly struck up a gay tune. The wild music seized the harvesters, the men letting out yells and swinging their arms. They drummed with spoons on the bowls and cups, gobbling their food.

The effect of this music on Tedescu was to stir up his hope. His eyes caught Ileana's but the girl was absorbed in herself. Tedescu concluded that the gaiety around Ileana fenced in, as it were, her hidden thoughts, increasing her secret happiness. Yet his hope did not sag.

When the gipsies stopped playing, Tedescu took up Tache's fiddle. He tuned it. "I'll play if a certain body will sing," he said. He did not look at Ileana, but Nicutz

the gipsy went over to her with that air of unbending
pride which in a gipsy becomes dignity, and said: "Lend
your voice to Tache's fiddle, beautiful girl."

Ileana looked at him as if awakened from a dream.
"I?" she asked.

Several voices cried: "Yes, yes, Ileana." The peasants
were willing to forget the devil or at least set him aside
to hear her sing. Tedescu touched his bow to the strings
and said to her: "I will trail with the fiddle after your
voice to the tune of 'See the swallows fly away.'"

Without standing up, just straightening her back, she
began: "See the swallows fly away, the nut-leaves falling
to the ground." Her voice, deep at first, rose clear and
even, and remained poised on the lament closing the
stanza: "Why do you not come, my beloved?" Tache's
violin, an old instrument which survived the outbursts
of four generations of violent-tempered gipsies, sounded
thin and dry compared to the girl's voice. Several young
men took courage and hummed softly. It was like the
murmur of the forest.

Nicutz picked up his cotton-covered hammers and
ran them over the wires of his *cembalo,* his eyes half shut.
The closing words of the song, "Why comest thou not?"
were repeated by all the harvesters.

After the meal they rested. Tedescu made a shelter
of sheaves, crawled under and closed his eyes—thinking
of Ileana. But in his reckless happiness he had drunk

more than usual, so he fell asleep. When he awakened all hands were at work, only the gipsies slept under the wagon that was being loaded.

Tedescu climbed on the wagon, setting to ranging the sheaves as if he were building a wall. The peasants admired his skill, especially the way in which he placed the long pole over the load and tied it to the front and rear axles. An unevenly loaded wagon with such an huge bulk could easily get turned over on the road. A sudden sinking of the wheel in a rut would throw it out of balance, and there are no longer men, even among the strongest peasants, who could steady it with the push of the shoulder. As Tedescu ranged the sheaves and tied the pole down, that danger was lessened considerably, so the peasants praised his work.

25

O n the evening of the third day the priest's wheatfield looked like a shorn sheepskin. Swarms of sparrows were gleaning the stubble. After the last wagonload left, the harvesters formed in double file, preparatory to the traditional ceremony of carrying home the cross made of wheat stalks.

"Pretty" Suzan was the villagers' choice for the honor of carrying the cross. They would have preferred Ileana "the Beautiful," but for the suspicion of her alliance with the Evil One. Tedescu, however, had his own mind. When they made ready to hand the cross to Suzan, he came forward and took it. He said: "Friends, good weather favored us; our work is done. Our venerable priest will thank you in better words than mine for your help, but I want to thank you all, in my own name, for the privilege of working with you at this beautiful task. I might say, a holy task. So, friends, I offer you each and all my hearty thanks."

"Our pleasure, our pleasure to have you with us, Teacher," answered the peasants.

"Now," resumed Tedescu, "we shall carry this cross to the house of our venerable host, to remain there until next harvest, when another one will take its place. As it is a girl's duty to carry it, I am giving it to Ileana. She will get home drenched," he smiled, "but she will forgive us, I hope, for if the embroidery on her shirt should run, that won't be our fault." He placed the wheat-cross into Ileana's hands.

The assembly was silent. No one moved, but all eyes turned on the priest. The priest stood aghast, watching the girl take the cross. "If she is in league with Satan, she will drop the cross," he thought. But Ileana held it against her chest. The priest hesitated for a short time; then, going up to her, he blessed the cross, holy emblem of their faith and symbol of God's blessing with bread. Tedescu, who was near him, caught the unsteadiness in the priest's voice.

Singing, the procession wended its way through the village. At each house boys and girls waited with buckets of water to sprinkle the wheat-cross, a ritual of blessing the harvest and of forecasting the rains of next year. When the harvesters reached the priest's house Ileana was drenched from head to foot. The pink of her arms showed through her sleeves, from her hair the water ran over her face and neck. The cross was dripping and heavy with water, but Ileana held it close to her.

Veronica met the harvesters in the yard and was about to take the cross from Ileana, when she turned very pale and, instead of taking the cross, she stared at the fence and crossed herself. Everybody turned to look. They were no less shocked, for over the fence projected the black head of a goat, with long, twisted horns, looking at them. A woman spat out so suddenly, crying, "May the holy cross kill you, Satan," that Ileana dropped the cross. She bent down for it. Everybody was edging away, but Tedescu went to her. Then he looked and saw the goat. Tedescu hurried out of the yard and into the school yard, which was only separated from the priest's by that fence. The gate was open. The black goat was there, with its front legs on the branch of a plum tree, nibbling at the leaves. He did not disturb the animal but ran back. He called out, laughing: "It is our mayor's buck—come and see. He is trying to get at the plums."

At first nobody seemed to believe him. They whispered; then talked loudly among themselves, the women still under the spell of fright. Then two young boys went to the fence, and after them others, and they climbed up to look into the school yard. "It is the mayor's buck," they cried, "true as day." Now the women ventured to the fence. The goat turned and looked at them "like may the holy cross kill him," they said.

Some of the peasants joked about the occurrence, but only half-heartedly. Tedescu alone laughed, mocking any one who looked doubtful.

Veronica regained her composure so that she even

smiled, in her motherly way, when she took the wheat-
cross from Ileana.

After the meal—which was a feast—the harvesters
danced. The whole village was gathered in the priest's
yard. The first dance was a *hora,* in which young and old
participate. So many did that the circle was big enough to
go around the house. Swinging and rocking, the circle
moved first to the right, then to the left, slowly; then the
fiddlers livened up and the dancers rushed concentrically,
reducing the circle to the minimum and, hopping back-
wards, widened it again. After the *hora* came the *reel.*

One-eyed John danced with his wife, but he was
watching Ileana. Presently he saw Tedescu leading Suzan
by the hand towards Ileana, and the three started the first
slow steps of the *reel.* Tapping the ground the hunchback
moved to the right and to the left, circularly, a girl on
each side. Then his strong voice rang out, reciting to
the music:

> "Green leaves of the oak,
> Listen to my longing
> Told to the night.
> Listen to my plight.
> For the dear one is my yearning,
> For her soothing voice.
> Tell her, oak leaves, of my pining,
> Tell her of my pain,
> And sing to her my choice."

Now, as the tempo of the *reel* quickened, Tedescu placed his hands about the girls' waists, they clasping hands on his back, and the three commenced to spin round. Their feet close together, the tips of their boots almost touching, they resembled a large cone revolving on its tip.

In the *sirba,* which is also danced in a circle, like the *hora*—one man one girl holding hands, except that they skip and hop—Danila took courage and danced on Ileana's side, Tedescu holding her other hand with Veronica next to him. Danila tried several times to speak to Ileana, but she looked straight ahead, as if he were not there. But when the circle broke up he did not release her hand. "I want—to—to say something—to you—but—but I cannot." In a sudden outburst he bent over Ileana's hand and kissed it.

It was late. The peasants were leaving. At the gate One-eyed John turned and called: "Where is Ileana? We are going home, girl!"

"I must go, Danila," Ileana said hastily, pulling her hand away.

26

T ED E S C U did not go home. He roamed through the
fields for hours. She has someone in the city. I can feel
it. She goes to the city for that, I feel it, he said to himself.

He could not remember how he got home. The sun
was high when he awoke. He heard voices in the street
and the clattering of wagons. Repeatedly he picked up
the violin, only to lay it down again. I have no right to
pry into her life, he told himself. But his heart said: you
must. You love her. You are not prying, you are loving.
You must tell her your love. You deserve her. Your love
deserves her love. And you are not certain that she has a
lover in the city. But I am! How can you be? Because she
betrays it. In words I cannot say how she betrays it, but
I feel it. He tortured himself, unable to find the shred of
a soothing thought. At length he decided to ask Ileana
frankly. "Tell me the truth, Ileana,"—that's how I will
say it. But the next moment he felt he could not do that.
Besides, what justified his feeling about her being in love
with someone in the city? Well, it was this: she was
happier now, that he could see, despite her trying to hide
it. It revealed itself, her happiness, in her becoming more
beautiful than ever, more graceful even. As one whose
happiness is settled. There was that ease in her earnest-

ness which said: all these who surround me in the village are beside my real life.

Then again, out of his despair and his struggle to get some light as to what to do, came this: I must face my rival. But, in the tangle of his thoughts, the idea formed itself that his rival might be the devil himself. At this idea he stared dazedly. "Am I going crazy?" he cried suddenly. "These peasants, with their dark beliefs, have upset my reason."

He picked up the violin, furiously snapping the strings. There was loud knocking on the door. "Who is there?" shouted Tedescu.

"Will you come out—for a walk?" Danila called, without opening the door.

The hunchback threw the violin on the bed, as if this thought of a walk had been his own, and ran out.

Through the village they walked silently. When they got to the fields the warm light and the fragrance of the open, productive land calmed Tedescu. He even felt compassion for Danila, who was pale and looked as if he had not slept the night. Understanding that the youth wished to speak to him, yet was unable to begin, the hunchback said: "Well, Danila, speak."

Danila, as if waiting just for these words, began talking quickly. "Tedescu, you are my only friend. My good friend. I must tell you—to no one else. I can speak to no one else. Only to you—I must tell it to you—I can live no longer. No—Tedescu—I—I am going to kill myself."

Tedescu stopped. He put his hands on Danila's shoulders, looked into his eyes. Deeply, searchingly. He was relieved. He found in Danila's eyes fearful indecision, but no despair. Almost tenderly he took his hand, saying: "Come into that little grove, Danila."

They went into the birch grove on the knoll and sat down on the moss. Tedescu took his hat off and deliberately, as if talking to himself, told Danila his life story. My misfortune is greater than his, that will make him bear his own more easily, he thought. He told Danila of his childhood—a happy time, when the hope of becoming a great man was already in him. Of the joy of his parents, whose only son he was, and of their plans for his future. Then came the unexpected misfortune—the accident that not only crippled his body but turned his life off the road of his dreams. The premature death of his father, because of his boy's stunted life, which made a living corpse of his mother who could never look at him without crying.

As Tedescu spoke Danila's feelings turned to him with the warmth of his youth. Indeed, his misfortune is as great as mine, he thought. He listened without moving.

Tedescu told his story in that even, colorless voice in which alone great suffering can be expressed. Danila began to feel that it was this poor hunchback who needed help. Yet, finishing his own story, Tedescu said: "You, Danila, you are the hope of your parents—you are their life. Not only must you live but you must live up to their hope and trust in you. They give you all and you must use it dutifully. You must be a man. You must study—you can. This is the first wound to your heart, but you must let it heal. It will heal."

Danila grasped his hand. "Yes, yes, you are a true friend. I am sad for you, in my heart."

Tedescu should have been content with this, but he also was young and intensely sincere. Therefore he could not refrain from saying: "You may well be sad for me, Danila, for I also love her."

This avowal of Tedescu did not at first disturb Danila. On the contrary, it increased his compassion for the teacher so that, in a momentary outburst, he said: "Tedescu, we are brothers."

27

ST. PETER's day was nearing. The village resembled
an ant hill. The last of the wheat was being hauled from
the fields. Everywhere the threshing was going on. The
better-to-do peasants had the machine, the poor ones
threshed with flails and winnowed the wheat by throwing
it, with sweeping motions, high above the ground to
allow the breeze to blow away the chaff. They used for
this purpose large wooden shovels, scooped deep, which
looked like huge, elongated ladles with the tip cut off.

The women were shaking the sacks, patching them
up and cleaning the bins. These bins were smooth as
glass, redolent of wheat and aged pine. The children were
helping a little, but mostly playing in the straw and
watching the threshing machine, where they were allowed. The mayor, for instance, did not let them come
into his yard.

The village looked gilded. Everywhere there was
straw and chaff. Straw in the yards, straw in the barns
and straw in the wagons moving through the streets.
And over it all the ripening midsummer sun.

At the mill the wheels were not turning yet; the
water flowed uselessly in the large sluice, diverted from
the sluices where it drove the wheels. Miller Sandru and

his son were the busiest men in the village. They were replacing worn out wings on the wheels, driving large wooden pegs here and there in the clumsy grinding structure, greasing the huge axles and cutting ribs in the stones that had "worn out their teeth," as Sandru said. As they worked they sang and whistled. They were happy, for soon the mill would be the liveliest spot in the village. Sandru and his son will look like albinos, like very healthy ghosts moving about in the shadow of the mill.

Sandru would be going from trough to trough, hold his hand under the wooden funnel, catching the warm flour in his palm and knowingly rub it between his fingers. He would run here and there, slowing the wheel if the flour was too hot, lowering the stone if it was too coarse, and controlling everything with the air of a general.

He would only relax when, bending over a trough, he would breathe the tepid fragrance of the powdered kernels, saying with a beaming face: "The kidney of the soil, the flesh and substance of the earth." And on St. Peter's day each household will have fresh bread from the new wheat, milled by Sandru. The peasants, young and old, will take the first bite of the staff of life, that year's blessing, according to old custom. Man, woman, child, will take a piece of the new bread in the right hand and passing his arm back of the head bring it to his mouth from the left side. With some of the older folk it takes considerable twisting and turning, and there is much laughter.

During the week preceding St. Peter's the street is alive with women, girls and boys carrying some of the new wheat to the mill. They carry sacks, each according to his or her strength, the men busy with heavier work. While waiting for their flour the women spent the time with some handiwork: spinning, sewing or embroidering. They sat on the canal bank, in the shadow of the willows. The endless noise of the wheels encouraged their chatter. Many generations of women folk had sat on these banks, talking over, ranging and pigeonholing every occurrence in the village. Many a woman had sighed then as now: "If these old willows could only talk."

On this day a group of women were talking about Ileana. One of them brought up the savory bit of the hunchback teacher's serious interest in the girl. "He would be a good one in bed, hunch or no hunch on his back," a broad-hipped, red-faced woman was saying.

"Of course he would. He don't sweat the life out of him as our men do," answered her neighbor.

"He has broad shoulders," put in another woman.

"And hands, did you see? Large enough to carry you on his palms," tittered a young one.

"He could slap your—with that big paw of his."

"Oh, now—that stings."

"And tickles, too," a lively matron said, laughing.

"You ought to know!" several women cried in one voice. The cheery one blushed.

"He is no man's fool, he isn't," spoke up a dark young woman.

"You may swear to that, Marina," sing-songed a buxom young widow.

"Well, if he loves the girl, he keeps it in his gizzard. He don't trail after her like that poor Danila," one woman said.

"He is only a—a baby at that, Danila is."

"A baby? Don't you trust such babies in the dark, little one," advised an elderly woman, touching the arm of the speaker.

"No, no, not even at dusk," chimed in another.

"If I had a daughter of age, say sixteen or seventeen," said a middle-aged woman, "I should hand her over to the teacher, on top of a chestful of new linen."

"Well, what's that? Sixteen is a ripe enough age. I had my John, my first-born, before I was sixteen. Three months before, to the day."

"And that was just eight months—to the day—after your marriage," specified an all-knowing gossip.

"John is no worse for that—is he?" snapped the mother of John.

"No harm, darling," soothed the gossip.

"The full time is nine months," put in a sharp-nosed, thin woman.

"What? Are you going to sharpen your tongue on my affairs?" cried John's mother. "Fie on you, Miriam Dan, for shame! I was young when I met my man, that's gospel truth, but I knew things."

"You knew enough to get out of the cold those biting autumn evenings, and Pavel's sheepskin was big enough for two," the sharp-nosed one said.

"Your eyes are gimlets when it comes to other people's doings, Miriam. What you did in the cold nights the Lord only knows, but you got flatter and flatter, front and back, like an old shingle. But I wouldn't have your tongue for all the treasures in the world. Not I, God forbid! You can bite the half of it off and it will be as long as a lizard's still. You will be dead and stiff as frozen cow's flop, but your tongue will keep wagging about your neighbors. Yes, Miriam Dan, may the holy host of saints protect us from it," whimpered John's mother.

"Now, now, you two, don't you get to snatching your turbans off. We started out at one place and landed—God knows where. For shame—you two! This is a neighborly chat." This from an elderly woman who could use her tongue as well as any of them.

The other women were silent, hoping the quarrel would lead to something. And it might have, for Miriam was raking her brain for the most stinging words, but one of the women whispered: "Hush, there comes Ileana."

Ileana had turned the corner, coming towards the

mill. Carrying a bag of wheat under his arm Tedescu walked by her side. The women watched them until they entered the mill, then they turned to each other. Each pair of eyes expressed the same meaning, for they all got up, deciding it was high time to go into the mill and see about the flour. Like a flock of geese they made for the mill.

Ileana was asking the miller: "When will my turn come, Uncle Sandru?" The miller, his eyes bright under powdered eyebrows and lashes, began counting on his fingers: "Miriam one, Sara two, Nutza three—you come the eighth, Ileana. A full two hours yet. You see, I keep those big wheels at a slow trot. No use heating up the flour. Women folk can keep their fingers busy, waiting a little longer. The bread is that much better—for the cool milling." Sandru turned to the teacher for approval.

Tedescu nodded. "Sandru," he said, "if I weren't a bookman I would like to be a miller."

Sandru laughed and bending over a trough caught the flour in his hand. He turned his head to Tedescu, saying in a loud voice: "Well, I am not the man to be surprised at another man's thoughts. A miller's work is good and wholesome, Teacher. He grinds the grain— good and well—but is that all? Oh, no! He gets the soul of it. Sure as you're standing there. The stones crush the body of the wheat, and the miller—he sniffs up its soul. Sure as day. Come here, Teacher. Bend over, bend close to the flour. Smell it. What do you smell? Well, I'll tell you what it is—the soul of the wheat. That's what your nose is drinking. And see here"—he banged his chest with his fists—"good lungs, eh? You never see a miller spit red —never! That powdered wheat, that fine, white dust of the staff of life—that cleans your lungs like good mountain air. When the wheels turn, they sing. When they stop —the water sings, and the miller sleeps like a stuffed goose. If he snores he won't awaken his wife either. No, no. True, Teacher, a miller is more than a man—oh, yes, he's a man and a half." And Sandru shook with laughter.

Tedescu smiled, but the women laughed with Sandru. They heard but half of what he said, but they knew their miller. He was a gay bird and they laughed heartily. The women knew Sandru; yes, and Sandru knew them. He knew them, in their kind, as he knew the mill. With this one, just a word; this one, you can pat her cheeks; this one, grab her and kiss her. And he practiced all these means when alone with the particular kind of woman.

Still, much of a man that Sandru was, he was no more than mortal, so he made his mistakes. The whole village knew that Sandru's round, jolly face was slapped occasionally by feminine hands, but he took it with good grace, without even checking up on his discrimination. That would have been useless for this reason: no woman ever complained to her husband about him. So Sandru lived in peace. He admired the peasant women's discretion. He himself was a man who had seen much but said little. He was, really, the eyes of the village.

The banks of the canal were cool on summer evenings, the old willows a fine shelter to lovers. They came there in pairs. And in the spring, when the ground was damp, the young men brought their sheepskins for the girls to sit on. Sit on! When the willows were in bloom, their beaded tassels spreading a bitter-sweet fragrance, there were as many young couples on the banks as there were May-chafers, Sandru said. And he added: "But the chafers buzzed and droned, while the youngsters only whispered or twittered softly—most of the time being as silent as the grass."

28

TEDESCU had met Ileana by chance, though not entirely so. He had started out from home, walking slowly towards her house. He knew that someone from John's would be going to the mill that day and, as the men folk were in the fields and Chiva busy about the house, it would be Ileana. He wondered, however—was even anxious—whether she had left already. He kept watching the gate as soon as he caught sight of it. Once he thought the gate was being opened and he hurried—but it was not.

Reaching the corner of the house he heard Ileana say: "I am going, mother. No, it is not heavy." Tedescu counted one, two, three, aware of his heart beating faster and faster. On the count of nineteen the latch clicked and the gate opened. Ileana came out, a sack over her shoulder divided like a saddle-bag.

"Good morning, Ileana," Tedescu greeted.

"It's more day than morning, Teacher Tedescu, so I will say good day," returned Ileana with a serious mien.

"You are right, Ileana, the sun is high. Will you let me carry your bag?"

"It is not heavy, not at all," she answered.

"Then you can trust it to me, I shan't drop it," he

smiled. Ileana let him lift it off her shoulder. He balanced it over his arm, carrying it as if it were a basket.

They walked in silence, Tedescu embarrassed, trying to think what to say. And so, in silence, they got to the mill.

When they were coming back the sun was nearly at midday. The heat rippled in flickering wavelets over the walls and fences. The dust was hot under foot. Tedescu was happy to be near Ileana. Her love has made her more beautiful, he thought. Even her walk is different. I would give my life to be the cause of this change in her. Why don't I tell her? But how? That question he could not answer. Perhaps words were not necessary. Only the evidence of his devotion to her. In time she will feel this devotion as part of her life, and she will need it. Then it shall reveal to her his great love, without a spoken word, and make her happy. Yes, but Ileana is happy—now. It was all useless, all this thinking of his. Then, unaware of how it happened, he asked: "Will you go to town on Saturday, Ileana?"

"Yes," she answered simply.

"You like the city, don't you?"

"I like to cross the plains—best of all. The city is too crowded and noisy."

"But there are many people there—all sorts."

"They are too pale, most of them—those who live there."

"That is true, Ileana. They are always in the shadow of the houses. But sometimes, by chance, one meets an interesting person there. Say this"—he blushed terribly but could not stop talking—"for an example, somebody meets somebody like—like yourself."

Ileana did not answer. But Tedescu noticed a change in her eyes. As if they suddenly descried an object which interested them. And she thought: that is true. This thought of Serafim flew into her mind, like a spark flying up the chimney. What did the teacher ask me just now? He cares for me. What the people say—he is not afraid of that. Serafim is not afraid either—but Serafim don't know about me. Would he—if he knew? I must answer the teacher. "What did you ask me, Teacher Tedescu?"

"I? I haven't asked you anything, Ileana. I said only —about people in the city, meeting sometimes a person, a very—a lovely person—like yourself." Tedescu blushed, not daring to look at her.

Ileana also blushed, was annoyed at herself for it and kept silent. After a while, however, she wanted to punish herself for blushing, so she said: "But you know the city so well, you must have found somebody there, somebody very nice." She glanced at him.

"No. I have not. Not like—in Aciliu," he said.

"Here in our village?" Ileana asked and again she blushed.

"Yes, Ileana, here in Aciliu. But I did have a great

friend in the city. A teacher—a professor, a great man. Him I loved with all my heart—a long time ago."

"And now, you don't love him any more?" she asked.

"It is so long ago, and now he is gone away—to Budapest. He lives in his books. He is a great, learned man."

"But do you think of him now, Teacher Tedescu?"

"Yes, often. I envy him, because he is happy."

Ileana thought for a long time before she asked: "Why do you envy happy people, Teacher?"

"I don't envy all the happy people, Ileana. I envy this man, because he can be happy—alone."

They were approaching Ileana's house. Tedescu was sorry. "How do you know he is happy?" she asked.

"That is hard to tell, Ileana. I can't say how, but I know it. I know it, you see, as I know that—that you are happy yourself."

Ileana was startled. She looked at him. She saw, for the first time, that this hunchback's eyes had a penetrating light in them, and yet were sad. They were strong eyes, friendly, eyes that one can trust, she felt. His mouth was large, but the lips were firm. He seemed handsome. Yet—she thought—beside Serafim he would be—he would be like the others, and clumsy. Serafim, graceful in his strength, would laugh at him. And inwardly she almost laughed at Tedescu herself.

At the gate they parted. Ileana thought no more of Tedescu. Serafim, the man of all men, Serafim filled her thoughts. She sang to him as she sat embroidering. She smiled at the little stitches that made up the design; as her hand moved with the needle, she smiled at the needle, shining like her joy, thinking that all these—embroidery, needle and the very light of day—were part of Serafim. She wondered where he was then; and, as by witchery, with the wondering about Serafim she saw suddenly Tedescu's sad eyes.

29

T E D E S C U believed himself free of all superstition. Nor did he believe in miracles, he thought. Yet he would never put on his left shoe first, nor step over a door sill with his left foot when entering a house the first time. But these he considered childhood habits, inculcated in him by his mother. "Right foot first, son, always right foot first," she used to say when they went somewhere. His mind dwelt on these things in connection with Ileana.

Leaving her he went into the garden. He walked between the rows of grapevines. Several times he stopped, looking interestedly at the forming grapes. Then he counted the clusters on one vine. There were more clusters than he thought. It was a tall plant, the vines branching from a thick butt just a few inches out of the ground, but there were five main branches, so long that they were looped several times, tied with straw to the pole. The Guarnesh grape, he said to himself. He was unaccountably fascinated by the pronged shoots, groping for an anchorage. Where they found one they curled around it, their tips forming a ring. These shoots behaved like the living antennae of an insect. He put out his finger against the tips of a tendril and waited to see how it would act. He was thinking of miracles and in his thoughts he linked Ileana with miracles. He wanted to reason about miracles, but his mind was lazy. Yet he arrived at the conclusion that what we do not know in the light of cause and effect belongs to the world of miracles. What we know is like a grain of sand; what we don't know is like the rest of the sand on the whole beach. That is the awful extent of the realm of miracles. Sometimes from that vastness a miracle sends its tendrils out into our world. They are mysteries. They come to lead us to trace God's work to its source. There is a God—no doubt. Even Professor Nemety is devoting his life to the building of a bridge, made of numbers, on which our understanding could cross the—the abysmal rift and join with God. Ileana is the tendril of a miracle. Wait. Here. Let us see. If this shoot from the grapevine will take my finger and wind around it, then that shall mean that Ileana will accept my love. Here, he whispered to the oracular tendril, you see, I am marked, as the peasants say. A hunchback. Ileana is marked also. She is marked by beauty. So great that it marks her. The peasants say that because it is so great it comes from the devil, because the devil is less mysterious than God. As one who discovered a deep truth, Tedescu exulted.

Affectionately he watched the tendril. The delicate prongs quivered on his finger, as if testing it. Then with infinite slow caution the plant-tentacles began gliding over his finger to close around it. "It is true, it is true!"

he cried. He kissed the plant-shoot. "Ileana—it is true!
We belong to each other."

Carefully he released his finger, bending the tendril
close to a branch on which it caught.

30

ILEANA was at the mill when Tedescu got there. She was talking to a young woman who, sitting on a sack, was suckling her baby. The mother's breast, white and full, rested against the infant's pink face. One of the baby's hands was on the breast, the other hand played with his toes. When he dug his fingers in the breast, the mother admonished: "Gently, little man, gently, my angel." As Tedescu came near, the woman covered her breast with a handkerchief.

Ileana bent over the infant, touching his face with her fingers. "Little lamb, lambkin, his Mummy's sweet angy—angel," she murmured, her lips puckered as if kissing him. The young mother watched Ileana timidly. There was fear in her eyes. She was sorry that she did not cover the baby's face when Ileana came. Turning her head to one side she spat out three times, whispering the invocation against the evil eye.

Several times, pretending to caress the baby, she covered his face with her hand, but she feared that it was not enough. As soon as Ileana left, the woman ran home to "quench embers in water", that being the remedy against the evil eye in case her abracadabra, pronounced while the girl was looking at the infant, proved ineffective.

Her heart sank at the frightful augury of the embers, for as she dropped them into the water, chanting, all the three sank heavily to the bottom. But she continued the soothsaying, dipping her finger in the water and tracing crosses on the baby's forehead and in his palms. Her hand trembled as she dripped some of the water into the baby's mouth. The little fellow screwed up his face and slobbered it out, but the mother wiped it back into his mouth, until she was certain that he swallowed a few drops.

Presently the baby started to cry. The frightened woman coaxed, cajoled, laughed and sang to him, rocking him in her arms, but the little fellow only cried the more. Soon the woman began to cry also. Wailing, now crying, now smiling, she talked to the baby: "Hush, little angel, mother is with you. Hush, mother's treasure, Mummy is taking your pain to herself. Hush, my dear heart, the angels will close your eyes with their hands." In her distress she rocked the baby up and down. The infant cried pitifully, choking, his face purple. The woman grew frantic. She was sure that the eyes of the possessed girl had drilled into the heart of her baby. She put him on the bed and, patting his belly, his back, she moaned and mumbled every word of incantation she knew. At length, exhausted by crying, the little fellow was seized with hiccups. At each hiccup the mother cried out: "God bless my little boy—good health to mammy's darling—God protect you." But the baby did not quieten.

She picked him up and ran to the gate. Anxiously she scanned the street for someone to send for the midwife. A woman came along. "Here, Stana, for God's sake, come quick!" cried the young mother.

"Mercy, Oana, what's happened?" asked the woman.

"The evil eye, Stana. My little one—that witch, One-eyed John's girl—she looked at him with her devil's eyes —run quick, run for the midwife."

"God preserve us!" Stana yelled, starting on a run.

When the midwife arrived the baby was asleep. They bent over him. They heard noises in his belly, like the gurgling of water. The midwife went to the shelf, took two earthen pot covers and put them on the tripod over the embers. When they were hot enough she took one, wrapped it in a piece of woolen cloth and placed it on the infant's belly. The baby stirred feebly but did not wake up. When that cover cooled they applied the other.

"It's wind colics," whispered the midwife. The young woman insisted it was the evil eye, saying: "I saw with my own eyes how the fire from her eyes went into the eyes of my little angel and he couldn't turn his face from her. He was tearing at my breast as never before, like a vampire, poor little angel—God forgive my sinful words."

"Now, you just be quiet, Oana, or you'll sour the

milk in your breasts," advised the midwife. "Whatever
the cause, your little one will be well as ever, very soon.
But those gases, they got to come out of him. Hear, hear
—how they boil inside him. Now, and—you heard it?
That relieved him—a great deal. You'll have diapers to
wash, but he'll be a soldier yet, never fear. Now, my good
one, I must go. Next time when he cries like that, just
heat up the pot covers and put them on his belly. See that
you bake your bread for St. Peter's. I must hurry and
look after mine. The dough must be running over the
trough. God preserve you. Don't forget—hot pot covers
for wind colics." And the midwife ran off.

Before evening the whole village was buzzing about
the terrible misfortune that came to Oana. The gossips
had so added to the tale that now the rumor was that the
baby won't live through the night, for against eyes like
Ileana's there was no cure.

Even more than by this gossip—which was in one
respect belied by the fact that Oana's baby not only did
not die but was as well as a healthy baby could be—Ileana
was pained by the women's behavior. When they saw her
coming they exchanged glances, whispering and nudging
each other. If there were babies in their arms they covered them up carefully. They even called to the tots who
were playing about and made them turn away from the
girl. They also repeated aloud the words against the evil
eye as if they could be hurt themselves by Ileana's eyes.

Not only that, but now they dug up the prattle of the two women who had said that Ileana could disappear as she pleased "from before you", because "she did vanish like a ghost when we got to the city with her, in the blinking of an eye," the two young women kept saying.

Little by little the teacher was also dragged into the gossip. At first they spoke pityingly of him. "An innocent prey to the girl's witchery," they said. But as they saw him with Ileana quite often now, and never a sign of fear in him, they began to whisper: "The hunchback must be something to the devil—God save us. How else?"

31

TEDESCU paid no attention to the gossips. His concern was with the suspected rival in the city. He planned to go to the city and face him. But for that he must know who it was. He could find out only by spying on Ileana. He could not bring himself to do so. He decided to win Ileana in another way. First, to deter her from going to the city by interesting her in the development of her voice. Once this idea lodged in his head, he set about putting it in action.

The notary had many city friends who came each year to the grape-harvest festival which he gave. That was always a great holiday in the village. It lasted three days, with banqueting, dancing, singing and much gaiety. It would be the best opportunity to bring Ileana to the attention of the outsiders as a singer. Tedescu was certain of her success. What he was uncertain of was whether Ileana would agree—first to let herself be prepared by him and, second, to sing at the notary's. However, these uncertainties did not deter him. So, one evening, when Ileana and Chiva were sitting in front of the house with the boys, he took courage and told her. "Ileana," he said, "your voice is very beautiful, you can do wonders with it. But you must train it."

Chiva listened, understanding only half of what Tedescu was saying; yet she nodded approval all the time. For she felt that the teacher's interest in the girl was an honor to the house.

Ileana did not answer for a long time. He will be with me a good deal, she was thinking. Do I want that? As to singing—I can sing enough for myself. But—if I should sing so that the city folk, as he says, admired it? And it occurred to her that if she sang like that, Serafim himself would admire her for it. That decided her. "What have I to do then, Teacher Tedescu?" she asked.

"That is simple enough, Ileana," answered Tedescu, beside himself with joy. "I will teach you to read music —the way one reads a book, and then you will sing some of the folk songs which are written down, words and music."

Chiva bent over to look at Ileana, as if she were already a being to be wondered at. She beamed all over, shaking her head. "Oh, there are such things in this world, such wonderful things," she said.

When Stan came she told him everything. The old man listened attentively, then said: "Well, daughter, you take a nightingale, a wild bird of the air, eh? Well, you clip its tongue loose and what happens? You can teach it to whistle any tune you want. You whistle to it—she stands perched in the cage with its head cocked to one side and looks at you, sort of gurgling in its throat, like a child moving its lips when you teach it a new word. Good. You do that once, twice—several times—then one day you come up to the cage and start the tune and lo and behold, the bird whistles it, clear as snow water."

This long speech of Stan was meant to be a hearty approval of Ileana's learning to sing, as the teacher had proposed. The family was a little concerned about One-eyed John, as to what he would say. But they knew that he liked the teacher; he would not mind, they decided.

Ileana surprised even Tedescu. Her memory was good and she had the gift of perfect pitch—"a rare enough gift", as the teacher said. Ileana did not know what it was until explained by him. Yet, though she learned well and applied herself earnestly, neither her achievements nor her application brought the result desired by Tedescu. Just the contrary. The more she advanced in her work, the more eager she became to go to the city. And it was the pupil who urged the teacher. Not with words, of course, but with a tireless devotion to her task.

In less than one month they had a "trial concert", as Tedescu called it, at the notary's who had an old harp-sichord in his "large room" or salon. Ileana sang several folk songs, which she knew since childhood, to Tedescu's accompaniment on the harpsichord. She had to learn the few modifications made in these songs by Zamfirescu, a talented and accomplished musician who devoted his life to collecting and recording folk songs. She also sang a modern song by a young composer who used the elements of folk music in his compositions. It was in the evening, and no sooner did the first neighbor hear the singing than she immediately spread the news, so that presently the street filled with peasants. They huddled against the notary's house, packed like sheep in a *strunga,* hardly breathing. Such singing they had never heard in their lives. The *doina* Ileana sang to Tedescu's violin obligato; it was like the voices of two angels, the peasants said, and they cried. Only they knew that it was not angels who produced such wonderful sounds, but a girl of their own village and a hunchback, "God preserve us." And when they heard the last piece, the romance, in the singing of which Ileana's voice revealed itself fully, reaching "so high that it was like the whistle of a bird and low as the wailing of the forest", the peasants crossed themselves, surer than ever that no human being could sing like that. And they went home, whispering among themselves "how great the power of the Unclean One is, what tricks he has for the snaring of human souls."

That singing of Ileana furnished them the strongest proof that she was possessed. And as it happened that a thunder storm broke over the village that very night and the lightning struck the only poplar in Aciliu—and in the notary's very garden—what more evidence did they want?

Another thing happened also. Some peasants went to the priest to speak to him about their concern regarding Ileana. To find if something could be done to obviate possible danger to the entire village. They spoke in a round-about way, with much hemming and hawing and crossing themselves. But what did they hear "from the mouth of his Reverence"? They heard that on the very day when Ileana sang at the notary's, Danila fell sick and it was the jaundice. "The jaundice, the jaundice," repeated the community.

Not that this illness was uncommon, nor that they did not know a sure cure for it—crushed embers drunk in gold-colored wine—but that it should come to poor Danila on that very day, that was the thing. The thing to "consider and reconsider".

Then also this teacher. They saw him some days so happy that he "was bursting with it", and again, at other times, he would be "as sad as death". And all this since that evening. The village was buzzing like a swarm of bees.

32

ONE-EYED JOHN heard all of the gossip: heard it in the fields on weekdays and at the inn on Sundays. In his heart he was sure that the Lord was meting out punishment to him by letting Satan take Ileana's soul. But against the teacher he could not believe the gossip. The teacher was a good Christian; more, he was the son of a venerable priest whose piety and good heart were known far and wide, John reasoned. As for Ileana there could be no doubt. Day and night he tormented himself, trying to find a means of cheating the devil and save the girl's soul. "But how? Good Lord, show me a way," he groaned.

He went to the priest, but that poor man had no advice to give. All he said was: "Look at my Danila, look at him, John. He melts away like a taper on the stove, and is as yellow, just because of your daughter. God only knows how she bewitched him. We hear him cry in his room and we hear him call her name. All we can do, John, is to pray. God will help us, in some way, I am sure, even when we don't expect it."

That was all the consolation John could get from the priest. In regard to Danila John did not very much blame Ileana. "She is a strong, healthy girl—apart from the other thing—and she has a head, too. But this youngster, he has sour milk in his veins—God forgive me if I slander," concluded John, slapping his mouth three times. Then he chuckled and called himself a fool for it.

Then, several nights later, something happened to John. It was a warm, sultry night. The sun had set in a bank of black clouds that stood unmoving, like a rock, against the sky. Lightning flashed in the distance and thunder rumbled heavily. John went to sleep on the barn floor, the house being "like an oven."

During the night he awoke suddenly, "as if shaken by a hand". It was pouring. From the roof the water fell in sheets. He stared into the dark rain. Then came a flash of lightning and, in that blinking of the eyes, "as if I had waited for it,"—John told the priest—"I saw in the middle of the yard a naked woman, standing there in the rain, with her arms stretched out. But when another flash came, there was nothing. I can swear, Reverend Father, that the unholy ghost, for it could be no other, was stretching its arms towards the house, as if calling to someone. It blinded my eyes, your Reverence, so beautiful it was, if beautiful one could call the devil. This is gospel truth, your Reverence," he concluded.

The priest shook his head and advised John to pray. John did pray, between long outbursts of heavy swearing. The swearing seemed to relieve him more and had a direct and quick effect. It goaded the oxen, drove his sons scurrying on their errands, and made Chiva stop up her

ears. If he happened to be in the house, his little daughter
Maria would run and stick her head under the pillows.
Only Ileana "never blinked an eye". When he thought of
that, John cursed again.

As to the gossips, John let them prattle, because now
the whole matter remained a thing between himself and
the devil. Occasionally, of course, when drunk and surly,
he would turn upon either man or woman who spoke
about his troubles, with such fury that he shut them up.

John's nights became more and more troubled: he
had fearful nightmares or he would toss for hours before falling asleep. In those hours his brain worked "like
a churn", he said. On such a night from this churning
resulted a question. "Might as well settle it now," he
mumbled, getting up. He glanced at the dying embers,
spitting on them. Everyone was sleeping. He threw his
sheepskin over his shoulders and walked out quietly.

The night was clear, a multitude of stars "up there".
John walked along the silent houses noiselessly, for his
*opancze** made no more noise than bare feet. Yet, near a
gate a dog barked. "Shut up, cur," John growled. He got
to Tedescu's house, where he stopped under a window
and listened. Examining the window he noticed a narrow
streak of light. Then he heard, or seemed to hear, a noise
inside. He tapped on the pane. There were steps in the

* Rude sandals, made of one piece of cow's hide.

room, then silence. John tapped again, a little louder. The
curtain lifted, Tedescu appearing in the window. John
put his head close to it and whispered: "It is me, Teacher
—open the gate."

Tedescu did not hear, so he opened the window.
"Good evening, John," he greeted.

"Good may be your heart, Teacher. Will you let me
come in at this hour?"

Tedescu nodded and went to unlock the gate. They
entered the house without speaking. Tedescu closed the
window, dropping the blanket over it. A thick brown
blanket hanging on two nails, serving for curtain.

"Well, John, what good wind brings you at this
time?" he asked, pushing up a chair. "Sit down."

"I will, Teacher. It's hot in here—and I with this
wolf on my back." John jerked the sheepskin off his
shoulders, coughed a little, cracked his knuckles and
smoothed his hair with both hands. He glanced about
the room, at the books piled on the bench and at the
violin hanging on a peg in the wall. He coughed again,
then he began: "Well, Teacher Tedescu, I came, but as
we say, the coming is easier than the errand. My legs
are, so to say, more nimble than my tongue—but I shall
speak. The matter is simple. Plain as my palm. I am a
peasant and you are a teacher, a gentleman. You went to
school and you gleaned learning, I worked all my life and
gathered callouses in my hands and, if not for this stout

belt, I might have ruptured myself too. That is so, that is
settled. Now, as we simple folk say, the difference between
man and man, in the eyes of the Lord, is what their sins
make it, no other; but in the eyes of the world, you and I
are different, apart from counting our sins. You are a
gentleman, entitled and honorably deserving to be; on my
part, I am a peasant—no more, no less. Yet I come to
you, to talk my heart out as man to man." John coughed
again.

"You are very welcome, John. Man to man, as you
say," Tedescu answered, smiling.

"Then, Teacher, I shall speak," continued John, "and
with your good will, declare before our Maker my heart
is as heavy as a boulder. And you will answer me, Teacher,
wisely and in truth, so I shall be soothed by your words,
answering to my rough words, for you know us, who
are simple folk. Well, now, here it is. You come to my
house; you talk to us, to Chiva, my wife, to the boys, to
the little girl and to me. To all of us. Very good and very
well. But now, with your leave, by the testimony of my
simple mind, Teacher Tedescu, I ask—are you not coming for Ileana? Now, I said it." John clamped his hands
on his knees, looking straight into the hunchback's eyes.

"Yes, John," Tedescu replied in a firm voice, "you
are right. I come for Ileana."

"That now is a man's answer, straight and true. So,
I know positively now, that what I felt is true. Good. But

I must speak more. You see, where there is smoke, there is fire also. That is true, we all know that. So, when people talk a lot, there is, so to say, the smoke, so at the bottom of it is the fire. You see where I am pointing, Teacher? Well, the people talk about my daughter, this way and that way, but they come always to the one thing, and that, Teacher, you know what it is. They come to that. Good. But the girl is flesh of my flesh, bone of my bone, she is my child. This matter about her is a punishment from God. I am a sinner, I am her father, that we know. But here is a thought of mine: suppose my child fell into the river, would I not jump in to save her? I would, sure as it is night. Well, that makes it plain." His face darkened and he burst out: "My girl's soul is lost to the Unclean One. He, God save us, grins at me with her soul in his claws. Good, honest man that you are, Teacher, you understand me now. I must—I must cheat the devil and save the girl's soul. This I must. I must do it, Teacher." He smote his chest, staring at Tedescu wild-eyed.

"How will you do it, John?" Tedescu asked gently.

John remained silent for a while, then slowly, quietly he answered: "Teacher Tedescu, good friend, that is just what I came to see you about. How shall I do? How am I to do it? Do it I must—but how—that I don't know. So, I will ask you now, good friend, in plain words, tell me, how shall I cheat the devil to save the girl's soul?"

Tedescu became anxious. He had spoken to John before without result, trying to drive the thought about Ileana's being possessed out of the peasant's head. And now the man's request frightened him. Explanations, he felt, would be useless. He decided therefore that plain speaking was the best. So he said: "John, I cannot answer your question, because my belief is not like yours. Please listen to me. I am telling you the truth. I do not believe —I never did and I never will believe—that Ileana has anything to do with the devil, or the devil with her. Never! Never, John! It may be hard for you to understand me, John, but what I say is the truth."

John stared at him in horrified amazement. He never moved but stared at the teacher for a considerable time. Nor could Tedescu utter another word.

Suddenly the peasant jumped up, his dumb mouth open, his jaw moving as if he were to speak, but no word came out of him. He began to tremble, unable to take his eyes from the teacher. With a great effort he slowly raised his hand and crossing himself began to mumble: "May the holy cross kill you, Satan," his eyes riveted on the teacher. And so muttering and crossing himself he backed to the door, groped for the latch, his hand behind him, opened the door and ran out.

Tedescu remained dumbfounded, staring at the open door. After a long time he turned and looked about the room, as if to ascertain where he was. He noticed John's

sheepskin on the floor. Picked it up and hung it on a
peg behind the door. Went out and fastened the gate. He
stood in the yard, the great silence of the night heavy on
his ears. He looked up. He stood there, looking at the
stars. After a long time he muttered: "It is hardly be-
lievable that they are so far away. Space expands with
distance—and objects diminish. Good God—ever these
incomprehensible opposites. Is that *the law?* John's in-
sanity and his wife's simple faith. Ileana's beauty, the
hag's ugliness—God, God!"

He returned to his room. "John wants to save her
soul. The belief of the peasants grows daily. It threatens
her." He stared, tormented with anxiety. "What will he
do? He is her father! The whole gruesome legend is cen-
tered in him. Her own father! He will—would he attempt that? No, no! But he is crazy with fear of the
devil." Suddenly he cried: "I am the devil, John! I am
your devil. It is I who will take Ileana, soul and all."

He paced the room, his brain chasing now one
thought now another. Then a strong, an intense longing
for Ileana overcame the madness of his thoughts.

33

SERAFIM also was troubled in his mind. "She is creeping into my soul. She has the trickeries of all the women put together. Now she sings, with that voice of hers, keeping me boiling; now she lets me take her, scorching me with her passion. Are they holy, her beauty and her voice?" He was afraid of her, yet the desire for the girl he was marrying was only the shadow of Ileana's beauty. Nevertheless, he tried to wean his passion for Ileana through Saveta. But he could only kiss her with his eyes closed. When she trembled in his arms it was not her desire shaking her, it was a fear about Serafim's behavior—because he fondled her "with cold, heavy hands". She was like a "water-soaked log" to Serafim. She could not wholly awaken him. The male in him remained turgid, resentful. And Saveta could not respond to his caresses except with that fear-tremor. She did not know how those cold hands, those tight lips that kissed her—and it was as if a stone were pressed against her mouth—she did not know how they burned when Ileana was in Serafim's arms. Had she known it, her heart would have stopped cold.

Ileana, in those great passion unions with Serafim—in those moments when he was no longer the mate only but the fire that swallowed her—in those moments she had no other feeling save that of expiring with passion. Before she had met him she used to look in the mirror occasionally, as other village girls do, while now her eyes, her mouth, her hair, her skin, her breasts—every part of her—cried to her with Serafim's words. As he had admired them, as he kissed and fondled them. She went to bathe in the brook, often twice a day. The smooth creeping of the water over her body, the tingling of its chill, seemed like a living being. Or as if it were Serafim turned into the brook by his own witchery.

She went about humming by the hour, because Serafim admired her voice and Tedescu had told her that humming would make it more beautiful.

None of the other girls in the village acted as she did. Before she had met Serafim she was, in the ways of life, as they were. Thinking of the village girls she felt she could not be like them, yet she envied their community of life, their unitedness. Often she felt the need of confiding to her mother, to unburden her heart, to share with another woman her feelings. But she could not do it. She loved her mother deeply, yet she could not speak to her.

On her side Chiva was beginning to worry about Ileana. She watched the change in her, day by day. She heeded not the gossip; it was this change, this difference between Ileana and the other village girls that grew daily, it was this that worried her. She said to herself: "Ileana is beautiful—thank God for it. She is gifted—the Lord be blessed for it. She is as good as sunlight—but, where is she going? She's taken a path—where that leads—God help me to understand." Her mind, habitually half-asleep in the security of her faith and the humdrum of her work, awakened and it tormented her. She decided to speak to her father.

So when Stan came, in his usual hearty good humor, Chiva asked him into the guest room. The days were getting shorter, but this room, on the southern side of the house, held a pleasant warmth and was redolent with sweet mint and the fragrance of new linen and virgin wool. With mock surprise Stan asked: "Well, daughter, am I the district judge or what, to be shown in here?"

Chiva smiled, motioning for him to sit down on the bench near the window. "Father, I want to talk to you," she began, sitting down beside him.

"And weighty matter it must be, daughter, shutting my mouth to spitting, by bringing me here."

"Weighty enough, father. It is Ileana I want to speak about."

"Oh, well, daughter, she is a nice person to give our time to—yes, yes, truly she is."

"Father, please listen to me. I am her mother. She is in my heart, that girl of mine, all the time. And now I suffer because of her. More than anybody can know."

Stan lifted his eyebrows. "I understand you, daughter. Those tongues, venom and thorns—I understand."

"Father mine," interrupted Chiva, "it isn't the gossip I am thinking of, it is the girl herself. I've tried hard to understand her, but I can't make her out. She took another road from ours and is leaving us. God forbid—leaving us—This breaks my heart." Chiva wiped her eyes.

"How, how is that, daughter?" Stan asked, greatly surprised.

"I can't say just how, father, but I feel it. It is what she does. Now, this—she washes her hair every week, twice sometimes, and bathes every day in the brook. I caught her making eyes at herself in the mirror—God save our souls—and she goes about humming like a bumblebee. She even walks differently. At the meals I am in mortal fear for John, because he glares at the girl's hands —they are always so clean to the very nails, and the way she's got to holding the spoon or the fork, like nobody else. Then she goes too often to the city and—you see, father, a mother can feel that about her daughter—I feel that she has somebody there. To be sure, I know she is a healthy girl, strong, ripe for marriage—she's a woman since the age of fourteen, maybe a little earlier. I know that well. But you see, father, here in the village she scares away the young men, the best of them who asked her in marriage. Then, for her to go and maybe take a

man—in secret—I—well, it's beyond me. I am old enough,
father, to say it, so excuse me, a woman needs a man just
as he needs a woman, I know that. But what shall I do
with Ileana? How am I to manage her to take a man of
her kind and marry him and settle, and give her father
and mother peace, as a Christian child should? How shall
I manage that? I've never said so many words at one
time in all my life, father, but—but my heart is just
flowing over. Because, you see, father, I am also worried
about John now. He goes about talking to himself and
I've seen him turn around suddenly, crying, 'Get thee
behind me' and cross himself. The other night I heard
him groaning, then he said: 'But how shall I do it, to
save her soul, tell me, good Lord.' He is sure that the
devil bargained Ileana's soul for her beauty. Now, father,
I've told you what's in my heart."

Stan had listened attentively until the end. He was
about to spit out, but glancing at the clean floor he checked
himself and only coughed a little. Deliberately he took his
hat off, scratched his head, and as slowly put the hat on
again, looking the while steadily at Chiva. "You see,
daughter," he began, "I have given a lot of time looking
up to heaven, at the stars, thinking and thinking about
them. Now, this teacher of ours, this Jancu Tedescu, he
has a hump on his back, but his head is straight as a
judge's. You can take the *pasca* on that. Now, he is of
one mind with me. He believes as I do—listen, good

daughter—we both believe that those stars have something to do with us. Sure as day, daughter, they have. Don't look at me like that. Those stars don't come out at night just to twinkle up there, like fire-flies. I am old enough to measure my words. I've heard old folk say that there is good reason for calling a person who is touched in the head a lunatic. Such a one is moonstruck. Then we say that a lucky person is born with a silver spoon in his mouth. Why? Because the new moon is like a silver spoon. So you see, daughter, all comes to us from above, from the stars."

He took the pipe out of his mouth, looked at it and put it back again. Chiva watched him anxiously, wondering where he was leading her with that talk. Stan resumed: "Now, daughter, you speak about Ileana. Well and good. She is a girl, beautiful as a queen. More than that even. Good again. Why? Then she has that warm blood of hers. Why? Do you know why, daughter? Does John know why? Does the priest know why? As to the viper-tongued gossips, let them go to the devil, the whole pack of them, they surely don't know why. No! But I, old Stan, your father, I know why. I have spoken to the teacher. I told him the whole story—the way I figured it all out, and he said: 'Good, Uncle Stan, very good, you have reasoned it out like Solomon.' Hear that, daughter? Like Solomon, from the teacher's mouth—to me. Yes! And one single word from him is worth a whole bushel

of them from—from most anybody." He paused, took off
his hat as if to air his head, put it back, then continued:

"Now, daughter, we come back to Ileana." (Chiva
sighed, leaning forward eagerly.) "She is your child,
therefore my grandchild. Good! Now, the story goes back
to her birth. Just let me talk, daughter, and you shall see
the light. Follow my words, one by one, until they make
meaning in your head. Listen well. First: Ileana is your
first-born. Keep that in your head, daughter. Second: you
were a young girl, John was a young man, when you
brought her into the world. Add this to what I said before. Third—and this is the key to all of it—third: when
she, just born, opened her eyes in this world, what did
she see, the little creature? What was there, right on the
window pane, looking straight into the baby's eyes? You
must remember, daughter, because when the midwife
called me in you looked at the window yourself and you
said: 'Look, father, the queen of the evening in our window.' You said that to me. Good. Now, you add all these
things together, and you'll understand what I will tell
you. What you saw in the window was indeed the queen
of the evening—the blessed evening star. It was this very
window here—I remember the cross in it and the carving
on the bars. Listen carefully, daughter, for now I shall
piece the story together for you. One: Ileana is your first
child. Two: you were young and John was young.
Healthy, strong, happy—both of you. Three: the baby

comes into the world, opens its eyes—straight at her blessed godmother, the evening star, and—the star looks at the baby. This is the whole of it, to the last word, true as the holy scriptures. God forgive me for taking it as witness. So, daughter, this is the meaning of the whole: whatever Ileana has, in beauty, in—in whatever it is, is the gift of the star. No more no less. Is she beautiful? Yes! Is she healthy and full of life? Yes. Is she bright? Yes! Has she a voice like the nightingale? Yes! Has she eyes clear as spring water? Yes! Is her hair like the rays of the sun? Yes! Who gave her all these? The star! Yes, daughter, the star. And now, let us cross ourselves, daughter, and take the next step." (They crossed themselves reverently.) "Who made the star?" the old man asked solemnly. "God!" he answered almost in a whisper. "Who gave all those gifts to the star? God! Now, Chiva—is it all clear in your head? Think hard if you must, but say: 'Yes, Amen—for the hand of God is in it.' More I cannot say."

Chiva looked at her father with loving admiration. She bent and kissed his hand, pressed her forehead on it and began to cry. Tearfully she said: "Father, father, I don't want to cry, but I can't help it. My heart is too full."

Stan put his hand on her head. "Cry, daughter, cry, my child, tears are good. They melt and wash away our sorrow." With his gnarled finger he wiped away two tears in his own eyes.

34

O u t of consideration for One-eyed John, Tedescu did not come any more to Ileana's house on Saturday evenings. He came on other days, for her singing lessons, when John was not at home. They also met—Tedescu watching for every occasion—when Ileana was going to the fields or to the spring, in the evening. To Stan's inquiry, "Why do you forget our council bench?" (meaning the bench in front of Ileana's house) Tedescu answered that he had to look into his books, now that autumn was near and the school season about to start.

There were days when Ileana was almost affectionate towards him, while at other times she was reserved, with that simple detachedness of the peasant girl which would become a "grand lady". Tedescu became aware that Ileana's friendliness fell regularly on the days before her going to town, when she asked for a "general rehearsal", so to say. He put two and two together, concluding that she wanted to carry the results of her work to—to him. So he decided to go to the city. He decided to go to his friend Oancia, who knew all the gossip and scandal in town, he being a young man who climbed by mixing, gathered the gossip as field mice gather the grain, in a memory as accommodating as their subterranean granaries. But he postponed his going until after the festival at the notary's, fearing that if Ileana discovered he was making inquiries about her, she would refuse to sing and be angry with him. That would shatter his hope of winning her.

Tedescu hoped that having tasted success with the outsiders, Ileana would more readily listen to him, and devote herself to become a singer, for success craves success. He knew that folk songs, as she would sing them, would bring her renown. Once launched upon that career, she could no longer dispense with him. Unintentionally the teacher conspired, and as conspirator he became politic.

The big day came. The notary's house was like a bower. The stairway was hung with leafy branches, the rooms were covered with vine leaves on the walls and floors, and the large room where the dancing was to take place was hung with garlands of oak leaves and clusters of grapes. But the floor was left clear.

Dumbrava, the notary, was managing everything, his face beaming and sweating. Then he called Tedescu "to look and wonder—eh." Tedescu approved and he even wondered, because Dumbrava had improvised a small stage, about two feet above the floor, at the end of the large room. The stage was set up in front of a door that led into a small room. They were to wait in there, Ileana and Tedescu, and come on the stage through the door, which was hid under green branches. "You will come like two birds out of a bush," Dumbrava said, laughing.

The harpsichord was on the stage, two candlesticks with huge waxen candles at each side of it. "Those will be the only candles burning. I shall have all the others put out and lower the wick in the lamps," Dumbrava said. It was he who told about Ileana's singing.

"She bewitched us," he said, "with her first song, but when she sang the *doina,* we could no longer hold back the song that woke up in our insides; we burst out, each and all, stood up, some on chairs, and sang, rocking ourselves. Somebody must have grabbed one of the garlands, for suddenly the whole ceiling of them came down on us, leaves, grapes and all. Yet," he continued, "above the hullaballooing her voice was like a burning torch in the darkness."

The peasants who listened from the street and the yard (some bold youngsters climbed to the top of the stairs) whispered among themselves: "Listen to that girl —good Lord, is that a human voice she has?"

Late in the night, after much feasting, even the *protopop* danced with Ileana, the priest watching his superior cleric dumbly.

Tedescu, on whom Ileana's success naturally reflected some of its glory, was in the seventh heaven. Not because of that, but because whenever he could reach her Ileana

would dance with him, radiant, answering every one of
his whispered words, never once closing her face in that
expression of detached coldness which he knew so well.
Two young city men, both handsome, were ever trailing
after Ileana, and Tedescu was beyond himself with joy,
seeing that when she danced with either of them, her
face did not open as it did to him.

35

SINCE the night at the teacher's One-eyed John became outwardly more sombre and taciturn; inwardly his torment increased. Jealousy sprang up in him, joining with his other feelings. In moments of emotional upheaval he saw his daughter and his wife as one being, the two merging, yet the composite creature preserved the identity of both. But the teacher, with his beliefs and his avowed attachment to Ileana, was become his enemy, in the shape of the defiler of his home. His affection for the girl went to the mother also, so John believed.

There were nights when the devil prodded John to go to his daughter. "She is yours to take," Satan whispered to him. "This one here is the other one and that one is this," he heard the devil say. John groaned, cursed and even prayed, tossing as in fever. Then Chiva would awaken and try to quiet him, whispering soothing words, praying for him, and run about the room in her long night shirt, bringing water and "a drop of *rachiu*". "Drink, John, quench the fire in you, John, it is your overworked body," she would say. And as she came towards him—there, suddenly, it would be Ileana's haunches he saw and that swaying of her body.

It was true what Chiva said regarding his tired body,

for John worked in a frenzy at whatever he did. He had grown haggard, the marrow in his bones was burning. The devil at his ear, most of the time.

One evening, coming from work, he met Tedescu face to face at the gate. John stopped dead in front of him, barring his way. He glared at the hunchback for several seconds, all tense, ready to spring and tear him to bits.

Tedescu made no move, but looked at the man calmly, his eyes sad, pitying. John, instead of hurling himself on his enemy, jumped suddenly to one side, mumbling and crossing himself. The teacher walked away without a word.

That evening John sat at the table so very calm, never uttering a word and seeming to see no one around him, that Chiva dared not speak. They ate in silence. After the meal Ileana and Chiva cleared the table, John sitting as if nailed to the bench, smoking his pipe. They went to bed, John never moving from the bench, for Chiva dared not disturb his peace.

It was nearly midnight when John got up from the table, walked deliberately to the cupboard, drank several draughts of *rachiu* and went to Ileana's door.

He stepped carefully, stopping to listen and to guide himself in the darkness. At the door he leaned against the jamb, bent forward and put his ear to the door. The room was perfectly quiet. Yet he listened for a long time, as if astonished at the stillness and at his own calm. He could move his arm without the slightest tremor, with amazing control. As if he were a machine, wound up and set to perform a number of preordained movements. Yet he felt the silence pressing against his ears like two hands. Suddenly the awful stillness shook with the crowing of the cock.

It came on John like a thunderbolt, shooting through his frame, upsetting its perfect adjustment. He began to quake, sweat broke out over his whole body. His head, as if suddenly ignited, throbbed, a roaring noise in his ears.

Grasping his head he forced himself to stand up against the jamb, but the ground sank under him and he fell. It was like a fall by stumbling, not from fainting or because of a stroke, for John remained conscious and felt the pain in his shoulder. He began to mumble, "Get thee behind me, Satan," the usual fear in him. Crawling on the kitchen floor, colliding with something, groping with his hands, he got to the door and into the yard. He walked to the barn—that roaring still in his ears—and lay down on the straw.

In the morning Michael could not wake him. Chiva came. Seeing her husband's pale, exhausted face, she bent over him. "He is breathing," she said. "Let him sleep and rest, son." She brought a blanket and covered him.

36

T E D E S C U was now planning a great future for Ileana. The district judge and the *protopop* spoke to him about her. Both said that this peasant girl was the true genius of her folk. Never had they heard such a voice or such singing. They said also that bringing these folk songs before the world was a service to the nation.

Tedescu did not need this encouragement, but he was glad to hear what they thought about folk songs. It reassured his belief in Ileana's success. So he spoke to her, telling her that the world would be open to her, if she but followed his advice. They would work together through the winter—then, out into the wide world. "You will bring glory to the village and help your parents, because you will be rich."

Listening to Tedescu, Ileana had beautiful flashes of the future, with Serafim the central figure, sharing with her the splendors spoken of by the teacher, whom she seemed to forget entirely. Indeed, she sat facing him now, without seeing him, despite the fact that his own words were conjuring up those visions for her. When at length she answered, what she said was so unexpected that Tedescu came to himself, observing her. "I am a peasant girl, Teacher Tedescu," she said, "what can I say?"

These words and her manner of saying them revealed to Tedescu of whom Ileana was thinking. He did not betray his suspicion. He only said: "You have time to consider, Ileana, and in the meanwhile we will continue with the work."

But he decided firmly to go to the city, to find the man and—"and I shall see," he concluded, unable to foresee what he would do. Two days later he went.

Tedescu found Oancia at the bank. Oancia was an ordinary-looking fellow, if one saw his head only, but when all of him was seen, his clothes almost saved his face. So at least thought Tedescu. The young man dressed well and had a flair for novelties in ties, collars and silk handkerchiefs. He was the son of a village notary, had studied law and was employed in the bank to attend to small legal matters. Of course he told everybody that he was the bank's counselor.

Seeing Tedescu, Oancia burst into exclamations of delighted surprise, repeating: "Well, well, what pleasure, what pleasure!" It was the noon hour, so they went to the White Horse, a good restaurant, where Oancia paid at the end of each month.

Oancia's eyes danced on Tedescu, all over him, while he prattled, gesticulating and raising his head to look at himself in the mirror. Tedescu tried to appear interested, waiting his opportunity to say what he wished to say. Towards the end of the meal the moment came. But as soon as he revealed his errand to Oancia, he was sorry. Sorry and ashamed. He blushed at the thought of having brought Ileana before this gossiping coxcomb. He mentioned her as "an unusually beautiful peasant girl".

Presently it was anger that drove the blood to his face, because Oancia repeated, "An unusually beautiful peasant girl," winking slyly and nudging him with his elbow. Tedescu was burning to box the fellow's ears, but he checked himself, assuming a serious mien and waiting for the prattler's answer. He did not have to wait long, for after a little hemming and hawing Oancia began: "Friend Tedescu, you've come to the fountain-head of information. I have seen, yes—the lovely creature—during the summer, on a market day. How could I forget that market day? Not until my last breath. On the square, in front of the cathedral it was. She came, she stopped. She stopped because somebody met her. They spoke a few words and walked away. I followed them for a little while; then—I could have strangled the fellow—I had to return to the bank."

Tedescu felt his blood run cold. "A fellow—" he said, trying to speak simply.

"Yes, what then, Friend Tedescu? Of course, and I know him. But let me ask you this, do you know the beauty?"

"Yes. Who is the fellow?" Tedescu asked curtly.

"Friend Tedescu, the fellow is no common rooster. He comes from the depths of maledom. Yes! I am sorry, but it's true. No stag or stallion, ram or turkey-cock, none of God's male creatures is better provided. One must give the devil his due and—"

"Surely, surely," cut in Tedescu impatiently. "But who is he?"

"He is Serafim Corbu—the Raven—as the peasants call him," answered Oancia.

Tedescu gasped. "What! The wheat merchant!" he cried.

"Yes, friend. The very Raven himself. Do you know him?"

"No, I don't—but I have heard of him," answered Tedescu, rising.

"What's your hurry, friend Tedescu? I have a full hour yet. It's a long time since we have seen each other. Let us take coffee at Rieger's and watch the ladies. Are you no longer interested in them? Come along. Let's take our coffee at Rieger's."

Tedescu refused and left him. Oancia remained in front of the restaurant, watching his friend until he turned the corner. Then he tapped his head with his gloved finger, shrugged his shoulders and sauntered off. By the time he had reached Rieger's, Oancia almost forgot his friend.

Tedescu walked fast, as a man with a firm, well-thought out plan. In truth, however, the only definite part in his plan was to go to Serafim Corbu. What he should say to the townsman peasant, and the manner of dealing with him, that—that he had to think out on the way. His thoughts were in a turmoil, boiling in his head. He was furious. In rage he saw himself assailing the man with abuse and physical violence.

Presently he found himself in front of the cathedral, in a crowd that slowed his steps. The sight of it quieted him somewhat. Enough to make him stop and look at it. Memories surged into his mind. Of the days when he lived in a mystic state, when his own life was as vast as the universe, and the possibility of every achievement open to him.

The cathedral greeted him, friend of his past days. Here were the wide, worn stairs; here the dent in one of them, which in his boyhood made him think of the wooden brakes on lumber wagons.

Tedescu walked up, putting his foot on the dent, and entered the church. The aged marble columns stood there, supporting the arches reaching into the obscurity above them. From the height he turned his eyes to the altar. He advanced towards it. He sat down in a front pew. Through a side door young seminarists came and knelt before the altar. Tedescu watched them for a long time. He could see himself doing as they—when he also was a seminarist. With this fixed point in time, as he visioned himself, his thoughts dwelt but an instant. They rushed forward—to Ileana. With her, the tumult in his mind started. He got up, bowed towards the altar and hurried out.

Tedescu walked fast. Crossing the bridge he heard the rush-noise of the river, as he had heard it years back.

In front of the gate, at Raven's Nest, he stopped. He was agitated and yet not certain of how he should deal with Serafim. He walked into the yard. The gate clanked behind him. A dog barked and ran towards him. Tedescu stopped. The dog remained at bay, barking. Then he heard a woman's voice calling the dog, and soon he saw her coming towards him, scolding the dog, "Shut up your muzzle. Get hence!" and she swung her arms at the dog.

It was Sandra. "What may your errand be, gentleman (*domnule*)?" she asked.

Tedescu greeted: "Good day," then added: "I want to see Serafim Corbu. Is he at home?"

Sandra looked him up and down as she answered: "Yes—he is at home. Please come with me. I will tell him instantly. He is in there," she pointed. She led Tedescu through the kitchen into a large room. "Please, *domnule,* sit down, I will call Serafim," she said. Tedescu looked about the room, breathing the clean odor of grain. Two

walls were half hidden by large bins, partitioned into
equal sections, all full with wheat, oats, barley, corn,
buckwheat and lentils.

"Come, Serafim, there is a gentleman, a hunchbacked
gentleman, who wants to see you."

"What gentleman? A wheat merchant, is he, in German clothes, or what—that you call him gentleman?"
asked Serafim. He was making his accounts and at such
times he assumed an important air. As he spoke he put
the pen behind his ear.

"As to what he is—I can't tell you, but he is a Roumanian, that I knew as soon as he greeted. The German
clothes, about that—they are not his Sunday clothes
merely. He looks natural in them. A gentleman, then, as
I said. Come!"

"He has a hump on his back, you say, *lele* Sandra?"
inquired Serafim with the same important air.

"I am sure it is a hump, or do you think he carries a
bag strapped on him, under the coat? What are all these
questions? He is there to see you and if you don't close
your eyes, you will see him yourself—Mother of the
Lord," answered Sandra.

"Good, good, I'll come," Serafim said. He put the
pen in the book, the point sticking out, and closed it. He
pushed the book in the centre of the table and followed
Sandra.

Entering the room he did not notice his visitor's face

turn pale, nor the sombering of his eyes, because Tedescu stood with his back to the window. Serafim said: "Welcome, *domnule,* be welcome. Please sit down."

Tedescu did not sit down. He measured the man from head to foot. He could not help admiring the handsome face, the pleasant, virile voice, even though he was annoyed at this tribute wrested from him.

Serafim approached him, repeating the invitation to sit down. He pulled a chair nearer Tedescu. I have never seen him before, he is not a merchant, Serafim thought. I should have made up my mind how to act, thought Tedescu. Then, decisively, he said: "I come to speak to you about—about a girl from our village." He felt a cramping tightness in his chest saying these words.

"A girl from your village, *domnule?*" asked Serafim.

"Yes. And what I wish to know is—is your relation with her."

Serafim looked at him sharply, then he smiled, as he answered:

"But, *domnule,* I don't know which—what girl?"

"You do; her name is Ileana," Tedescu said.

It was Serafim who changed color now. He did not pale—he flushed. Then, as gradually the color subsided, his nostrils swelled out as he breathed. The rush of air hissed into him. "Now—we'll talk, *domnule,*" he said, each word like a square paving stone, fitting to the other. "First—you are of her village, you say. You are not the priest—I say. Second—you are in my house—speak straight—who gave you the right to meddle in my affairs?"

"I can hear very well. Don't shout. I am not the priest. You are right. I am, as you can see—a man. The right to speak to you, I took it myself. And—"

"Then you can keep that right to yourself and leave me in peace, *domnule*," interrupted Serafim.

"And," continued Tedescu, a tense, ominous evenness in his voice, "you shall answer me. What is your relation with her?"

Serafim turned white with rage. Glaring savagely at Tedescu, grinding his teeth, he shot up from the chair. He did not shout, yet his voice could pierce the wall: "You threaten me in my own house, *domnule*?"

But his words were like hailstones against a rock, for Tedescu, seeing his anger, became master of himself, never moved, nor did one line on his face change. Only— and this he alone could feel—the force in his body increased. The sight of his eyes intensely sharp. He felt as if with them alone he could overpower the raging peasant, for with his eyes he held him riveted to the ground—at bay. So he uttered no word.

Serafim stood his ground, threatening to spring, his eyes on Tedescu's. Then, as if the effort of inaction were too much for him, he began to relax, like a slowly released bow. Tedescu observed every slightest change in

him. The peasant's face began to light up, culminating
in a smile. And as he spoke: *"Domnule,* we have played
this—I am angry, you are angry, good—we two, grown
men, forgive me, *domnule,* you are my guest," he sat
down again. "You see, *domnule,"* he resumed, "I am a
ready sort of fellow—you can see that, *domnule,* and my
best thought is the last one—Roumanian that I am, gen-
uine, stock and roots. We can talk—surely we can—but
not with dry mouths. That's not Roumanian. Sandra,
lele Sandra," he called. Turning to Tedescu, who watched
him almost fascinated, he continued: "I behaved like a
city man."

Sandra entered. *"Lele* Sandra, be good and bring
some *tzuica* and olives." Sandra closed the door behind
her. "But we shall understand each other, no doubt. You
see, *domnule,* it is men's business to understand each
other. You have your affairs to look after, I have mine.
Then, one day I come to you or you do me the honor of
coming to me. Then, of course, we must understand each
other—" Sandra brought the plum brandy, olives and
thin slices of bread. She put them on the table, placing
small glasses for the two men. She made a perfunctory
motion with her apron over the clean table and walked
out.

Serafim poured out the *tzuica.* "Please—and here,
they are meaty" (he pointed at the olives and pushed the
plate nearer to Tedescu), "and a little bread. We are

Christians—woe is me—to have set that aside. Please,
partake."

While Serafim spoke Tedescu gathered his thoughts.
He was ready to meet his man on this new ground. He
took the glass. Instantly Serafim reached out for his.
Raising it he said: "You are welcome in my house,
domnule," and touched Tedescu's glass. He only drank
after Tedescu took a sip and put the glass down. Tedescu
took an olive and a slice of bread. Serafim did likewise.
They were silent, each waiting for the other to speak.
Serafim spoke first, suggesting they take another drink.
Then he fell silent again. Simultaneously, each raised his
head—their eyes met. Serafim smiled genially. Tedescu
merely answered with a glint in his eyes. He appraised
the peasant's cunning, which had won Ileana. But he ad-
mitted that Serafim was handsome, also intelligent. He
was jealous, yet envious only of his sway over Ileana, not
of his personal gifts. He decided that his question had
remained unanswered; it was Serafim's part to speak, so
he remained silent. Serafim took an olive, held it up and
looked at it, as if meditating on its form. Then, without
looking at Tedescu, he said: "So we shall get to understand each other—if we just talk it over, leisurely. You
have time, *domnule,* and—what did you ask me about
this girl, about Ileana, let us call her?"

"Ileana *is* her name. She has parents in the village.
Are you going to ask her in marriage?"

"Marriage—*domnule?* Marriage! That is what you want to know? I see. Her parents are in the village and they want to know if I am going to ask her in marriage. Now, *domnule,* they have a right to know that from me. Truly, positively—they have the right. The father and the mother—both of them have the right to ask me: 'Serafim, are you going to marry our daughter?' But, *domnule,* they did not ask me. You see, so I didn't answer. How could I, if they never asked me? You understand that, *domnule?*" Serafim spoke deliberately, regarding the olive in his fingers.

"I am here to ask you that, Serafim Corbu," responded Tedescu.

"Yes, yes! Of course. They have work to do now, so you—you came in their name." At the conclusion of these words Serafim glanced at Tedescu.

"No! I came on my own decision. It is I who put the question to you," said Tedescu.

"That is good, too, *domnule.* Proper, for how do I know but that you may be her first cousin."

"I am not her cousin. We are no blood relations. I am Jancu Tedescu, the teacher in the village."

"So! That I understand also. I have a friend—we are, so to say, no blood relations, but I love him as a brother. Can there be nearer relation than brothers, *domnule?* Still, you see, I love him as a brother, as if we were blood relations. So, I understand. You are a friend. So much, as if you were brother and sister. Please, take another drop of *tzuica*. And, please, a bite of bread, an olive."

"Then what is your answer to my question, Serafim Corbu?" Tedescu asked, rather curtly.

Serafim lapsed into a leisurely manner, answering: "That's just what I should ask myself and you, *domnule,* —saying, now, what should be my answer?" He raised his brows and shoulders, utterly at a loss. A man who really needed help.

Tedescu felt his anger rising. He clenched his fist, advising himself: hold yourself in hand—play his game. And he burst out laughing. So suddenly that Serafim started. He roared laughing, shaking with it, looking at Serafim as if his nose were climbing to the ears. Serafim actually drew back, dodging the impact of Tedescu's sudden hilarity. He stared at him dumbly, baffled, truly at a loss now. And Tedescu thought: if he gets angry, I win.

But the old peasant in Serafim—stock and roots— came to his aid. He started to laugh also. They were guffawing together so that Sandra, hearing them from the kitchen, stopped her work and listened. She went to the door. After standing there for some time she almost burst out also. Throwing up her hands she walked away, chortling. "Mother of the Lord," she mumbled, cackling again.

Tedescu stopped as unexpectedly as he had started. Damn the cunning fox, he thought. It is I who must speak or get away before I strangle him. Serafim calmed himself also. "Teacher Tedescu," he said, "you have a good heart. Only with a good heart can a man laugh like that."

"True—very true! That goes for both of us, Serafim Corbu. So I will tell you now what you will do. You are going to ask Ileana in marriage and—marry her. You see, how I can read your heart? What your mouth says is—what you want it to say; but your heart—your heart tells the truth. And—"

"Wait, Teacher Tedescu," interrupted Serafim, "what is this reading in my heart?"

"And," continued Tedescu, "when you meet Ileana next, you will tell her that you are going to marry her. Don't deny your heart with your mouth. I am right. I know it positively.... That is very fine. She is poor, but you have enough. You are rich, Serafim Corbu."

"By thunder, Saint George and the dragon—Teacher, what is this? What are you saying, to my face? I said— wait, *domnule!* I am my own master!" cried Serafim.

"Of course—who denies that, Serafim Corbu?" said Tedescu quietly.

"Deny it? Nobody can—but, *domnule,* you tell me what I should say to Ileana," said Serafim sullenly.

"Serafim Corbu, calm yourself. I don't tell you what to say to Ileana. I read it in your heart."

"Aha, *domnule,* you read it in my heart, eh? A

peasant's heart, and yours the eyes of a learned man. So! I'll tell you, Teacher Tedescu. Not one word like that will I say to Ileana. Not one breath of it."

Tedescu was glad to see Serafim's anger. He had waited for it long enough. Having caught him, he decided to hold him. "Then how will you tell her that I spoke to you? She will ask: 'What did Teacher Tedescu say and what did you answer?' What are you going to tell her then, Serafim Corbu?"

"But—by the dragon, Teacher Tedescu, who says that I will tell her you spoke to me?" snapped Serafim.

"She will know it from me," Tedescu answered quietly.

Serafim's face hardened. He watched Tedescu sharply, his clenched fists on his knees. What is the purpose of this man? he asked himself, his eyes drilling to fathom what he could not reason out. Tedescu, however, received his scrutiny without a twitch of his features. Then the thought that Ileana must not know of this encounter stood out in Serafim's mind. That—yes, that is what he must prevent, by all means. But, by which means? By winning him to my side, he concluded. So determined, Serafim relaxed, a genial smile coming over his face like an illumination. He leaned forward, touched Tedescu's knee and began:

"Teacher Tedescu, you are—I see that plainly—a man. A man! You know that 'crow and crow don't pick their eyes', as the saying goes. Ha-ha! That's true. So, you are a man and I am a man. Settled. You came to me as I might have come to you. Man to man. Good! Now: as man and man we got to understand each other. I say: Teacher Tedescu, I won't breathe a word of this to Ileana. You say: 'I will'. We must straighten that. Why? Because we are both men and Ileana is a woman. We have our thoughts, she has hers. Why would you or my-self meddle with her thoughts? You say to me: 'You are going to marry her'. I say to you: No, Teacher Tedescu, that I shan't do. You will ask me why? I will tell you the truth: I am engaged to a girl, a good girl, a fine girl, a rich girl. You see how I tell you everything? Because we must understand each other, man and man that we are. Crow and crow—ha, ha! This makes it this way: Ileana is free as the air, with her own thoughts—we shan't meddle with them; you are free and I am free. And—you see, Teacher Tedescu, all is settled—fine and clear. Have I spoken a single word amiss, *domnule?*" Serafim was beaming, waiting Tedescu's answer.

Tedescu, without soliciting it, by a slight trap, caught Serafim, making him reveal what he wished to know. First, that he would not marry Ileana. Second—and he would have used any means to obtain this—that Serafim would not tell her about their meeting. This was of great importance to Tedescu, because he feared to arouse Ileana's distrust. Because of this gain, he submitted to the peasant's shrewd putting them together, as twin kernels in a fruit. Crow and crow. Then, also, with the knowledge that Serafim was marrying, he would be freer to choose his way of winning Ileana from him. But as to this, he would have to think about carefully. So he answered: "Serafim Corbu, I see you are a man, as you said. I understand that it is for Ileana's good that you ask me not to tell her about my coming to you."

"Of course, Teacher Tedescu, certainly, for her own good; how otherwise would I figure it," interrupted Serafim cheerfully.

"Now," continued Tedescu, "I shall leave you. Thank you for the hospitality." He got up.

Serafim could not hide his joy. He felt that he had downed his man. Was the victor. *"Domnule,"* he began, "do me the honor and stay to supper. It is getting late, surely, but I would be honored to shelter you for the night under my roof. Yes, yes, do accept my humble offer, *domnule."* He was all heartiness. But Tedescu had to go. There was work awaiting him in the early morning. So they parted, Tedescu rushing to the inn without noticing the streets or persons, and Serafim bursting with his triumph.

37

Tedescu found his driver awaiting him. "I am late, Pavel," he said to the peasant.

"The time is yours, Teacher, no worry about that. We'll get home in good time. I fed the mares a full peck of oats. They'll trot. Are we ready?"

"I am ready. Have you settled with the innkeeper?" asked Tedescu.

"Settled, closed accounts, all in good shape, Teacher."

"Closed accounts? How do you mean, Pavel?"

"Well, like this, Teacher. I owed him for sheltering the wagon and horses, twice last month. Not to forget a pint of *rachiu,* a stingy pint, if the truth be told. I paid— he pocketed the coin and—wiped the slate. That's the long and the short of it, Teacher, thank God."

They got home in good time, as Pavel said. The moon was up, its livid light fell on the roofs and spilled over into the street. The air was chilly. Tedescu lit the fire in his oven, undressed to the waist and washed in cold water. Then he threw a knotted chunk of oak on the fire, dressed and went to the next-door neighbor, an old couple, where he had his meals.

Varvara, the old peasant woman, had no children; she took to the teacher from the beginning. She cooked

the choicest bits of meat for him, inquiring of the priest's
wife about the best way of cooking cabbage, because she
knew that the teacher was fond of it. This evening she
had for him a fine lamb stew. While Tedescu was eating, Varvara went and brought several mushrooms. They
were like miniature parasols, with delicate pink ribs on
the inside. "See, Teacher Tedescu, what my man brought
from the woods," she said. "Watch their skin come off.
Now, a pinch of salt, a taste of pepper and on the embers
they go."

"And fit for a king's mouth," spoke up old Phillip,
from his hearth-bench.

Tedescu listened to the sizzling of the broiling mushrooms. Presently Varvara brought them on a round plank
and offered them to the teacher almost solemnly, as if it
were the holy sacrament. "When you get married,
Teacher Tedescu," she said, "bring your little wife to
Varvara. This old one will teach her a thing or two about
cooking. No shame to learn, for anybody. Besides, how
should a young wife know her husband's relishes? She
can't know, and just don't. So she feeds him into a bad
temper, poor innocent creature, and has to purr to him
to straighten his eyebrows and curl up the corners of his
mouth. Ugh, Teacher Tedescu—he can look sour, such a
husband. Enough to curdle fresh milk. You just bring
your little wife to Varvara and, God bless us, you'll see."

"Yes, yes! The old woman has fed me nigh on to

sixty years, Teacher, and I am still here," chuckled Phillip.

They laughed, the three of them. Tedescu took one mushroom on the point of his knife and carried it to the old man. "Thank you, Teacher, I've had my supper a good while ago."

"Take this little one—it's just a bite," urged Tedescu.

Phillip took the mushroom and stuffed it into his mouth. "It's tasty enough," he said, munching, "but I can't help thinking of burnt horse-hoofs when I smell them broiling." He chuckled again.

After much coaxing Varvara took one mushroom also, but she ate it slowly. First she drank the juice from the shriveled cup, then she bit small pieces from its pulp. Tedescu was very fond of Varvara. He ate the mushrooms in her manner. He smiled at old Phillip's comparing their smell to burnt horse-hoof; but he is right, he thought.

Varvara sat on the bench, watching him eat. Her wrinkled face reminded Tedescu of a frozen red apple, thawing on the chimney ledge. Age thaws people, he thought. He loved aged people. Varvara had young eyes —he mused—and good teeth. She spoke clearly and laughed heartily. She was no gossip, but she enjoyed every shred of news circulated and embellished by the "sharp tongues". And she had a lively curiosity. She gleaned every bit of news and ranged it, in a neat mass, stored away in her old head. Then she took now this part, now another, to ruminate. When she went about her work, her mind was busy with the things she had heard. At their evening meal she would tell Phillip some of the amusing news. She always made them so in telling. But Phillip was like a bottomless pit. Varvara's information sank into the depths of him and disappeared for ever. So that, when she would say, "as I told you last week, remember?" Phillip would look at her so empty of remembrance that Varvara would have to repeat last week's tale. As to his answers, when Varvara held forth, they were: grunting, chuckles, cracking of the knuckles and an occasional ha-ha-hee. Varvara knew the meaning of each of those expressions of her husband and was content with them. Her husband had no gift of the tongue, but he had a mind and a character—well, "a rock of gold", she said. Sometimes—rarely, of course—he was the rock without the gold, for his yes and his no remained yes and no, even in the face of Varvara's pleading and tears. But the days of pleading and tears were long past now, and the old couple lived like twin weather-tired trees, waiting for the end. Yet they did not grumble against life. They had had their spring and summer and a long, rather sunny autumn; now let the winter and its cold come.

This evening Varvara had something on her mind. Tedescu saw it in her eyes, in the bend of her head, as she sat watching him. He ate slowly, waiting. For long minutes no one spoke nor stirred—as if listening to the crackling of the fire. But as soon as Tedescu finished eating, Varvara moved a little and began:

"Well, Teacher Tedescu, autumn is here now. Nothing but crows in the fields, cawing already for winter. The days are getting shorter and shorter, and the nights —God bless us—keep stretching. They'll get to be very long soon. I am too old now to sleep all through a long winter night. So, after my share of sleep, I lay there, awake as the morning, my mind busy—with a thousand thoughts. They come like a flock of sparrows. Then, I catch one and hold it. Even now, the nights are too long for me. The days are shorter, that's true, but then, even in a short day many things happen and are told. Oh, yes. Well, the Lord be praised, I have good ears. So I hear this and I hear that and some more. Everybody talking. Then one evening I say to my old man—having considered each word in my head—I say: 'Phillip, you know what? Let me tell you: if that girl got married, she would be a fine wife to the right man.' 'What girl, woman?' asks he. 'What girl?' I say. 'Good Lord—Phillip, you ask me that? Why, the one everybody's talking about.' Then I flared up because he looked at me as empty as your hat over there, Teacher, and I say: 'Good Lord, Phillip, now that you've lived your days tongue-tied, now are you deaf and blind too?' I said those words —but no, he didn't know what girl. 'That angel-face,

One-eyed John's girl—what other girl?' I told him. Then
he understood and nodded. He meant yes; that is, he
agreed with me. But you see, Teacher, all this talk, all
this guessing, there is something of every kind in it. I
believe one thing, another body believes another thing,
and so, between all the people in the village, what this
one thinks and the next one thinks, everything they say
about the girl is held for gospel truth. The young men
want her well enough—that we know—but they are
afraid. They are afraid of the devil. That's a good and
Christian fear, to be sure, we all know that. So I thought
about it and I thought and I thought. Many nights. Then
I came to this: Varvara, I said to myself, there is deviltry
in every woman. In the pretty ones there is more. Now,
this girl, she is so pretty she is glowing with it, like a red-
hot ember. So, maybe—who knows—maybe the devil is
in it. I won't say yes, but I won't say no. But what I'll
say for sure is this: let her get married, to a good man,
and see if he won't chase the devil out of her. If it be a
real man—I say he will. What do you say, Teacher Tedescu? You have enough learning to fill all the heads in
our village. So, what do you say?"

Varvara folded her hands and bent forward, looking
steadily at Tedescu. He frowned, having understood that
she was not only speaking out her mind, but that she was
addressing him with a purpose. However, as he guessed
her meaning his annoyance lessened; besides, he would

not be harsh with Varvara, so he said: *"Matusha* Varvara, I don't know as much as you do about such things, but I do not believe at all in this devil business."

"Now, Teacher, that's just what I thought of you. You are young, God preserve you, and as you say, you don't know what we old folk do. That's as it should be, seeing you are not a peasant and therefore you are different from our young men. So, maybe—with your leave be it said—maybe it would be you—I am old enough to be your grandmother, excuse my presumption, so I can say it—I thought that maybe you would be the very man for the girl. Have I said too much, Teacher Tedescu, or have I spoken proper words?"

"You spoke kindly, Granny Varvara," Tedescu answered getting up, "but the management of our lives is in the hands of the Lord. I must go think about my school now. Good night to you both." He took his hat.

"Those are golden words, Teacher, we are in the hands of the Lord. Yes, yes, gospel truth," Varvara said.

"No hurry on our account, Teacher," put in Phillip, stirring on his bench.

"No, no, Teacher, stay a while yet," urged Varvara. She sighed, resuming: "And what you say about the Lord is the pure truth, God help us. Well, if you must go, you must. I wish you a good night, Teacher."

"Good peace to you, Teacher," Phillip added. And Tedescu left.

38

SERAFIM was in fine spirits. He had bought up a great quantity of wheat and forage. The prospect of good gains cheered him. His approaching marriage with Saveta and his affair with Ileana did not worry him. "Her I will marry," he said to himself, thinking of Saveta. "She will bring me her dowry, she will be the young woman in the house. Fine. She will bear my children. I'll give her as many as she can bear. She's young. She comes of good blood. I want many children. Only my own shall eat up my stores. When I'll be old there will be a lot of young life around me. When I die, my children will go on, each on his own. They will spread over the whole country, the seed of Serafim Corbu, getting richer with what I left them. They'll be the Corbus —branches and leaves of the same tree. The tree—I am it. (He slammed his chest.) The other one, Ileana—she's my playmate. She'll warm up my blood. She is fine for that. What breasts, what thighs, what skin! Fire, the fire of life! The wife is for bearing children. Good. I give you children, wife. What sin? Did I look for Ileana? No! She came into my path—like that. Temptation of the devil? Maybe. But would any man say, 'Get thee behind me!' if such a girl came his way? No! The best Christian, the bishop himself, would take her first—and pray afterwards to be forgiven. Good Lord, have you not made us all sinners? Christ loves sinners best because he loves to forgive. That's Christian."

He was sitting at the table, where he kept his accounts in a large book, which he carefully locked in the table drawer as if indeed the figures of the profits shown there were the real money. As he was putting the book away he saw again that folded, yellow paper which his father had given him to keep safely, "to show you, my son, that now we can walk with our heads up—true men that we are." He recalled again these words of his father. He took the paper and unfolding it he read, mumbling the words aloud:

"From the peasants of Szeceny to his excellent highness the Count of Toekely, their Lord and master with humble reverence, addressed in writing their respectfully humble petition. We the Roumanian peasants, by the will of our Lord God who is in heaven, in service to his excellent highness Count Toekely, ask audience to our humble petition from the honorable ear of his excellent highness, and our respectful petition is as we can, as simple peasants, put it in proper words. It is well known to us, the Roumanian peasants, that the Lord giveth and the Lord taketh as it was with Job of the Holy Book, but we are as poor as Job and we do not sit on manure with ashes on our heads, but we work hard until our flesh and bones ache and when the sharing of the crop comes we wait in hunger for the righteous sharing, but the hand of your gentleman overseer of your highness' goods and chattels is hard and heavy on our backs, because when winter comes we have to feed on beans for meat and on linseed oil for fat in the best days, for in the poor days which are many in the winter, and in the spring before the nettles and weeds that are eatable come out of the good earth, we dip our corn-bread in vinegar which we spice with rubbed garlic and sweeten with a few drops of linseed oil but it thins our blood to water which freezes in our veins when we chop the wood and haul it from the forest to the castle of your excellent highness who should live from the Lord God many years Amen in blessed health. So we the Roumanian peasants of Szeceny say to our good lord and master look to our misery with eyes of righteousness for there is a God in heaven who sees everything on earth and we thank your excellent highness from the depth of our hearts but the hand of the overseer is too heavy on our backs. Now we have no more words to tell to the winds which blow cold and to your high excellentness the gall-bitterness in our souls which flows over and so we end our humble petition and wait in peace which we ask our Heavenly Father to give to your excellent highness the same. Amen."

Serafim spat out with rage, smashing his fist on the table, shouting: "God's thunder and hellfire, damn that

Count's pussy soul. I would bury him in the cesspool if I caught him. He's palsied and paralyzed now, crooked and trembling and drooling and eats the bread I sell him, the spawn of Satan. My peasants—Good God, my peasants to beg like that! Ah, by Saint George and the dragon, but things have changed. The Corbus are come into their own. I'll marry and have children, and they'll have children, strong, proud—with clean blood in them. They won't beg, as I don't beg. If I went with that petition I would have stuck it in the bastard's heart on the point of my knife." He was raging in this way when Sandra came, saying a buyer was waiting.

In his fury Serafim drove a stiff bargain, patting his belt while haggling, as if to say: I have plenty of money here—take the wheat or leave it.

After that rage Serafim mounted into a lighter sphere of contentment. He was a conqueror. Master of his fate. In this frame of mind he planned his next meeting with Ileana.

39

TEDESCU was busy in his school. He was cheered by the readiness of the children to respond to his efforts. He had infinite patience with the small pupils who were learning the *a b c*. He drew objects on the blackboard for them, writing the names of each object in large letters. This coupling of the concrete with the abstract helped the little ones to memorise the letters.

To the bigger children Tedescu was a real companion. He organized games during the intermission and treated boys and girls alike in every respect, encouraging them to play together, helping the girls to forget their shyness, instilling in the rough boys—who were impatient with the girls' awkwardness—an attitude of indulgent sportsmanship.

The children loved him. They were eager to do some service for him. They would ask permission to walk home with him and vied with each other who should clean his room, chop his wood or run some errand. Tedescu thanked them graciously, always, but it was seldom that he walked home with any pupil. He loved to walk alone. The hope of meeting Ileana was ever with him. Alone, he enjoyed the autumn evenings, when nature seemed to shrink into itself. He also closed himself up,

with his thoughts, relishing his warm room, the soft light
of the candles and the endless mathematical exercises on
large sheets of yellow straw paper. He made cones out of
plasteline, taking infinite pains to shape them perfectly;
then he sliced them with a thin wire, obtaining every
possible section of the cone. He made also cubes and
cylinders out of the same material. Later he devised a
system of his own, with the aid of which he taught
geometry to the children. He would cut a piece of paper
in the shape of a cross, its tree consisting of four equal
squares; two similar squares, one on each side, completed
the cross. Folding the paper on the lines adjoining the
squares, he obtained the cube. By dividing one of the
squares into a given number of units of smaller squares,
he taught the children the measuring of areas.

These children, at work in the class-room and at
play with their gaiety and hearty joy, were a link between
him and Ileana. More than that, they brought her, in
spirit as it were, with them to school. So that even in his
moments of concentration upon a problem, when alone,
Ileana remained with him. As if his studying was no
longer a process of absorbing but one of imparting, of
sharing. But when he sat before the fire in his room,
watching the play of the flames, he thought of Ileana in
a very concrete way. He visioned her at his side, radiantly
silent, both looking with the same eyes on the splendors
of a future whose beginning was the present.

40

T H E village was buzzing with renewed gossip. Ileana
had gone to the city and did not return in the evening.
This she had never done before. Chiva waited up until
midnight, when One-eyed John sent her to bed, cursing
his ungodly luck.

The following day Tedescu thought of going to the
city and bringing Ileana back. It was his duty, he said to
himself. Facing Serafim again was easy; but facing Ileana,
if indeed she was at Serafim's—where else would she be?
—well, facing her, that was not easy, because he had no
right to interfere. This right was One-eyed John's. He
should go to the peasant and tell him: "Your daughter is
at Serafim Corbu's. Go and fetch her." But how could he
go to John and say these things about Ileana? That would
be to betray Ileana, to play the traitor and the coward at
the same time. This teacher had too much mind for his
heart, or—was it too little heart for the mind he had?
No, the heart was a stout one, but it was rendered, by
his love for Ileana, indulgent, patient, instead of being
tempered, steeled for vengeance. But the man who waits
is more tormented than he who acts, for action burns up
the fuel that torments. And so, inactive, Tedescu spent
that day in mental torment, and yet another day.

Ileana met Serafim as usual, in the market place. While driving outside the city he embraced her, saying: "You know, my little heart, we see each other very, very seldom."

"Twice a week," smiled Ileana.

"It is years—the time between. You know, my little heart, I've been thinking of something. Something so good, so very good. I have a small place—on the river—not far from here. There used to be a mill there, but now only the house in which the miller lived is in condition. The mill is just a big shed now, where I store the forage. We'll go there, my little heart. The big willows hide the place and no one comes there. All you hear is the noise of the river."

"No, no, I must go home this evening. Mother will die of worry," protested Ileana.

"Oh—mothers don't die so easy as that. They cry a little—but mothers always cry a little. You are not a child any more. Haven't you told her, as I asked you, that you may stay in the city overnight sometimes?"

"Yes, I told her, but she begged me to obey, to be good and come home, and she asked me so many questions about my friend that I blushed, my face burning so hard that I had to run out, because if I cried, for shame, I would have told her the truth."

"Well, you will explain better after you have done it.

We'll think it out. You'll stay and explain tomorrow. Today is ours, my little heart." He held her close, his ardor increasing with each word. "Today is ours," he kept repeating, passionately. Ileana hoped she would escape and go home, as before, but she feared she would not. Already her will was melting in his caresses.

They drove into a large shed close to the river. Serafim unhitched the horses, unharnessed them and tied them to the manger. Ileana watched him, sitting in the wagon. "Shall I stay—will I stay?" she wondered rather than asked herself. She heard the river near by. She looked and saw it through the foliage of the willows, floating, the sun scintillating on its face.

"Let us go in. Jump into my arms, little heart," Serafim said. He caught her in his arms. He unlocked the door—holding her embraced—and led her through a small room smelling of virgin wool and sheep-cheese. There were large bales of wool, up to the ceiling on one side of the room; on the other side there were three shelves, attached to the ceiling rafters with heavy chains, and huge cheeses ranged on the shelves. The next room was large and clean, but it had the peculiar odor of uninhabited places. The odor of sun-warmed dust and wasp combs. There was a large bed, covered with a snow-white blanket of carded wool, and a table near the window with a clean tablecloth on it. The chest and the several chairs were dusted, but across the icon hung a spider-web. Ileana picked it off on her finger, winding it as on a spindle. The fireplace exhaled a cool, sooty breath.

Serafim lit the fire in the large grate. He threw some chunks of oak on the kindling, then ran up to Ileana, embraced her and kissed her, whirling her around. He lifted her up, swung her around and took off her kerchief. Her heavy braids, coiled several times around her head, were live gold. A crown of live gold. He put her in a chair, placed her hands in her lap, saying: "Now my little heart will sit still and watch her Bujor prepare the meal."

He rolled up his sleeves and went to work. He set the table, carefully choosing the place for Ileana and himself. He put the loaf of white bread and the two bottles of wine on his side. He arranged the small leg of lamb on the grate and put half a dozen eggs in the hot ashes to bake. Each time he passed by Ileana he bent over and kissed her on the cheek or on the nape where the ringlets peeped out from under the braids.

They ate and drank, now embracing, now Ileana holding him off, then vehemently yielding to his kisses. They sang, danced and chased each other about the room. Ileana dodged him around the table, jumping over the bench, over the chairs, eluding his grasp like a butterfly. When he caught her he punished her by holding her tightly, fondling her, humming into her ear, biting her chin and with his lips pulling at the ringlets on her nape. She wriggled, laughing, moaning, at times feigning to cry. Again she escaped him and ran out of the house. He after her. She jumped through the high, tangled grass, hid behind the willows, until they reached the river bank.

Ileana sat down on a grassy spot in the sun. The river was rapid in the middle, but near the shore the water curled in whirlpools. She threw twigs in the water, watching them turn round and round, quiveringly, till they were sucked down into the throat of the whirlpools. After a little while the twigs emerged, upright, at the edge of the pool, then stretched out, as if lying down with fatigue, and again they turned round and round and were sucked under.

Serafim, sitting near her, threw pebbles at the circling twigs, missing most of the time. Ileana took off her boots and let her feet dangle in the water. The early autumn clearness made it look colder than it was. The smell of the river reminded Ileana of the watery smell of the first snow. That odor that seeps into one's clothes and is carried into the house. She recalled how, when she was a child, her cat brought that damp odor to her bed. She laughed now, seeing the cat when for the first time it went out into the snow; how it curled its body, stepping gingerly in the white chill; how it snatched up its paw and shook it.

"Will you bathe if I do?" Serafim asked.

Her eyes laughed. "How can I—without anything to —to cover my nakedness?" she said.

"You'll cover it with water," he laughed.

"And you cover your eyes then," she retorted.

"Of course I will—like this." He put his hand on his eyes, fingers spread out.

"No! I will tie them with a handkerchief," she said laughing.

"Then you will drown me," he answered, making a gesture of fright. He ran to the house and brought a long nightshirt for Ileana and a pair of drawers for himself.

"Here, my little heart, now you can bathe, covered as a ghost."

They undressed, hiding behind the willows, apart. Ileana emerged looking like a snowman. The shirt hung to the ground, shapeless, and she pulled her hands into the sleeves. Serafim jumped forward. His body was white up to where the bronzed wedge connected his neck and face to the trunk.

"Oh, the nice ghost!" he cried at Ileana.

"And you are like a goat," she said, blushing, but did not look away from him. Serafim's chest was covered with curly black hair, but on his back, from waist to shoulder blades, the hair was like a goat's. It looked like a fur corset, because his shoulders were white.

Serafim went in bravely, dove under in the middle of the river, and when his head emerged he blew noisily. Ileana walked in, step by step, with little shrieks; then she lay down facing the current. The shirt flared above her body. When she stood up, the water just above her knees, the wet linen clung to her.

Serafim asked her to come where it was deep. Ileana would not go. When he dove under again, she ran out and dressed quickly.

They sat on the doorsill, in the sun. "It will move away soon," Ileana said.

"Then we'll warm each other," whispered Serafim.

I must go home, thought Ileana, her mind only. Her body tingled, and now, in the sunshine, it was assuming mastery. Serafim had his arms around her. Close against his body, her own body held its supremacy over her mind easily. Now they heard singing, a woman's voice, close by; but the river sang with her and they could not say where the singer was. "She may come from anywhere," Ileana said.

"Let's run in," proposed Serafim. He pushed the door with his back and they went in. Serafim locked the door.

"If she comes here she will see the horses," whispered Ileana.

"Let her. It's often I stay and sleep here when the forage is stored."

Presently the song died away. The room was warm, the fire on the hearth was still aglow, a thick layer of embers in a wreath of white ashes.

"I should better go home now, Serafim," Ileana said.

"Yes, yes, my little heart, and I shall die here pining for you." He took her in his arms. They sat on the bed. The blanket was soft as moss. "We can rise before the sun, little heart. I'll drive you where the road dips into the village, on the edge of the plain," he said. Ileana did not answer. "So we must go to bed now—oh, I am so sleepy," he said in a droning, sleepy voice. He lifted her off the bed, pulled back the blanket and tapped the pillow. "Your head here, my head here," he said.

"Only one pillow," Ileana laughed.

"Our heads are small, little heart."

When Ileana awoke the room was bright with sunshine. Her eyes fell on the icon. To her surprise the cobweb was there again, a ray of light on it. The icon looked as if slashed across, the wound a ray of light. She crossed herself. Serafim slept, his face against her shoulder, his arm heavy on her body. She closed her eyes, yielding to the pleasant lassitude. Her mind was still as a deep well. She felt the weight of Serafim's arm across her chest. It rose and sank with her breath. The low murmur of the river was heavy on her eyelids.

She awoke to Serafim's caresses and the warmth of his voice in her ear. His lips in the shell of her ear. She was breathing with his own breath, her chest sinking with his and rising with it. It did not burden her, it enfolded her in warmth, a breathing wave of living warmth.

When they got up the sun was no longer in the room. The sun was going its rounds. They washed together, bending over the large basin, their heads touching. She spattered a handful of water on his face, and he blew it off noisily and rubbed his wet face against hers. They dried their faces on the same towel, each at one end.

"I will braid your hair," Serafim said. It streamed down, her hair, over her back and on her sides to the middle of her thighs. She parted it carefully with the comb.

"Now braid the right side first," she said.

His fingers worked swiftly, braiding the four strands as he braided the hemp into a whip. It looked like a golden chain, the hair braided in four strands. Then he braided the left side.

"They are too tight," Ileana cried.

"Put them up this way, little heart, so you will be different from all women, in the braids also," pleaded Serafim.

She stood in front of a small mirror, winding the braids around her head. She felt Serafim's eyes on her. She turned and met them, the light from them sharp and piercing. She looked deep into his eyes, then she thrust out her arms, crying: "Are you a dragon, Serafim? My

God—who are you? You are a dragon!" Cold horror
came into her eyes. Serafim grew pale, for at that moment her braids were snakes of flame and her eyes drilled
into his very marrow. There was a sound of wings outside, an instant's darkening of the window, the raucous
cry of crows in flight. They shuddered, facing each other.
Ileana was petrified with fear. It flashed through her mind
that this was an abandoned mill—the Evil One seduced
girls in the guise of handsome men—carried them to for-
saken places. She wanted to turn to the icon but could
not.

Serafim was staring at her, then—he knew not how
it came—but there rose out of his chest a sound strange
to his own ears, like a choked breath—a quick, tattered
laugh.

"My God—don't—don't!" shrieked Ileana, falling
into a faint.

That sound torn out of him and Ileana's cry and sudden fall sobered Serafim. The nightmare of fright left
him. He carried her to the bed, sprinkled her face with
water and rubbed her hands—ice-cold they were and lifeless. He watched her face, the shadow of death on it.
After a long time there was a faint tremor in the eyelids
and presently they lifted. The life was not in her eyes
yet, only a dull wonder.

Serafim dared not speak. He held Ileana's hands in

his, warming them. She seemed not to recognize him. At length she said: "I was very frightened."

He bent over her, put his face against hers, kissed her. He was about to say that he also was frightened, but he checked himself. Male pride served him well this time.

A strong wind blew up, shaking the willow branches against a clouding sky. The long willow leaves, torn by the wind, fluttered by the window like shingle-chips. "How dark it is—so suddenly," said Ileana. Her voice was yet quite feeble.

"It's going to rain, little heart—but we have a good shelter," Serafim answered.

"I must get home—let us start at once," Ileana said anxiously. She sat up.

"Yes, little heart, surely, but it is raining already. Look at the black clouds chasing up. We must wait until it passes," coaxed Serafim. The rain came on the wind, a few drops spattering against the window-panes, but on the willows the rain was lashing already noisily. Now it came, surge upon surge, buffeting the window and the door.

Ileana got up, in Serafim's arms, and they went to the window. They looked into the forest of rain-reeds. She leaned on Serafim, gazing into the rain. She reached out and wiped the vapor on the chilled pane. Now she could see the pools near the house, the bubbles on the trembling surface tilting like half-immersed glass balls. Some of them burst, others defied the rain, shaking with a drop of foam in the center of their transparent head.

"It will last long—look, the bubbles stay," lamented Ileana.

"It may not, but if it should—little heart, we'll have to stay here, together, by the will of God. It is He who sent the rain."

"We should have gone early, in the morning."

"Yes, little heart, but the angels would not wake us."

"Good Lord, stop the rain," prayed Ileana.

"Good Lord, Thy will be done, Amen," chanted Serafim.

The Lord willed the rain to keep up. Ileana became sad, thinking of her mother. She cried softly and was annoyed with herself for it; yet she continued crying at the window, while Serafim busied himself with the fire, preparing the evening meal.

The night came, a solid block of darkness, the wind howling in it, stray drops of rain tap-tapping against the panes.

Serafim had everything ready. They ate and the food and the wine cheered Ileana; so the night, holding this lighted, warm room in its dark lap, was a friend—she felt it so—its black, soft face pressed against the windows. She could hear it cuddle the house, humming to it, at times slapping the walls, playfully, then rubbing its heavy black body against it. "I heard it breathing," she said.

"Breathing—who, what—little heart?" asked Serafim.

"The night—hear—" Ileana answered. And there was a sound, as if a living creature, as large as the night, were breathing.

Serafim carried Ileana to the hearth. They sat in front of the fire, she on his lap, watching the yellow flames leaping along the sooty wall. Now and again the tip of a flame tore off, flew up the chimney and vanished. Serafim looked into her eyes and said: "There are two fires burning in your eyes, little heart," and he kissed them. Then they went to bed, and on the ceiling Ileana saw the ghost of the fire dancing, but in the very core of it they were together, Serafim and herself, breathing into each other, the black night cuddling the house in its lap.

41

O n the morning of Ileana's homecoming One-eyed John was in a fearful rage. He beat the oxen with a chain, shouted savagely at his sons, kicking everything in his way. Then he stopped suddenly—often he did so—as if rooted to the ground, staring wildly, listening. He glanced at the apple tree, the crazy apple tree that was shooting out blossoms, now, with winter at the door. "By the clouds and thunder, what a sign!" he muttered. He felt the wrath of Heaven in it.

When they got to the forest One-eyed John set to chopping down dead trees, hacking at them furiously. Hitting a knot the axe sang out sharply, at which John swore. The boys cut the branches off the fallen trees and piled them together for loading, after the logs were on. Once Nicholas got in his father's way and his father ran around him as if he were a rock. At another time, when John stopped suddenly to stare and listen, some animal stirred the dry leaves back of him. John swung around and hurled the axe. It crashed against the spot whence the noise had come. He crossed himself, livid, glaring at where the axe lay. Michael fetched the axe and leaned it against the tree where his father stood.

The oxen waited patiently in the yoke, blinking at

the wind, bending their ears. Around their muzzles the warm breath from their nostrils was thin vapor. The wind whistled in the branches, at times it howled. The trees felled by John crashed to the ground, splintering their branches. The stroke of the axes echoed in the forest as in a cave. The tack-tack rebounded from the wall of trees, slapping John's ears.

From where the axe strokes rebounded the forest was black. Now and then John would look into that blackness. The sky was a dome of lead, blasting its coldness on the shivering trees.

John worked in a fury, muttering: "God's will—it shall be done. I understand, Father in Heaven. I must save her soul."

Hot steam rose from his sweating body. His fury, his endurance frightened the boys. They tried to work fast also, watching him all the time. Then John would stop suddenly, shouting: "Get away, get away, may the holy cross kill you!"—and they, struck with terror, felt numb, unable to keep up the steady speed at work.

On the way home John drove the oxen without whipping them. He swished the whip, cracked it, but never touched the animals. The boys were glad to get home. It had grown dark. The unloading was left for the morning.

One-eyed John went into the house. He sat down on the bench near the window. Presently he looked around and jumped up. "I must wash my hands, woman. Give me good, clean water—look at my hands! Give me good, clean water to wash them. Where is the girl? Did the girl come home?"

Chiva nodded, running to fetch the bucket. She filled an earthen wash-bowl and handed it to John. He washed for a long time, noisily, splashing water on the floor. Chiva brought him a towel. She moved quickly, silently, her face red and perspiring.

Stan came, greeting them cheerfully. John grumbled: "Welcome, father-in-law." They sat down to supper. Stan said grace. When he came to "Thy will be done" One-eyed John repeated the words rapidly, in a loud voice. At the end of the prayer, when all said Amen, John sang out the word as the deacon does in church.

Chiva cut the steaming *mamaliga* with a thread, helping John first. He took a piece on his fork and blew noisily on it. Little Maria stared at her father, unable to eat. Her mother raised her eyebrows. Maria's eyes filled with tears—she began to eat.

"And how did the day's work go, John?" asked grandfather Stan.

"We worked—like that, and like that—this way and that way." John swung his arms, making the motions of hewing and loading.

Chiva dropped her fork. All were startled by the clatter. John stared at the fork lying on the table. He stared, kneading a piece of hot *mamaliga* in his hand.

Then he pounced on the fork and shoved it into Chiva's hand. "Hold it tight, woman, hold it tight now! Grip it! Grip it tight—like this." He clenched his fist.

Little Maria got up from the table. John glanced at her. "I've had enough. I've eaten all I want." Smiles and tears on her face.

"Go to sleep then, Maria," Chiva said quietly.

"I will, mother! Good night, dear parents, good night dear gran'dad. Good night, dear brothers and sister."

"A-a-a-men," sang out John. His face was gray.

The boys got up also and went into the hayloft. They slept there until the cold weather, when they moved into the stable, to the large bed suspended from the ceiling. There it was warm—and they changed the straw bedding often, to keep it sweet and soft. But not as often as for the cattle. "We don't soil our straw as they do," Nicholas would say, laughing.

As they were going out, John called: "Michael, did you bring in the axes? Bring them in, put them under the hearth-bed. Understand? I don't want them to freeze."

"The axes—freeze, John?" asked Stan.

"Sure! Yes! Don't you know, father-in-law, axes freeze? Once, many times, I stubbed my toe against frozen cow's dung. Hard as a rock. Frozen like that. Iron freezes too. It just freezes, you see. Take a frozen axe; you strike a knot—bam-bang, then zing, klank—it breaks."

The wind howled in the chimney. The window panes

sweated. The drops of water traced crooked lines on the glass, growing larger as they rolled down on the panes.

Old Stan took his pipe and started to fill it. Then he lit a match. John watched the sputtering sulphur match throw out tiny blue tongues, then it burned with a yellow flame, which sank and rose on the pipe with the old man's puffing at it. Then he looked at Ileana's hands, white and smooth, folded on the table. He kept his eyes on her hands for a long time. Suddenly he tossed his head as if to listen in back of him. Ileana started and got up.

"I am going to bed, mother. Good night." Saying good night she glanced at all the three persons seated at the table. She crossed the kitchen to her little room.

They heard the door close. No one spoke. Stan sucked his pipe, ejecting little puffs of smoke from the corner of his mouth. John was sitting upright, stiff and tense. Chiva cleared the dishes away, sleep weighing on her eyelids already. During the day she had questioned Ileana, and her answers, as she reflected on them while going about her work, seemed plausible enough. A girl like Ileana would win a friend easily enough, and that she should stay with her city friend who needed help with the sewing of her wedding clothes was quite natural, "though," Chiva added to her conclusion, "she should have in some way let us know about it." At any rate, until other thoughts should come to her mind she was at peace now about the affair, and sleep was coming over her as usual. She was anxious about John, but that anxiety had already become part of her daily life.

Stan finished his smoke and got up sighing: "Well, it's getting on. I am going home, children. Good night to you both. Rest yourselves well." He looked for his hat.

"There's your hat," John said, pointing to a corner. He went out with the old man and fastened the gate after him.

Stan stood in the middle of the street, looking up at the sky. It was dark overhead, but in the north it was clearing. A livid light, still as ice, shone behind the ridge of hills, the thick blanket of clouds sharply defined above it, like the high bank of a river.

"Good evening, Stan"—a voice came from the corner of the house.

"Good may be your heart, Christian man—but you sure put my hair on end."

"It's a Christian, Stan, and sorry to have startled you," said the voice.

Stan recognised it. "No harm done, Teacher, no harm," he answered, "I'd never thought my old hair could jump up so sprightly. There's life in it yet. Well, hair grows even on a dead head, God bless us."

"How are things in there?" asked Tedescu.

"There," repeated Stan, pointing to John's house,

"well, as I could see, Teacher, my poor son-in-law has a bad twist in his brain, to say it plainly. To my mind, God preserve us, he's near to—to cracking in his head."

"Is he very angry at Ileana?" Tedescu asked eagerly.

"He is, as Lord forbid, splitting in his head," repeated Stan in a low voice.

"Did he scold her? Has he—has he threatened her?"

"No, that he did not. Nor even looked at the girl. But he was like the black cloud before it bursts. So I figured him to be."

"He may sleep it off," Tedescu sugested.

"So he may, Teacher, and I for one trust the day more than I trust the night."

They walked together. The old man ahemmed several times as if on the point of speaking, but said nothing. Then he stopped. "Here we are, Teacher. You brought me home," he said. They wished each other good night and parted. Tedescu heard the old man opening and closing the door. He turned and walked homeward. Passing by Ileana's house he slowed his steps—stopped and listened. It was dead silence. Twice he turned back to listen, but the house remained silent. He went home.

42

A F T E R Stan left Chiva went to bed. She slept with her
little daughter, John sleeping on the hearth-bed. He
watched Chiva undress, and as she was getting into bed
he walked out. He went to the wagon and took one of
the yoke ropes, twisted it in two, and came back into the
house. He threw the rope on his bed, blew out the lamp
and sat down on the bed. He looked at the rope, picked
it up and twisted it tighter, then pushed it near the wall.
He undressed and lay down.

He lay for a long time, looking at the ceiling where
the light from the fire played. Then he turned to the wall.
It was very quiet, save for the occasional crackling of the
charred ends of the logs in the fire. John heard his wife's
breathing. "Nobody knows but myself. It's all here, in
my head." He spoke to the wall, pressing his fingers on
the forehead. It felt good to have his fingers pressing his
forehead. There was a great heat in the head, yet he
shivered and pulled up his knees.

Suddenly that heat in his head pervaded his whole
body. Red lights flashed in his eyes and he was seized by
a quaking that was from passion and a dull fear. "I will
go to her—I will—now—" but he did not stir from bed.
But the wall, flaming red, with blotches of black on it,

pushed on towards him. It moved on to him, and in back of him were voices. Pell-mell, mixed voices, yet all were whispering the same thing: "He is going to her."

He was moving now—he knew he was moving, the voices all about him. He felt the floor cold under his feet —and he was crossing himself mechanically, the voices whispering: "He is going to her." His head was bursting with the fire in it.

Stealthily, on tiptoes, his hands groping on the wall, he moved, figuring the distance to Ileana's room—its door at the further end of the kitchen—by the steps he took. "To save her soul," he muttered, stopping to cross himself. He stubbed his foot against the door-sill, stepped over it and got into the kitchen. In the kitchen there was a scaly light on the furniture, on the things there, a subdued scaly light, as at the bottom of deep water. He got to Ileana's door. He shook fearfully, but tightly gripped the latch-knob and turned it, slowly, very slowly. The latch lifted, the door gave, pushing against the blackness inside—gently, gently—pushing against it. He took a step into the blackness. Ileana was in it, in her bed, in that square of blackness—there, John figured, there—he took towards the right.

The black mass, the thick black mass in which he was, began to quiver—John felt it quiver all around him, but he stepped forward into its quivering body. Nearer, nearer to the source of its welling quivers—one step, another—his hands stretched in front of him, groping for that source. Now he heard it—breathing. He touched it —it was Ileana's bed. From here rose that trembling, warmly breathing, breathing life into the black mass.

John's hands were nearing it. Now—here, warm, soft, smooth, firm. It moves, it stops breathing. "Who is it?"—it calls, a sudden gasp.

"Hush-hush-hush, daughter. It's me—John, your father—here, my hands, here—hush, hush"— The hands touching, holding, releasing, gripping again, loosing hold of shoulder, arm—what they touched—because everything moves, recoils, struggles. "Father—father—" cries that core of darkness. "Hush, woman, hush—you are the woman. I come—hush—the man, I am the man—" "Father—Father—" the cry is sharp, anguished. "No—no! Oh God, no! Father—Help, mother! Serafim!"—"Hush, it is John—save your soul—devil take mine—give mine for your soul—hush—I take your—hush—"

The weight of the night, the black ghost of it chokes Ileana, holds her, her body crushed by it. It breathes fire on her, it claws at her, it tears—it tears her flesh. She struggles with the ghost, she cries, she strikes, she calls, "Help—mother—help!" But her cries don't move away from her, crowd about her, fall back on her. Suddenly the torturing ghost yells: "Hush—the devil is here—hush—he can have my soul—for yours!" The yell is raging—it rends the darkness. It made light—it is light. "This is

mother"—"I am here, mother—save me!" Chiva pulls at
John, crying: "For the sake of God—John, for the sake
of God!"

John gets up, Ileana's hair in his hands. "Where is
the rope—woman, where's the rope?" He rages, pulling
Ileana by the hair. Chiva shrieks: "Michael, Nicholas!
Boys—sons—help!" She runs out, calling, shrieking:
"Help, for the sake of God, help!" Michael runs to her.
"Help, son, your father—Ileana—call the neighbors!" She
runs back to John. He is staring at her, holding Ileana's
hair in his grip. "I want her soul—give me her soul—
Satan will take mine, for her soul."

Ileana is on her knees, on the floor, her face resplend-
ent in fear—her nightshirt torn off her shoulders, her
breast white, quivering. "God save us," Chiva prays, covering her. "Avaunt—it is mine, her soul—" John shouts,
pushing Chiva away.

Several peasants rush in. John pounces on Ileana,
strikes her with his fists, tries to choke her, yelling:
"Give me—your—soul—" he shrieks.

The men overpower John. He struggles furiously,
but they carry him out. In the kitchen they tie his hands
and hold him. They pour water on his head. "For the
sake of God—bring him to bed—good Christians, bring
him to bed," Chiva pleads.

They put John to bed, Chiva insisting on bathing his
forehead in cold water. Dipping both hands in the basin

she applied them to his forehead. "I must quench the fire in his head," she kept muttering. Several women came, in their nightshirts, with a *cojoc* * thrown on them. The peasants sat about talking in whispers and soon they started teasing the women because their nightshirts hung from under the *cojoc* over bare legs. In the corner, near the window, one man slipped his hand to the knee of a young woman. She turned on him angrily: "Shame on you, Vasili—in a troubled house," she whispered. "Let's go in the barn, Raveca," grinned the man. "Go cool off in the pond," scolded the young woman. But soon after, when the other people were gathered about John's bed, the two went out.

Chiva would not leave John's bed. She was tired and dozed sitting there, but when he stirred, groaning, she woke and laid her wet hands on his forehead. A neighbor remained with her, but Chiva induced her to lie down beside Maria and now the woman slept as soundly as the little girl. The house was quiet save for John's tossing and occasional groans. The lamp, with the wick lowered, burned the whole night.

Chiva thought of Ileana and wished to go to her, but she could not leave John. His face was ashen-gray, then again it became red, and he tossed about, groaning at times, without opening his eyes. It seemed as if the eye-

* Sheepskin coat, fleece on the inside, the outside embroidered.

lids were glued in the hollows, under his forehead. Chiva watched those hollows, murmuring her prayers, then her eyes would close, her head pitching forward; but even when she dozed her lips moved.

In the morning, she found Ileana's room empty. There was something terrible about the emptiness of the little room at that gray hour of morning. It froze Chiva's heart. "The girl's gone—God save us," she mumbled, wringing her hands. She felt that the room was so empty because Ileana left it—left it to go away. She hurried out into the yard, went to the barn, then to the garden, calling: "Ileana, where are you, daughter?" Everywhere she felt the same tormenting emptiness that was in Ileana's room.

When Tedescu came she said: "Ileana left us, Teacher —God save us," and she shook with the sobbing inside her. But it was John who needed their attention, for the midwife and some old women who were there said: "He is in the clutches of death." Tedescu hurried away, saying he would bring the doctor from Seliste. He helped Dimitri harness and hitch the horses and they started out without "a drop of anything", as Dimitri said.

"What happened to neighbor John, Teacher?" asked the peasant.

"I don't know, Dimitri. He can't wake up, it seems," answered Tedescu.

"He can't wake up? God preserve us! So he is in a

dead faint. Did you hold vinegar to his nose? Did you
burn some horse-hair near his face? Did you rub the
soles of his feet with garlic? Did you shout in his ears?
Did you press his ribs? Did you rub the shells of his ears
with hands warmed over the fire?" Dimitri put these
questions rapidly, almost angrily.

"No. They put hot stones to his feet," replied Tedescu.

"Well, that's one sensible thing out of a score you
might have done, Teacher," Dimitri approved. He spat
out, resuming: "You bookmen—with your leave, Teacher
—are good at squinting at the printed words, but when
it comes to real doing—basta! You stop dead and let a
poor soul sneak out of the body." He spat again, angrily,
crying: "Get up, Floare—you're going for the doctor."
The mare pricked up her ears and sped up. They fell
silent, Tedescu and the peasant. The blanket of clouds was
sliding southwards, pushed by a steady wind. Dimitri
coughed occasionally and grunted. Tedescu thought to
the rumbling of the wagon, welcoming the warm whiffs
coming now and then from the sweating horses.

The doctor drove his own horse. He took the lead, in
the light buggy, leaving Dimitri far behind. The peasant
grumbled: "I could drive faster than your doctor, Teacher,
if I had a horse like his, tall as a gate, all legs, hitched to
a toy wagon with rubber padding on the wheels. My good
mares earn their feed as I do, by hard work, not by can-
tering. Still," he added, "you understand, Teacher, a doc-

tor's racing with the archangel Gabriel; he must have a good horse. No doubt on that."

Tedescu found the doctor at John's bedside. Chiva sat at some distance, with the sewing in her lap, her hands idle.

"You can walk on your full feet, Tedescu," said the doctor. "The patient can't hear. It is brain fever. Still," he hesitated, twirling his watch chain, "perhaps it is better not to make too much noise. The brain is sick, maybe more sensitive because of that. In an independent way, I mean, keeping the shock to itself. Yes, it is brain fever. How did it happen, exactly? The women are incoherent about it."

Tedescu told what he knew. It was nearly evening when the doctor left. He gave instructions to Chiva and repeated them to Tedescu. At the gate, taking leave of Tedescu, the physician said: "It will take time, but he will recover. I shall come again soon. The wife is brave —very reliable. Help her."

The doctor's matter-of-fact manner of speaking was reassuring to Tedescu. As if John's condition were completely settled. He turned his mind to Ileana. He was thinking, figuring what to do about finding her and bringing her back. John being so very ill, her duty was to be with her mother, Tedescu told himself. He did not blame her for leaving the house after her father had attacked and beaten her. But—Tedescu thought—she should

be with her mother now. The man is on the verge of
death. Who knows what may happen despite the physician's prognostication?

He decided to go for Ileana. He was sure of finding
her. There was Serafim to go to first. Even if she is not
there, he would know where she is. When he told Chiva
of his intention, she kissed his hand in a burst of gratitude, crying silently. The following day he went to the
city.

43

D u r i n g the remaining hours of the night Ileana did not sleep. She lay at first in a stupor; the frightful calm that is as near death as ever a human being can get without dying. Then life began to assert itself with glimpses of thought; with tattered fragments of feeling and thought. The past began creeping forward, piecemeal, integrating, taking form, slowly, in a detached relation to her.

With the first glimmer of light on the window Ileana stirred. Wearily, dazedly, she got up and dressed. She was even deliberate in combing her hair and winding the belt around her waist. She put on her short *cojoc*. It was white as snow, the soft embroidered sheepskin, with the curly fleece inside, warming her as soon as she had it on.

All was quiet in the house. She saw from the yard that the lamp was lighted in her parents' room, and dared not look at the window but for an instant. She was not sad leaving her mother, because she was able, at this moment, to harbor only the determination to go away. Even the thought of Serafim, of her going to him, only came to her clearly when she reached the plain. The plain stretched out to the horizon, soft and silent, like a cross-section dividing the night and the day.

When Ileana arrived at the outskirts of the city, "the world" was alive. The people went about their business, talking very loudly—she wondered at this—and the sunlight was very bright. She heard the booming of the church bell, the sound rolling over the city in that flood of light. She saw the steeple in the distance, a sharp cone of congealed light against the blue sky. It was a new world, all these noisy people, the strong light and the sharp outline of the city. Even the pigeons above Serafim's gate seemed larger and taken with undue fluttering. The gate also, with its forged nails, had a particular significance. All this strong outstandingness of what surrounded her was to Ileana like a great noise that hammers one to diminutive importance. In the midst of it all Ileana felt small and lost. Being so near to Serafim, thinking that she might see him instantly—he also, as belonging to this world which was outside her, assumed a greater proportion. And because of that, Ileana felt now that her errand, her coming to him, was of slight importance. Yet it was imperative.

Serafim was not at home, but Sandra received Ileana as a friend. She made her sit near the window, where the flower pots were ranged, asked her to drink water with a little cherry jam, if she did not want to eat the plum cake and fresh cream.

Sandra watched her eat the jam and drink of the
"good spring water", talking to her about the work of
putting up things for the winter. "I have bushels of car-
rots in the cellar, buried in dry sand; two barrels of cabbage, white and solid as rock, pickling in brine, flavored
with cherry leaves, with thyme and a few roots of horse-
radish. Oh yes, that makes the brine a real medicine. It
cleanses the blood, oh yes, Mother of the Lord, how good
it cleanses." She told of all her prevision for the long
winter. And she talked continually, without putting a
single question to Ileana, save the searching with her eyes.
They told her enough. "The girl is in some trouble,"
Sandra said to herself, yet she kept talking about her own
work.

They were still sitting together when Serafim came.
He walked in, clamping over the floors, whistling. He
did not see Ileana, so he called: *"Lele* Sandra, I am as
empty as a bell." Sandra turned her head, saying: "We
have a guest, Serafim, fallen from the sky." Then Serafim
saw Ileana. He was startled, but he ran to her, crying:
"Welcome, welcome, little—little friend." He was going
to say "little heart" but checked himself because of
Sandra's presence. The woman smiled cheerily at Ileana,
saying: "Now I'll go scold my pots if they didn't cook all
by themselves."

Serafim watched her close the door, then he sat down
beside Ileana, embraced her and smothered her with

kisses. "You did fall from heaven, little heart. I am
happy," he said and kissed her again. He seemed not to
notice Ileana's apathy. He played with her hands, fondled
her and kissed her. "I could eat you. I could drink you,
my little heart," he whispered eagerly, crushing her with
his embraces.

Then, when he least expected, Ileana said: "Serafim,
I've left home." Simply, as if saying "good day".

Serafim drew back a little to look at her. "You left—
your parents' house?" he asked, surprised.

"Yes," Ileana answered.

As if searching to comprehend, Serafim looked at her
for a little while, then asked: "And what are you intend-
ing to do, little heart?"

"I left without thinking of that, Serafim. I dressed
and left without thinking of that, coming here, without
any other thought in my head."

"Yes—yes, very good, little heart. Welcome. You're
as welcome as the sun, surely. We will think—we will
find, surely, we'll find—but why did you leave home,
little heart?" Serafim's voice suddenly became colorless.

"Because my father beat me," answered Ileana. She
was angry with her weakness, for her eyes smarted with
sudden tears. But she checked them and, averting her
face, wiped her eyes.

"Oh, fathers are brutal sometimes—with daughters
who are not strong enough to defend themselves. But all

daughters, all girls get that sometimes—oh yes, little heart. Did he ask you? Did you tell him?"

The tone of his voice as he put these questions, startled Ileana. She looked at Serafim. Suddenly she understood. She gasped, her hands convulsed. It was as if she had found the house empty where she had expected to find her lover. Her heart was bleeding from the wound.

At that moment Sandra entered the room and taking her in her arms said: "We will sit down to table, Ileana —you see how well I remember your name. I have good stuffed cabbage with sour cream to smooth it—yes, and you shall see, a nice little tidbit. Come, come."

At table Serafim became gay. As if forgetting the circumstance that brought Ileana to him, he strove to enjoy her presence. After the glass of plum brandy which he swallowed at one gulp, he did really not think any more of anything but his being with Ileana. He joined Sandra in prompting her to eat, was even more persuasive than his housekeeper. He ate heartily, trying to cheer the girl with a torrent of prattling. To his surprise, Sandra, tenderly solicitous with the girl, never looked at Serafim, or smiled at his witty remarks. In fact, when he was saying his best she would cut in with: "Take a bit of this, Ileana," or "but your plate is empty, girl." Mechanically Ileana tasted the food set before her. Sandra watched her, said nothing. But when the meal was ended, she did not rush out to her work. She let the servant girl clear the table, and held Ileana's hand in her lap, patting it gently.

Serafim at first nodded smilingly on Sandra's motherly cuddling, but after he drank some more wine he was annoyed and wished to have Ileana alone with him. Several times he winked at the woman, and knitted his brows, scowling, but she faced him as if he were the icon on the wall, without a sign of comprehension, so that at length he grew angry. *"Lele* Sandra," he said, "maybe you want to go and see if those fellows finished measuring out the wheat."

"Maybe I should, Serafim. Maybe I should tire my poor, swollen feet. Oh, Mother of the Lord, they feel like millstones on the end of my bones, and I would jump up and run to see how the men fill the sacks, but as they work on their own time—why should I meddle?" And she did not budge, as if indeed her feet had suddenly become millstones. When Sandra needed reason she had it handy, and enough of it to befuddle Serafim. That heavy, earthy reason that moves like molten lava.

Serafim poured out a glass of wine for himself, was sipping it, when they heard footsteps outside and a man's voice. Serafim put down the glass and stood up quickly, when the door opened and a big man came in, greeting: "Good day, Christian household. I see my mother-in-law is on the down-grade, God preserve us," the man said, coming to the table.

"She may not be too badly stricken, *bade* Filimon,

for there is bread on the table and olives and plum brandy," answered Sandra.

"Well, at Serafim's table food is tasty, be the table set or half cleared. As it is not all empty, there's hope for my mother-in-law," laughed Filimon.

If anyone understood Serafim's uneasiness, that was Sandra. But she betrayed it with no word or gesture. She offered the bread and knife to Filimon and poured out a glass of brandy for him.

"And who are you, lovely one?" Filimon asked, turning to Ileana.

"She is my niece, *bade* Filimon," Sandra answered promptly, pressing the girl's hand under the table. Ileana blushed but said nothing. Serafim could have kissed Sandra.

"They have a good pattern in your family, Sandra, for girls," Filimon said, looking at Ileana.

"Those who marry, marry young—among my people," Sandra answered, smiling.

"That's the time to make lovely children," pronounced the big man oracularly. Then, turning to Serafim, he thundered out in his huge voice: "Well, son, to our good health, and to all the lovely children of our seed!" He emptied the glass of brandy in one gulp, put a piece of bread in his mouth and wiped his bristly moustache while munching.

He had a chest like a barrel and when he spoke the

words rumbled inside him, warming at his heart before they issued. When occasionally Ileana looked up, there was Filimon's gaze resting on her.

Serafim was trying to brace up, sipping the wine, because each time Filimon opened his mouth to say something, Serafim became uneasy. At length what he expected, wishing that it would not happen, did come to pass. It was like the caving in of the roof, as far as Serafim was concerned. For Ileana it was nearly as portentous.

Filimon, never taking his eyes from the girl, addressed Sandra: "Now that I have seen your niece, Sandra —and glad I am, too—I invite her to Saveta's wedding. Bring her along. Surely, lovely one, you will come. Saveta —the only daughter we have, her mother and I—will be a good-looking bride. Oh yes. As to the bridegroom— ahem—what shall I say, what could I say to his face? I would say—if I were not the father—I'd give a pair of oxen to be the groom." Concluding he clamped his thick hand on Serafim's shoulder and shook him.

Serafim almost bit his tongue and could taste the vinegar of his own smile—for he did manage to smile.

Ileana felt the pressure of Sandra's hand on hers and she clung to it as the only firm part of a crumbling world. She grew so pale that Sandra got up instantly and lifted her in her arms. "Come, girl, come! I should have known it—she could never eat stuffed cabbage," she said to Filimon, who stared at Ileana.

"She is beautiful, that girl, Serafim. She'll be some lucky fellow's heaven. By the thistles, she will! Ha-ha! The stuffed cabbage! Well, and she's as healthy as a trout. But, you see, that's a thing to wonder about what a stomach will get angry at. I was a bull for health, as a boy, yet one slice of onion pie would turn me white as potato sprouts, and I could eat a peck of green apples and not belch once," Filimon said after Sandra took Ileana with her. Serafim nodded, that same sour smile on his face.

Sandra took Ileana to her room, made her lie down on the bed. She pulled the girl's boots off and covered her with the blanket. "It may be the cabbage, Ileana—for all we can tell," she smiled. "Now you just sleep a wink, it will warm you." Ileana closed her eyes, but she did not sleep. Sandra tiptoed to the door, went out, told the servant girl about some work and came back.

Ileana lay with her eyes closed. Sandra sat down at the bedside. She thought: the poor girl may be with child —he had her, this wild buck. Yet she was not angry with Serafim, only sorry for Ileana. "I will talk to her," she said to herself; "yes, yes, the world don't go to end for that." She bent to Ileana and putting her face against hers, she whispered: "You should open your heart to Sandra, my child."

Then Ileana began quietly to cry. "That is good, child, very good," Sandra whispered, as she put her arm

over her, "it will melt the lump on your heart. Did you
run away from home, my lovely one?" she asked. "Tell
Sandra. Two heads are better than one and seeing that
one is twice the age of the other, we'll get at the end of
the thread and straighten the skein."

For a long time Ileana could not speak, but Sandra
waited patiently. Then she heard the girl's story, all about
her parents, about the village gossip and about her father.
Sandra did not blame anybody; above all she did not
blame Ileana. Nor did she attempt to justify anyone. "It
is life," she said, "and fate alone can tell why so many
things come to pass to one human being. But," she said,
"neither storm nor flood, nor any wrath of Heaven lasts
longer than its allotted time, after which comes sunshine
again. Our days are like a string of beads," she said,
"some being as clear as dew, others gray, and between
them black ones. But the black ones only make the clear
ones shine the more and they bring even the gray ones
nearer to the clear, so that, by God's holy wisdom, our
life is better managed than we could if the burden was
left to us." And so speaking she asked a question, now and
again, simply, as if it just came naturally to her mind,
and Ileana answered without hesitation until Sandra
knew what she wanted, at which knowledge her face
brightened, lit up entirely, as the morning with the sun
up. She found that Ileana was not with child. "The Lord
be thanked for it," she said. "Our sins should remain be-

tween us and our Maker, then we can get washed clean of them by His infinite grace. It is when our neighbors get to know our sins that they keep them for us, safely, and never let us be rid of them. If you were with child— God forbid—and brought it into the world, the innocent creature would be branded in his cradle and remain with it until his last breath, and the mother could never be washed clean of that sin."

Sandra builded and builded, with these and such words until, lo and behold, the issue was that Ileana was more fortunate than unfortunate. "I have a sister," she said, "a woman who is a rock in the waters of life. She is there, always the same. We'll go to her, my child, and —and we shall wait a little time, until these clouds clear away. You will see, Martha is a woman of gold. She is curt—she has yes and no—and a few other words, but they are like bricks to build with. Oh yes! We'll go to her."

44

SANDRA was making ready to take Ileana to her sister. She was changing her aprons for the Sunday garments, when Serafim came in. Ileana was sitting near the bed, waiting for Sandra. Serafim was pale and for the moment he was speechless, but he devoured Ileana with his eyes. In her immobility, sitting there, her face motionless as her body, she was more beautiful than ever. Serafim could have kneeled down before her with adoration, but he remained near the door, until Sandra said: "Serafim, shall I pull my shirt off in your sight? You see I am about to change my clothes."

"I'll turn towards the door, *lele* Sandra," he answered submissively.

"Good, good, turn your face away," agreed Sandra, touched by Serafim's meekness.

Ileana was now suffering keenly. The pain from a deep wound is not felt at once, but when it comes it is cruel. She could not look at Serafim, for if she lifted her eyes she would choke. It seemed an eternity—the few minutes that Sandra took to change her clothes. The woman came to her now, took her hand, saying: "Come, my child."

Ileana got up, but it was torture to walk. Serafim

turned to them. *"Lele* Sandra," he said, "I'll drive Ileana to the—to the plain, near the village," and he came towards Ileana.

"Say good-bye to her, Serafim, she is going with Sandra," answered the woman.

"By Saint George and the dragon," muttered Serafim, stretching his arms as if to snatch away the girl. "Serafim!" Sandra cried. "Can't you see her heart?" He remained awestruck, as if seeing now only, this image, stone-rigid, lifeless.

It was Sandra who put her arms around the girl and led her out. She closed the door behind them.

Serafim stood there, anger welling up in him until it broke out in an oath and the crashing of his fist on the wall. "The old witch," he snarled. He ran to the door, halted, kicked it and swore again. Sandra had snapped the rod of his will.—"The old witch," he growled, but it was all in him, that boiling. He could not force it into action. He jumped to the table and drank from the bottle —savagely—gripping the uplifted bottle as if to crush it. The wine gurgled into him, full flavored, smooth, rich. "The cunning old witch," he muttered, and broke into laughing. "She blinded Filimon with her tongue. Stuck it into his eyes. 'She is my niece, Filimon,' with her sharp witch tongue. Ha-ha, the cunning one. Say, *lele* Sandra, you old witch, you did that for me. You are a good old witch. Now I see you clearly. Ha-ha, for your Serafim.

Good old w— *lele* Sandra. Fine, fine! I see you clearly
now. Good! Save her for me! Put her away, like a grape
for the winter. Put her safely away for me. Thaw her out.
She froze—poor girl—lovely Ileana. Yes, *lele* Sandra, I
can't take her frozen like that. You thaw her out for me
—your Serafim. I see you now, clearly, you cunning *lele*
Sandra. Good old *lele* Sandra. You know your Serafim.
I'll kiss you for it on both cheeks. You are—if you were
younger—I would ... You just thaw her out for me. They
are all cunning, but the older ones are witches with it.
Ha-ha, Filimon. You got her tongue in your eyes—ha-ha,
Filimon, ha-ha, I'll marry your daughter—I'll give her
children—but Sandra—you don't know Sandra. She saves
my happiness—she puts Ileana away for me. The bread
I have, she saves the cake for me. Good *lele* Sandra, I'll
kiss you on both cheeks." He drinks again. Slams his
chest, shouting with joy: "Serafim, you are luckier than a
king, Serafim.

"It is good, fine, good—oh yes Ileana, sure, you ran
to me—you left the village. There is no Serafim there.
There is only one Serafim. Can I kiss—? Can I love—eh,
Ileana?"

He was getting drunk—more drunk. He was warm
and happy and certain.

"You will find a good place in the city. I know where,
too. Not a servant, no, no. They have a little girl and they
are rich. Halmayer and his wife make weak children.

Their little girl is white and thin. They want to save her.
You'll take care of her. They'll feed you on the best—with
the little one—and you will ... I'll see you Sundays and
then, the house is big. I'll come to you at night, in the
room, when everybody sleeps—the little one too. We will
miss nothing—I'll give the children to my wife, to Saveta,
sure. She will be big every year with a little Serafim. She
will nurse them and rock them in the cradle.

"Good *lele* Sandra, you take care of your Serafim.
Wait, *lele* Sandra—you just wait—Serafim don't forget.
No, no. I'll kiss you! Maybe, you just wait, maybe ...
You are not old, I only call you old witch because you are
cunning. Ha-ha, poor Filimon. Because of me, ha-ha, you
jabbed your tongue into his eyes—the big bull—moooh—
the big bull. You are a fine cow, *lele* Sandra. Wait, why
not? A slick, fine cow. Why not? Eh—*lele* Sandra? Why
not a cow? Wait, I am saying, I am speaking to you—
lele Sandra. Listen, you can hear me—moooh—the big
bull, Filimon, ha-ha—moooh—" He leaned over the table,
mumbling. Fell into drunken sleep.

45

MARTHA was at home. She was in the garden, covering the last crop of tomatoes, in case the night should be frosty. She earned her living as a vegetable vendor, was a strong, healthy woman, with a voice both pleasant and powerful. She kept it in good form, calling her wares in the market place.

Martha's house was in one of the suburbs, about two miles from the city, where the vegetable gardeners and the domesticated gipsies lived. The gipsies were for the most part fiddlers and *cembalo* players, the men traveling about, while their families lived in neat little houses in enviable comfort. The sons took to one of the two musical instruments at a very early age, the daughters merely growing up to be married.

On Sundays, in fine weather, the city folk came to this quarter for their walk, especially the young students, because the houses were quaint and the benches in front of them adorned with beautiful girls in their fineries. But with the gipsy girls they got no further than to exchange greetings and perhaps a few words. The young men were not even invited to sit on the bench in the street. They had to stand when addressing an old acquaintance among the bevy of girls. If ever a young man showed too much zeal, the girls would tell him to go his way. If his daring was such that he did not obey, the girl who attracted him would get up and go into the house. They maintained their aloofness, these gipsies.

In a manner of speaking, the vegetable gardeners and vendors, all Roumanians, observed a like attitude towards the city folk. Even in the market place, if ever a man became so bold as to pinch the chin of one of the girl vendors, he would receive such a torrent of scolding—if not a slap on his jowls—that he would remember it for a long time. They were spitfire, those lovely girls. The difference between these girls and the Roumanian peasant girls was that they wore skirts instead of only the two aprons, as the peasant women do. And because they had to sit in the market place on a small three-legged stool, in all weathers, they had several layers of skirts, wide and flaring, which made them look like pampered, overclad dolls. From the waist down they looked like very stout females, but above it, the bodice, tight over the crinkled shirt, brought out the maidenly forms enticingly. It was like the rarest flower on a cactus bulb. Indeed, they had thorns, these lovely creatures, the seminarists said.

In such togs Ileana could have sold cabbages for tomatoes to all the orderlies marketing for their officers. Whether Martha thought of this or not is difficult to say, but she never took her eyes off Ileana while Sandra was telling her story. In any event, she welcomed the girl heartily, and before Sandra took her leave, Martha served them cherry jam and spring water.

At parting Sandra kissed Ileana—she did not often kiss anybody—saying she would come very soon. "Just you keep your heart cheerful, my child, there is a God in Heaven," she said.

At supper Martha spoke to Ileana about her own life, about her work and about the small work in the house, such as cooking a little, a bit of sewing in the winter evenings, and the two-weekly washing of the laundry. She asked her a few questions about home, as for instance how many children they were, how the crops had been: such questions, but none of the intimate, concerning Ileana alone.

"For this night, Ilenutza," Martha gave her this diminutive of Ileana, a sign of affection, because she was half a head taller than Ileana, "I will make your bed in the guest room, in the big bed. Tomorrow we shall find a cozier place for you." A guest room is not considered cozy because it is large and crowded with all the fineries and best possessions of the women folk. Besides the many kinds of woven materials hanging on poles along the walls and over the bed, there are chests—the painted peasant chests—full with linen, and the bed is piled up to the ceiling with pillows in embroidered cases. This room is the museum of peasant and family art in every household.

Ileana went to bed, high up, on top of two mattresses. Before falling asleep, in the great silence of the night, she heard the hearth-cricket chirping, as if speaking to her. With her eyes closed she felt as if she were at home, hearing their own cricket, but knowing that she was not there she became sad. It was that vague night sadness of the young, which does not scare away sleep—it rather brings it on, so very softly that the two mingle in sweetness.

46

TEDESCU left his driver at the inn and went directly to Serafim's. This time he was resolved to deal with him straightforwardly. If Ileana was there, he would take her back to her parents.

Sandra received Tedescu as if he were already an old friend. She asked him in and told him that Serafim would not be back until late in the afternoon. But, seeing that the teacher was a friend of Serafim—so Sandra put it—she begged him to accept the hospitality of his home and to have a little something to eat, since it was nearly noon. Tedescu thanked her, saying neither yes nor no for the moment. He figured: if Ileana did come directly to Serafim's, Sandra knows about it. If she did not, he could find out where Serafim was, in which case he would leave and go to find him. At any rate he sat down, showing no hurry, nor did he question Sandra at once. He complimented her on the fine order about the house, the cleanliness that spread even into the yard. Sandra smiled, answering that she could only keep the dirt out of the house if the yard was clean, so she saw to it that it should be, for George swept it twice a week from end to end, "groaning or grunting, as he pleased," it was his privilege, but the sweeping was done.

Talking in this way, they came, little by little, to the children and the school at Aciliu—yes, and the school yard which the bigger children enjoyed sweeping every Saturday—and so closer and closer to the object of Tedescu's errand, until his question whether she knew a girl from Aciliu, Ileana by name, seemed natural. Yet, simply as he put this question, Sandra considered for one short moment before answering. It was not that she was deciding whether to answer truthfully or not; it was that her mind, in one of those flashes that come, told her, in plain words: Sandra, now you know why this man came the other day, when you puzzled about it, and she had the answer on the tip of her tongue. "Yes, Teacher Tedescu, surely I know the girl, surely, and not later than yesterday, this time, maybe earlier—yes, it was earlier— I saw her, yes," she said, speaking deliberately to prolong the relishing of her own words.

"She came to see you, then?" asked Tedescu. The "you" might have meant Sandra alone or the persons of the house, in the way Tedescu said it.

"Yes, she came to the house—that is, the poor child, like a bird with an injured wing. Yes, just so, she came here," Sandra answered.

"Then she went away? Where did she go, *lele* Sandra?" asked Tedescu, trying to hide his eagerness.

"Yes—that is—I took her away myself, poor girl— to my sister Martha. In the New World suburb, not far."

"I have a message for her, *lele* Sandra, from home, and I should like to give it to her."

"Of course, with your own mouth, Teacher, as we say, without cooling it by passing to others. I understand, surely, and Martha will be home also, since on other but market days she comes home for noon. Now, do us the honor of partaking of a little meal and I will go with you, seeing it is not far—and my work never runs away, it waits for me."

With these words Sandra got up, and in a short time the table was set and everything ready, as all she had to do was to warm up the left-over stuffed cabbage. The corn-bread was freshly baked that morning, and when she had the oven going Sandra remembered to slip in a cheese-cake or a *henklesh,* which is a loaf as modest-looking as the daily bread, but "it melts in your mouth and gladdens your palate with its flavor," as Sandra said, for she shortened the dough with milk and a lump of butter and kneaded it until she could dig her fingers in the dough and pull them out clean, because the dough was so smooth. It was the test of its being to a point, she said. On this day she had both—cheese-cake and *henklesh,* for she intended to take half of each to Ileana and Martha. So they ate, Sandra and Tedescu, like two old friends, chatting "between the bites."

After the meal Sandra changed her clothes and they left. Tedescu knew the suburb quite well; he would have found the place alone, but he was glad of Sandra's company. In fact, on the way he told her about Ileana's mother and about the sick father, and won her to his side regarding Ileana returning home.

They found Ileana and Martha at table. Martha received the teacher with all the usual hospitality of the country folk. Ileana paled when she saw Tedescu.

Martha invited the visitors to sit down, which they did, though they told her they had just eaten and could not touch—"not even the *pasca,*" Sandra said. So, after Ileana and Martha finished their meal, the two sisters— each one taking something from the table—went out and left Ileana and Tedescu alone.

When the two women had closed the door behind them the teacher spoke: "Ileana," he said, "I came for you." "I understand," she answered, her eyes on the ground. "To take you home, now, with me." "Yes, but I cannot go home. For the good of all, I must not go." "That's just why I came, Ileana, for the good of all, that is why you must come home. Your mother is breaking under the work, and she cries for you. Her heart is too full, Ileana." "I understand. God knows. But my father, how can I?" "Your father, Ileana, is very sick. He is in bed and recognizes no one. He is between life and death." "He—you say—my father, he recognizes nobody? He doesn't know anybody, you say, Teacher?" Ileana asked. "Yes, Ileana, he is very, very sick, so, your coming home

is best, is what you must do." She sat, pale, unmoving.
"He tells the truth," she thought. She looked at him, even
her eyes were pale and dry. Then she said: "Yes, I must
be with mother now, Teacher." "It is the only good thing
for you to do, Ileana," he answered. "God help us"—she
whispered.

Martha and Sandra blessed Ileana at parting; they
even managed to laugh—"with their lips" as the peasants
say—to cheer her. All the way home, now and again,
their laughing stood out in Ileana's recollection of them,
so vividly as to almost blur their visages. She sat with
Tedescu on the front seat, on the blanket, with another
one over their knees, looking over Dimitri at the backs
of the trotting horses, the harness and the reins jumping
on their smooth hides. Dimitri seemed planted on his
haunches, sitting on the board in front of them, his feet
on the pole, his back against their knees. On the plain,
where the wind met them full face, Dimitri shielded their
legs. Even the plain was sad, with a flat, endless sadness,
and here and there tufts of grass shaking in the wind,
and the wind unable to arouse the plain from its sadness.

The village clung to the bottom of the bowl, flat-
tened out like a scared animal, the evening rolling heavily
over it, coming from the hills to fill the bowl to the brim,
beyond which there was yet a tarnished silvery light.

As she came into the yard Ileana looked at the
lighted windows. The reddish squares were flat, seemed

pasted on the wall—not as before, with life in them, the life of warmth and light which stretched out into the yard like welcoming arms. But Chiva must have watched from behind those reddish spots, because she came out rushing to her, with a whispered cry, "My daughter, my daughter!"

In her mother's arms life asserted itself again, warm, caressing, enfolding Ileana, and the sobbing that rose to her throat was good.

47

"Your father is at God's mercy," Chiva whispered, leading Ileana by the hand. She did not cry, she only took Ileana to the sick man's bed.

"His poor face—as if the soul had left him already," she said, bending over him, holding the girl's hand. "But he is breathing," she whispered, "God is good. He will save him."

Ileana stifled her crying, looking at her father's head, sunken in the pillow, the thick eyebrows rendering black the hollows of his eyes.

Chiva embraced her with a wan smile, saying: "God is good, He won't take him from us. We must have faith. I sent for his Reverence, he will come soon," she whispered.

The several neighbors who came to ask about the sick man were sitting in the kitchen, talking quietly when the priest arrived. They all rose and the women kissed the hand of his Reverence.

The priest answered their greeting with a few words and entered the room where John was, crossing himself at the door. The peasants crossed themselves also and resumed their seats. They listened in silence for a while, their heads turned towards the door.

"It will make it easier for his soul, poor John," said an elderly woman at length.

"The holy sacrament has turned many a soul from the very door of death," remarked another woman.

"The ways of the Lord are hidden from our sinful eyes," an old peasant said.

"Nobody can tell the end."

"No, no," agreed the others, nodding.

"We must live and be ready. When the Archangel comes we must be ready," observed an old woman.

"That's so, Granny," answered a young peasant, "but we never think of the Archangel until we hear the flapping of his wings."

"That is why we sin so much," the old woman explained, "because we think of the Lord only when we are in trouble."

"As to that, Granny," resumed the young peasant, "no fear of our forgetting the Lord—for troubles are never missing to any of us."

The old woman was about to answer, but the door of the sick-room opened and the priest stepped into the kitchen, followed by Chiva. The peasants rose again. The priest motioned them to be seated. Chiva took a chair, wiped it with her apron and placed it in the middle of the room, saying: "Be seated, your Reverence."

The priest sat down. He looked from one to the other, at all the peasants, by way of a personal salutation to each, thus establishing the community feeling. He was a man who could not endure isolation, being himself as much of the herd as he was herder. He lived not by his own breath alone, so he welcomed the stuffy air of a crowded church, an air warmed by the herd, drenched by the sweated bodies packed together like sheep in a *strunga,* and a room crowded with peasants was to him a slice of the church. As if more of God were present in proportion to the number of persons. His was the Lord of hosts.

"It is beautiful to live in neighborly closeness," the priest said. "That warms our hearts and the Lord blesses us."

"That is the veriest truth, Reverend Father," answered the peasants.

"And, my good people," continued the priest, "a kind word gladdens the giver and the receiver and the Lord puts it down in His golden Book. A kind word leads to kindly deeds—which is the Christian way. Thus we follow our Savior Jesus Christ, for He said, 'there is no sin in that which goes into the mouth but in that which issues from it.'"

"We understand and we bow, Reverend Father," answered the peasants.

After this preliminary the priest addressed each one by name, asking of one how his corn had been, of another about his potatoes, of a young woman how her aged mother was, and so of each. This led into a neighborly chatting that took in Chiva also, for several women asked how her hemp had yielded and when she intended setting up the loom. They agreed that winter was near, "just behind the hills." "It will soon be here, with short days and long nights. We'll rest our bones, God help us," said the men.

"Yes, and there'll be *clacas* at corn husking, wool carding, spinning," suggested the women. They almost forgot John in this community of interests.

The priest got up to go. The women kissed his hand again and Chiva held the door open until he went out through the gate.

The neighbors asked Chiva if John had taken the holy sacrament. "John did not hear his Reverence," she said, "not one word did he hear." She had tears in her eyes, concluding: "His Reverence will come again."

Being Sunday, other peasants came, and those who had come first left, one by one. The women kissed Chiva and some of the men were cheerfully assuring her that her man was young yet, strong too. "Why does a woman of good sense pull such a face?" they asked. Chiva smiled mournfully, answering, she wished it was as they said.

48

FORTUNATELY, because of the change in the house owing to her father's illness, Ileana could not connect her present life at home with the past of only a few days ago. She could not bridge the gap. The past receded so rapidly that it left her stranded on the present. She helped Chiva as before, but worked even harder now, the variety of familiar tasks leading her on.

Ileana seemed tireless and never noticed that the more work she took upon herself, the more Chiva found new things to do, because Chiva herself could not remain idle for one moment. The two women worked, side by side, silently, hours long, communicating merely by glances.

Tedescu spent his evenings with the family. Chiva and Ileana would sit at the table, in the circle of the lamp-light, doing some handiwork. The boys stretched out on the bench near the wall, and Maria, seated close to the hunchback, her head on her arm, her eyes glued to his face, was all attention. Clustered together thus, the family would listen to the teacher. He told them interesting historical events or read a book. He lowered his voice so as not to disturb John; and, to Maria, Tedescu's face with the light on it and what he was telling or reading

were one and the same thing. When her eyes closed Chiva
took her quietly and put her to bed.

They were all interested in *War and Peace* by the
great Tolstoy, waiting for the evening with eager anticipation. Once the reading started nobody uttered a word
nor moved, and if Chiva had to see to John for something
she would walk on tiptoe, Tedescu waiting for her with
the reading.

Ileana would occasionally look up, her eyes resting
for a few moments on Tedescu's face bent over the book
as he read. And one night, when Chiva was thanking him
for his kindness, Ileana came up and said: "Yes, Teacher
Tedescu, you are very good to us and I thank you also."

But usually, Ileana remained bent over her work,
while Tedescu read to them. As they were all gathered
in the large room where John lay, they spoke in whispers,
as if the family were in some secret plotting. This de-
meanour brought them closer to one another. Maria went,
now to Chiva, now to Tedescu and Ileana to whisper
into their ears.

It was a boon to Ileana, this hushed living, and while
going through her day's work she looked forward to the
evening. Tedescu was happy. For him, the evenings at
Ileana's were life itself. The light of the lamp and the
whisperings enveloped him and Ileana in an intimate
closeness, and Maria's running from one to the other,
quietly, made the union tighter.

49

WINTER came and settled upon the village. The street was a padded tunnel: thick snow on the ground, a dark, heavy vault over it. The children's voices echoed in the thick air and remained there, walled in.

The pigs had been slaughtered. The lard in wooden tubs was stored in cellars; in the attics hung the sausages, hams, loins and strips of bacon—the thin bacon from the hog's belly—drying and browning in the smoke that came in thick clouds from the opening in the chimney. It was a rich, scented smoke that rose continually, for when the fire lowered, the peasants threw punk, nut-leaves and the bark of walnut trees on the embers, all of which made a rich, fragrant smoke that roared up the flue. Thatch and shingles of the roof were crusted with a shiny, black varnish, from the smoke of many years' belching out into the attics, with no escape but the cracks—here and there—rolling, beating against the inside of the roof with its ghostly body. This coating protected the roof from the sparks that flew up—for it was like glass, and the spark hitting against it lost its fire.

The hams and sausages hung in the smoke, imbibing it until, in the dead of winter when such sausage or bacon was fried, the house was filled with a delicious

odor that made one's mouth water. Coming in from the
cold, the frost in their hair and clothes, the children
danced around the frying pan, sniffing with delight and
expectation.

From the rafters in the kitchens hung inflated blad-
ders; they were like huge eggs of parchment, drying
slowly, to serve as tobacco pouches. And every cellar had
a large vat filled with cabbage that soured in brine spiced
with cherry leaves, thyme and dill.

The looms clattered in varied rhythms, according to
how many treadles the woman at the loom was pedaling.
The shuttle ran madly between the threads, the woven
fabric coming like a miracle in its wake. They had hemp,
wool and linen, weaving every kind of texture, from thin
linen for women's shirts to the coarse woolens for men's
trousers, winter coats and blankets. Some women had
cotton thread, bought in the city in packages bearing an
English mark, for they said that the English thread was
stronger and better spun. But cotton is a luxury, for it
has to be paid for in ready cash, and when the peasant
changes his produce into money and then buys with the
money some such material, he can see the loss very clearly.
Even when he makes a straight exchange as in the village store, where he gives two eggs for a box of sulphur
matches in the summer and one egg in the winter, even
then he can notice that there is a something in the
transaction that is always controlled by the tradesman.

The *clacas* had begun. The first one was at the priest's, carding wool. The priest had no sheep, or only half a dozen or so that he kept in the cemetery from the time the first shoots of grass appeared until the snow came. But by the end of the year his wife Veronica managed to accumulate quite a bit of wool, all washed and clean, ready for carding. The peasants paid the priest mostly with ware, every kind of article being acceptable to Veronica, who was a fine manager indeed. She received eggs, butter, cheese, chickens, sometimes a goose, a suckling pig, a few yards of linen, a load of fire-wood and a day or two for chopping it up and piling it in the woodshed. A village priest performs a multitude of duties and every household is indebted to him for one or more of his holy offices. Veronica had very simple book-keeping, but that she attended conscientiously. "Pavel Podure: Holy unction, baptism of his 3rd child—three pounds of wool, one bushel of potatoes and two dozen eggs." The entry after the sign of "equal" she put in when she received payment, being unable to say in advance how the payment would be effected. Once the statement of the articles received was made, the account was closed, until next year, but that was for another page.

Practically all the young people of the village came to the priest's *claca*. They filled two large rooms. There was much talking and gaiety. Chiva considered it her duty to send Ileana, for One-eyed John was well on the

way to recovery. He was not yet his former self, but he
could be about and even do some light work. There was
no reason why Ileana should not go, at least none that
Chiva could see.

At the *claca* Ileana worked silently. She had hands
adaptable to every kind of work, and what she did was
well done, gracefully, to boot. Some girls remarked that
her movements were "unpeasant-like," and they snick-
ered. One girl whispered to her neighbor: "See the airs
she's picked up in town."

"How does she bleach her shirt like that?" asked
another girl. "There is no sun these days."

"We don't know those things, Dina," answered her
neighbor, laughing wryly.

"Did you see the hunchback teacher? Just watch him.
His eyes glisten like a cat's in the dark when he looks at
her," whispered one girl, the homeliest.

When the work was done and the singing and dancing began, Ileana remained sitting alone. But once, when
Veronica sat down by her, the girls noticed her smile.
"She's putting on airs. She won't dance or sing yet she
laughs—and her father with one foot in the grave," commented the gossips.

50

SINCE John's illness Chiva managed everything alone. The children obeyed her, the boys consulted with her about the outdoor's work and seldom quarreled among themselves. Ileana had changed towards her brothers. She answered promptly their silliest questions. She was always ready to mend their clothes and extract splinters, very skilfully, from their dirty hands. She could dress a wound neatly, "painlessly." "You never feel her touching you," Nicholas said to a boy whose finger was festering from a splinter under the nail. He urged him to come and have Ileana attend to his finger. The boy came. Ileana had him wash his hands in three waters, then she made him soak his finger in hot water for a long time. Then she took and belabored the festering finger, hammering it with the side of her palm, took a needle which she passed through the flame of a taper and pulled the splinter out. She bandaged the sick finger with a hot linseed-meal poultice, warning the boy not to get it chilled.

The boy remained sitting on the bench, gaping, following Ileana with his eyes, his head turning this way and that way after Ileana, like a weather-vane. Chiva had to send him home. "Go, Nicutz, go with God, my boy, your parents will be worrying about you," she said, leading him to the door.

Nicutz told everybody how wonderfully Ileana healed his finger. "As soon as she touched it there was no more pain. She just took it away, with her hand," he said. The gossips looked at each other wisely, nodding understanding heads.

Michael and Nicholas also felt very close to the teacher. They consulted him about farm work, for Tedescu seemed to know all about it. They learned many things from him. He taught them how to tie a sack with the smallest piece of string, securely, yet so it could easily be untied. He showed them how to lift heavy things, the strain on the legs instead of on the arms and back. He showed Michael how to sharpen the razor and how to mend his *opancze*.* He taught the boys to grease the scythes, the sickles and other implements put away for the winter, to prevent rusting. He made for them the best axe handle, from ash, and showed them the easiest way of twisting the rope around the horns of the yoked oxen. He explained to them the signs of the weather, about which they already knew something, and told them the names of the principal constellations, for of these they knew only the big bear and the small

* Primitive sandals, worn by the peasants.

bear—that is, the two dippers, which in some communities are called "the Lord's chariots."

"Teacher Tedescu knows everything," Chiva would say, with frank admiration. And one evening, in a teasing mood, she asked him how much leaven she would need for so and so much flour. Tedescu answered promptly: "That depends, Chiva, on how old your starter is. How sour it is. Then it depends on whether your flour is cold or not—and also on when you want the dough ready to put in the oven. Another thing, Chiva: if you knead the dough thoroughly, so that when you turn it and flop it, it raises bubbles, it will get leavened quicker. Well, have I told you?" he concluded, laughing.

Chiva crossed herself, staring at Tedescu with wondering eyes. "Well," she said, "Teacher Tedescu, this one thing I never expected you to know, God forgive me, though I do believe you know everything."

Ileana smiled with a sense of unaccountable pride.

During all this time she could not entirely hide her suffering, and Tedescu needed little to notice it. He understood and suffered with her, the more because he dared not speak to her about it. Yet so much did he wish to see her happy that once the thought came to him to intervene, to help Ileana—even, if need be, to help her see Serafim. For he guessed that she was longing for him. But the next instant his jealousy rose. And it prodded him into self-esteem, into realising his own worth, holding him up as the man for Ileana.

She suffers, yes—but I—I suffer even more, he would tell himself. She must forget him. When in that state of mind, Tedescu was full of courage, deciding to speak to Ileana. Occasions came quite often, when they were alone, but he only sat dumbly, observing the girl quietly doing her handiwork. She was always friendly towards him, but it was a neutral friendship, as if he were neither man nor woman—just friend.

At his evening meals Varvara would buoy him up, talking to him about women in general and about young girls in particular. About the very pretty ones, most particularly. "They are difficult to read, Teacher Tedescu," the old woman said, "those pretty ones with eyes that look at a man as if he were the wall or the door. But they are not as cold as those eyes of theirs, behind which they hide. Oh no, you should know that, Teacher. The truth is that they wait for the man to speak, all warm inside, whenever they lay their freezing eyes on him. Oh yes, I am a woman and I know—yes, yes, Teacher Tedescu. You see—and who don't know this?—love is like a seed. You plant it—and plant it good, and it grows. That's sure. But it's the man's business to plant it in the girl's heart. No fiddling, just straight planting." Varvara was not a woman who talked to the winds. Even her husband, after half a century of listening to her, would not stick his fingers in his ears when she spoke.

So, one evening, Tedescu left Ileana, sure of having planted the seed. How well he had planted it he could not tell, but it was done, and now "God help it." It happened in this way:

John and the boys got home late from the woods because they upset the sleigh twice, the snow was deep and the boys would not let John help with the reloading. Chiva was with them in the kitchen where they were eating their supper. Maria had gone to a friend who was ill and had sent for her. The little girl would have liked better to remain home with the teacher, but Chiva dressed her warmly and sent her off, saying: "Go, my child, go, cheer up your friend. She is lonesome, she is alone all day long with no one there to play." Tedescu and Ileana were alone in the large room. Ileana was embroidering while he read to her the story of an old couple who had lived many years "yoked to the cart of their common life", unaware of the passing of time. Late in life they realized that they had almost forgotten each other. They had forgotten the meaning of love because they considered each other as "the other" in the yoke. And now, at the close of their life, they both felt they had missed the most beautiful part of it.

When he had finished, Ileana hesitated, then said: "I feel that it is not true."

"Don't you think, Ileana, that many people go
through life just in that way?" asked Tedescu.

"No," she answered simply.

"Then what do you think, Ileana?"

Ileana worked on, faster than before, reflecting. At
length she said: "How did they get married? Why did
they get married at all? The writer does not say why.
So—we figure it out. If they got married as other people
do, they wanted each other. People want each other when
they are in love. This is what I think." She only glanced
at Tedescu once while she spoke.

"Even so as you say," Tedescu answered. "They loved
each other; good, but the burden of their life was such
that giving themselves to it, love was left aside."

"That's what I can not believe, Teacher Tedescu.
Two people living together can not forget love. I have
no book learning, but I feel that way. You asked me and
I said it."

"In this story, maybe," pursued Tedescu, "the man
loved the girl when they married, and the girl, say that
she only liked him enough to marry him. In such a case
it could happen as the writer puts it, don't you think?"

"I think," answered Ileana, "that if she liked him
enough to marry, she would get to love him afterwards.
The man could make her love him. He could by his own
love make her."

These words went to Tedescu's heart. Gave him the

belief that she spoke so freely because she felt for him something that was more than friendship. He almost jumped with gladness.

He rose and went to Ileana, but was seized with embarrassment. "It is lovely to be able to do such beautiful things with one's hands," he stammered.

"I learned to sew when I was very little," Ileana answered. "As you say, my hands do it now by themselves —I don't have to think."

"It is fine, that way your thoughts can be elsewhere," he said.

"That is the way, surely," she agreed.

"I am sorry I did not learn some useful trade, like carpentry or making shoes."

"Your work is very useful, Teacher Tedescu."

"Yes, but during the evenings—I would like to do some work with my hands, while thinking about something—something else."

"When would you read then? You love so much to read."

"If I were skilled in doing something really well with my hands, I would not read. I would work and think."

"Could you stop reading books?"

"Well, not altogether. I would read some, but I would read much less than I do now."

Ileana was silent for some time, thinking. Then she

asked: "Is it really better to have book learning than
to live, as we peasants do, learning from other people,
by word of mouth?"

"That is difficult to answer, Ileana. We would have
to know first whether living a peasant's life is good.
Don't you think so?"

"It is good—for many people," answered Ileana.

"If it is, then they need no book learning," Tedescu
said.

Ileana fell silent. Slowly, as the light dims when the
sun is setting, the color vanished from her cheeks. Her
hands stopped altogether, and she grew pale. Tedescu
watched her, thinking she reflected on what he had said.
In his exalted mood he attributed her outward change
to their conversation and to himself. Had he guessed
that Ileana was thinking of Serafim, his hopeful joy
would have lessened. Indeed, at that very moment, she
was tormented with longing for Serafim.

As it was, he kept repeating to himself all the way
home: "The seed is planted, the seed is planted."

51

CHRISTMAS was approaching. The children were busy
learning carols and making stars out of pasteboard. They
glued gold-paper on the stars to make them as nearly
real as the stars in heaven. The bigger boys were preparing their Magi vestments, crowns and wooden swords,
and on the Sunday before Christmas they rehearsed in
their regalia at the school. The noise was not less than
in the market-place, for several groups rehearsed at the
same time and some of the boys, confused by what the
Magi or Herod said in the next troupe, answered amiss.
So they quarreled and started all over again. Each group
consisted of five boys, representing the three Magi, Herod
and the Shepherd who carried the star that guided them.
The performance opened with a song in praise of the
Savior—Herod singing as lustily as the others—but after
the song came the dispute, and Herod drew his sword,
to which the Magi responded by drawing their own.
Herod, heathen that he was, got angry and charged, his
sword striking those of the Wise Men, making them
clatter against each other. But in the end, as every Christian knows, he was defeated, for he did not find the
Infant presaged by the star.

On Christmas day, from early morning until evening, the boys would go from house to house to perform "Herod and the Magi". They were paid, or rather rewarded, with sausages, pieces of cheese, a slice of smoked ham or bacon, a corner of spiced bread and even with eggs—and the Shepherd, being the humblest, carried the bag and would inquire timidly, "Are they boiled, the eggs?" For if they were not, he would have to put them in his shirtbosom and that was embarrassing, to say the least.

Tedescu helped the boys in their preparations. The whole village was busy. The women were cleaning their houses, scouring kitchen-ware and everything that needed it, such as buckets and the vats in which they stored the snowwater for washing their heads, because snow-water is soft and good for hair.

52

ONE-EYED JOHN had recovered his health, but he seemed yet so absorbed with his own thoughts as never to notice Ileana and Tedescu.

Sometimes he sat on the hearth, smoking his pipe and cracking his knuckles, while Tedescu talked about folk music. He spat on the fire, the boards of the hearth seat creaking under him as he turned. But sometimes he walked noiselessly in the room, like a shadow, passing the table where Ileana and Tedescu were sitting.

On Sunday afternoons when One-eyed-John went to the inn and stayed until supper time, with the older man, Ileana and Tedescu sang together. Her voice had now a richness that surprised even Chiva. When she sang one of those sad folk songs, Chiva always cried. But she cried at the gay ones also, with happiness, because Ileana "could make a stone cry," Chiva said.

When she sang the exercises which Tedescu now made her do, Chiva commented: "All this warbling must be good for something, oh yes, but God help me, I don't know for what. Forgive me, I am old and my head has its habits, God help us, and this is new to me. We sing when the heart is full, be it with sadness or with joy. We sing our sorrows or our happiness, from the heart, so

I can't understand this thing. Ileana has to gurgle in her throat like a bird and it makes my head turn. She goes up, up, until her voice is as thin as a thread, gurgling in her throat, God help us! But you surely know why she must do it."

Tedescu smiled, explaining to her that a singer must train her voice in order to do with it what she wanted. Chiva nodded as if she understood, but she only agreed with him, trusting in his wisdom.

This "warbling" Ileana did when John was not around. It happened, however, that he came once—he was in the yard—while she was trilling. Chiva saw him stop dead and gape at the house, whence the sound came. She ran to Ileana, motioning to her to stop. "Your father is out there," she said. After a little while John came tramping in. He shook the snow off his sheepskin and cap, his eyes on Chiva, questioningly, then he said: "What's this screeching in here, woman?" Chiva, never stopping her work, mumbled: "She was hoarse this morning, a frog in her throat. I said: 'Daughter, scream it out of your throat, just scream it out!' That's what it was, John." The peasant grumbled something and went to warm his hands at the fire.

53

THE winter holidays had passed. The days were growing longer, but the sun still "had teeth," the peasants
said. During the latter part of Lent the sun was warm
enough to melt the snow. By noon the water was streaming from the roofs, though towards evening it began to
congeal into icicles, the drops gliding along them, chilling on the way, and by the time they reached the end
of the ice-torch they were caught and turned into ice.
The air was good, however, with the sun combing and
carding it, combing it clean of those dark clots of fog.
The children's voices rang clearly in this air. They were
large-bellied from feeding on beans and lentils and linseed oil or the black oil of pumpkin seeds. They were
eager to reach the end of Lent, with Easter opening the
larders for them.

And now the last week of Lent—the last week of
fasting, more exacting than the other weeks, for this one
had the Holy Friday in it, a day when they must let the
stomach cry and gnaw its own substance. The women
folk were as busy as ants, each household an ant-hill.
They were carrying furniture—the lighter pieces, bedding, clothes, icons—out into the yard, so they could
whitewash the walls freely. There was the baking of

holiday bread and the boiling of eggs in colored water.

The sun "ate up" the snow save on the mountain-heights where the winter was climbing—slowly, to be sure, for it lingered in shaded ravines. The earth was thawing out; it began to breathe again, you could see its breath, a thin, warm vapor. The air was drenched with its odor. From the birch-grove on the hillside the wind brought the fragrance of new sap into the village. On the border of the marsh the willow-reeds were budding, their russet coat adorned with silver buttons.

One-eyed John went about with a lightness in his step, as if the approach of spring were renewing his life also. Yet there was determination on his face. And now he noticed Ileana and Tedescu. Sometimes he stood looking at them, cracking his knuckles, staring. They saw him, Chiva and the other members of the family, walking briskly in the yard and stop suddenly as if to listen. At times he muttered to himself, but they did not hear what he was saying. On Saturday before Easter he was especially lively and went to bed at sunset, so as to be rested for the midnight mass. Chiva sent the children to bed also, saying they could sleep soundly for she would surely awaken them in time. By nightfall the village was as quiet as the cemetery.

One-eyed John was asleep also, despite the fact that the approach of holidays, since his sickness, excited him. "There is holiness everywhere, in the street, in the yards and in the houses," he had told Chiva. More he did not say. Chiva did not wonder much about his words, for she too, as all peasants, felt that way about holidays, but she did momentarily have "a sort of flutter in my chest" —as she put it—about the manner in which John spoke.

Tedescu had a light supper at Varvara's and he too went to sleep, Varvara urging him to go to bed "as for good. Sleep like a stone to rise like a loaf," she said, laughing. "I shall wake you up in good time, Teacher," she continued. "I have never missed the miracle of Resurrection, never in my life. The Lord only knows if I shall be here next Easter. This one may be my last, so no fear my missing it. No, no. Some people count their years by other holidays, but I say—this is my seventy-fourth Easter, and if the Lord takes my soul next summer or next winter, they'll know my age." She talked all the time, accompanying Tedescu to the gate.

Chiva awoke with the first tolling of the bells. She called at Ileana's door and went to the stable to arouse the boys. John was dressing when she came back, near the window, looking out now and again. It was pitch dark— only the booming of the bells, and small squares of lighted windows appearing on the black screen, two here, two there. John put his face close to the window, watching for them. "They are all up," he said, turning to Chiva. She understood. Now they were in the street, John walking ahead of his family—all, everybody, walking in the dark. Voices sounded muffled in that blackness, but neighbors recognised each other by the sound of the voice.

The peasants would not light their way to church, for the Savior was yet in the shadow of the dead. The light would only come when He arises from the tomb. And when He rises, the candle on the altar shall ignite, by itself, and the peasants will take light from it on their tapers and carry it home to the icon-lamp, and guard it on the tiny wick floating on oil until the following Easter.

Every person carried a taper, coiled into a ball, for that purpose, and careful they were to shield its little flame, on the way home, for it bode misfortune if it went out. But such foreboding could be avoided by relighting the taper from another one that had the flame taken from the altar candle.

All the villagers, every person save the infants and the sick, were now gathered in front of the church. The priest in his full vestments stood in front of the closed doors. Two candles in tall candlesticks were burning at his side. There was not a murmur among the people. Now the bells began to ring for the third time. The priest led the congregation around the church, three times. He was chanting, assisted by the deacon and the choir. Now he stopped again in front of the door, praying alone, the choir answering only "Amen".

Suddenly the doors opened wide. The priest bowed

reverently, entered, the congregation following. He mounted to the altar, kneeled down and prayed. The multitude knelt also, bowing to the floor, rising and bowing with the priest's prayer.

Now the priest rose, faced the congregation and with arms raised to heaven he repeated three times: "Christ has risen!" The multitude answered in one voice: "Verily He has risen!" The choir burst into song, "Christ has risen from the dead, with death upon death treading, giving life to the entombed." The congregation sang with the choir. Three times they repeated the ritual, ending it with "Light up New Zion," then the ceremony began. The priest officiated solemnly and many women cried, because verily Christ had risen.

After the ceremony the congregation moved towards the altar, where everybody took the *pasca*. They crossed themselves, opened the mouth, and the priest put the morsel of hallowed bread and wine on their tongues. The grown persons waited, each his turn, but the children, sometimes five or six in a row, opened their mouths at once, so excited they were.

Tedescu received the *pasca* soon after Ileana. He lighted his taper from the altar candle and left the church.

The night was turning gray. Dawn was coming, but was yet far. Passing some peasants, Tedescu was greeted with the cheery "Christ has risen!" to which he answered, "Verily He has risen."

He looked for Ileana among the people in the church yard. She was not there. Small groups stood in the street, others walked slowly homeward, shielding carefully the quivering taper-light they were carrying. Tedescu was careful of his own, holding it close to him, his palm cupped around it. He could not walk as fast as he wished; but, then, everybody else was in the same condition—Ileana too—and that consoled him. He watched for her. Suddenly there came a little eddy, a puff of freshness that curled around him, and he stopped because the flame of his taper trembled. He put his hand closer to it, ready to hold it with his fingers, if he could. The plume of fire shuddered again; it bent to one side, cowering before its enemy; then it shrank to a wee blue tongue and disappeared, as if sucked in by the taper.

Tedescu gave an involuntary "Oh," standing near a fence, in that grayness, alone. Then he started off, walking rapidly towards two women, a good distance away. He came up to them and recognised Chiva and Ileana. Chiva was moving along slowly, a few steps ahead of Ileana. "Ileana," he called, barely above a whisper.

Ileana stopped. "Has your light gone out?" she asked anxiously.

"Yes—I don't even know how it happened, Ileana—but—just suddenly, it went out." Chiva was going her way.

Shielding her taper, even more carefully now, Ileana said: "It is nothing, Tedescu—you can light it from mine

—it will be right again." She spoke gently, concernedly.

He put his hand on Ileana's to better protect the light, and—but his hand trembled—raised his taper to the little flame. The air was perfectly still. He raised his eyes to the girl's face. For an instant the two tapers burned together, molten wax dripping on their fingers. "Ileana—I," Tedescu stammered, "I—I love you, and—and Christ has risen."

Holding the taper, their hands were united, and the two flames burned in one, united also—and the wax dropped warm, like tears, on their hands. For one moment Ileana faltered, then answered: "Verily—He has risen." More she did not say.

And they walked together now, careful of their tiny flames, slowly, side by side, the grayness melting in a light that opened the world before Tedescu's eyes.

Ileana's last words whispered themselves in this slowly growing light. Tedescu heard them, endlessly whispering themselves, with a new meaning for him. And, when at the gate he took leave of her, he walked home with the same slow steps they had together kept. But Ileana's word: "Verily, He has risen," whispered themselves ceaselessly. Hope grew in Tedescu. She walked at my side. She did not run away. Step to step she walked with me. Verily, verily, Christ has risen. Repeating these words, Tedescu relit the icon lamp in his room. Then, the glorious Resurrection sun rose, filled his room with light.

54

W H E N Ileana entered the yard, dawn was there already. A beautiful dawn, a gentle holyday light. As she walked towards the door, her father emerged from the shadow of the barn, coming towards her. Ileana greeted: "Christ has risen."

"Verily He has risen—verily—verily," John answered, standing now beside her, a rare smile on his face. He glanced at the taper in her hand. "There you have it, the light of Resurrection—protect it well, daughter, carefully —(he cupped his own hands)—a little breath, a tiny breath can blow it out. The gates of Heaven are open now, child—wide open, for the Son of God to enter. Yes, yes, verily Christ has risen, daughter—the angels opened the gates of Heaven for Him." He spoke solemnly, but that smile kept reappearing on his face.

"Come with me, daughter," now he spoke in a lighter tone, "come, we will go to see the sun rise. It is the holy morning of the great day. The holy morning, the sun coming into it. Let us go and see it come in." He spoke gently, but now and again one of his words rushed out of him shrilly, detached from the others. He took her hand. "Come, girl," he urged, "let us see the sun rise."

"Father, I'd better help mother with the Easter breakfast," Ileana said.

"It is well, daughter; she will tend to that. We must not miss the open gates of Heaven. You see—Christ has risen. Come, girl."

"But—this light, Father," Ileana said.

"Oh, yes, this light, one puff"—he blew in the air—"one puff will put it out. Take it to your icon lamp. Take it there and come. I am here, waiting. We must not miss the open gates of Heaven." He released her hand. "Go, and come quickly," he urged.

Ileana went to her room, blew out the tiny light of the icon lamp and relit it from the taper, then extinguished the taper in the oil. She came out—Chiva did not see her, for she was not in the kitchen: she was changing her clothes in the large room.

John was standing where she had left him, waiting. He took her hand again and led her through the garden into the vineyard. "It is a pure day. Yes, clean and pure. It is Easter, and we are going to see the sun come in. It comes in, the sun too, new and clean, this morning. The whole night the angels were washing its face—and they were singing, washing the sun's face. Hosanna, Hosanna —they sang—Glory to God!" Speaking continuously, ex-altedly, he led her to the birch grove above the vineyards. Twice he stopped—Ileana felt his hand chilling on her own—as if to catch his breath. Ileana prayed inwardly and the flutter of misgiving vanished from her, because of the freshness of the morning which was as her own prayer, and she linked her father's conduct with the dawn of the young spring and with the miracle of Resurrection. The holy light of it wrought a miracle in her father's soul, she thought.

"Here, girl," John said. "We have reached the place. The sun rises there!" He stretched out his arm, pointing. "We are here! Now, sun, rise!" he sang. A faint glow showed where he was pointing. The odor of mossy earth lingered in the air.

Ileana felt her father's hand tighter. "You hurt me, Father," she said.

John turned to her. "Lord, Lord up in Heaven! Hear me, Lord! Thy gates are open wide. Rise, sun, rise! Oh, Lord—receive her soul—oh, Lord—my child's soul." He said these words with his eyes now on her, now looking up to the sky. He was very pale, his eyes burning.

"Father—dear, good Father—" Ileana cried, seized with terror. She struggled to free her hand.

"No—no, girl—Jacob and Isaac—no, no, not that—the open gates of Heaven, up there see—come, come, sun— see, girl, your soul will fly to the Lord—through the open gates—clean—this holy day, Resurrection—Lord, help me, oh Lord, Thou help me—"

Ileana struggled frantically, but the man became steel, his eyes wildly turned to the sky. "Hear me!" he yelled, "hear me up there—Thou Lord—Thy open gates—John, 'tis John—I, her father—Jacob and Isaac—"

He clutched at her throat. "Lord! Lord!" he cried. Suddenly, above the crest of the hill, appeared the sun. "There, there, your holy eye, Lord. Thou seest me. Thou seest me!" shouted John, stretching out both arms to the sun. Ileana fell to the ground, but, fear driven, she rose, ran into the grove.

"You have accepted her soul, Lord," John thundered, "from me . . . my hands, John, her father, her earthly father. Alleluia."

Ileana's kerchief lay on the ground. "I will bury you in the earth. Here in a new grave. A new grave," he said tenderly to the kerchief. "Flesh of my flesh, blood of my blood . . . bury you in the earth . . . new grave . . . your soul is with God . . . Alleluia! Alleluia! All-ha—lows."

He kneeled down. With his hands he dug the moist earth.

Chiva had set the table. The room was bright with the first rays of the sun. Clean shafts of gold across the table near the window, gilding the colored eggs in the bowl. Old Stan came in, greeting: "Christ has risen!"

"Verily He has arisen," answered Chiva. Maria clapped her hands, crying: "Grandfather Stan, look, aren't they lovely?"

"They are, child, very lovely—and Christ has risen." He bent down and kissed her on both cheeks.

"Verily He has risen," piped Maria. She put her arms around the old man's neck and kissed him also.

"Where is John? Where is Ileana? Where are they?" asked Stan.

"Where could they be, I wonder," repeated Chiva, going to the window.

"You didn't come together from church?" the old man asked.

"John was here, out in the yard, when I got home. Ileana was two steps behind me," answered Chiva.

"So, so," exclaimed Stan, nodding.

"I wish we could eat," Michael said. Nicholas clicked his tongue, winking towards the quarter of lamb in the pan on the hearth. Maria sniffed "Uhm," bending over the brown roast.

"I'll go look for them," Stan said, walking out.

Chiva sat down, pensively stroking Maria's head. The little girl fondled the colored egg in her hand, chirping at it. Presently she said: "You love Easter too, dear Mother, don't you?"

"It is a happy holiday, child," Chiva answered.

In the yard Stan called: "John, Ileana—where are you? Breakfast is waiting!" He saw the garden gate open, so he went into the garden. There were fresh footprints on the path. "The two of them," Stan muttered. He followed the tracks into the vineyard and through it. As he came in the open, near a little knoll, he thought he heard something. He hurried on, over the knoll, following the tracks.

He saw the edge of the birch grove and John kneeling on the ground. "God help us! What can it be?" he cried, running up.

"John. . . . Ileana . . . Almighty God . . . What's happened?" The old man gasped. He bent over Ileana's kerchief. John glared at him, halted his chanting. "Don't touch her mortal— Flesh of my flesh. In the ground. New grave. Her soul, God has her soul. Alleluia, Alleluia! All-ha-lows! Sing. Lift your breath. Sing. Alleluia . . . Alleluia!"

Stan crossed himself, awed by the demented man. He could utter no words. Petrified, he stood, crossing himself, his eyes staring at John's hand, scooping the earth.

At length he looked about him, to find Ileana's body. He feared she was dead, at John's hands. "She is nowhere," he muttered. "John—where is she, John?" John answered not, nor looked at him. He dug furiously, chanting. He was livid, his body drenched in sweat.

Tearing himself from the scene, Stan ran to the village. "Come, for God's sake, come," he urged his neighbors. Several men left their Easter breakfast and followed him.

They overpowered John, rolled him in a blanket and so brought him home. He raged in the swaddling, then sang, Alleluia, Alleluia! and again roared.

Women and children met them as they entered the
village and more came out from the houses. The street was
full with the procession. And now the sun was seen from
the village and the sun was big and red. "The sun of
blood," an old woman said. The peasants looked up,
crossed themselves, murmuring: "The sun of blood, the
sun of blood."

Varvara called Tedescu: "Hurry, hurry, Teacher,
there is—there is the whole village in the street." They ran
out into the crowd. "He lost his reason. One-eyed John.
Killed her," voices told them. "Killed," groaned Tedescu,
pushing insanely into the throng. He rushed forward, ran
ahead to John's house, ran through the gate, stopped dead.
There was Ileana, as one risen from the dead. He ran to
her. "Ileana . . . Ileana. Thank God!"

The peasants streamed into the yard, a hushed crowd,
packing closely as dammed ice floes. From their midst rose
John's voice: "Alleluia . . . All-ha-lows," raucous, throat-
strangled.

The priest came, prayed over John, now laid on his
bed, bundled in the blanket and the blanket tied around.
The large room was filled with incense smoke, the murmur of the priest and women's sighs. Into the room came
the sound of crowding people, of shuffling feet, subdued
words; then more words, then the breaking out of clam-
orous voices: "That girl, the bewitched, the possessed, she
did it. The unclean one in her. The Easter sun is red. Sun

of blood. God save us. She must expiate. The village is
cursed with her. . . ." Their clamouring grew, jamming
against the house as flood waters against a dam. The
creaking of the door as the priest opened it was like the
breaking of rafters. Tedescu shuddered. With grim determination he led Ileana to the open door. The multitude
hushed. The girl and the teacher stood like ghosts in the
door-frame. Numberless eyes focused on them from strain-
ing faces.

Tedescu raised his arm. "Good Christians," he cried,
but his voice trembled. "Good Christians . . . Christ has
risen. God bless you all with His holy blessings. I am taking Ileana away. I am marrying her. We are leaving the
village. Your Reverence, unite us to each other," he concluded, turning to the priest.

"No—no—no holy marriage," rose the peasants' pro-
test. "Away . . . Away . . ." they shouted.

The priest could not quiet them. "Away, away—now
—at once. No marriage in our Church . . . away . . ."
clamoured the crowd.

"Away . . . away . . ." thundered the Teacher. "Away!"
He was insane with chagrin. "Away! You burst your lungs
yelling. Bring a wagon, bring horses, we are going. Now
at once. Bring a wagon." He was ashen gray, his eyes wild.

"He lost his reason," the peasants cried. "He too . . .
he too. . . ." Old Varvara pushed her way to the door and
stood beside the teacher. She faced the crowd. Tears in her

voice, she said: "Is there not one heart among you—good Christians? I am old! This may be my last Easter on this earth. God only knows. If I could, I would myself take these young people, in God's name. . . . For the sake of my soul. . . ." She could say no more. Her voice was broken by sobbing.

The peasants remained silent. Silent all. All save Dimitri. He came forward. "I will!" he said. "In the name of the Father, the Son and the Holy Ghost. . . . Amen." He crossed himself.

Like wooden images, Tedescu and Ileana, sitting together in the wagon, saw not the peasants: through the streets lined with peasants, the wagon went. The peasants watched. Strained faces, eyes, eyes. Not a whisper among them.

But when the wagon had gone out of sight, they raised their voices: "Christ has risen. He delivered us of this evil. . . ." And returned slowly to their houses.

During the next three days the peasants feasted. This was the happiest and noisiest holiday in their remembrance.

But John's house was silent as the grave. Only now and again the awful silence was broken by John's voice howling: "Alleluia, Alleluia! All—ha—loooooows!" And whoever passed by the house, crossed himself, hastening his steps.

THE END